PRAISE FOR

The Witches of Willow Cove

"This atmospheric debut is a nail-biting story of local history, sinister magic, and what it means to be a true friend. With narrow escapes, rising tension, and secrets aplenty, good luck trying to put this one down!" —Diane Magras, *The Mad Wolf's Daughter* (*New York Times* Editors' Choice)

"…a delightfully spooky, action-packed adventure full of heart, friendship, and page-turning suspense! With vibes similar to *Goosebumps* and Roald Dahl's *The Witches*, it's the perfect book for readers who love to read under the covers with a flashlight! A truly magical debut!" —Kim Chance, *Keeper & Seeker*

"A spellbinding story of friendship, teamwork, and the perils of coming of age in a modern-day coven." —Kurt Kirchmeier, *The Absence of Sparrows*

"Fans of Harry Potter have a new series to fall head-over-broomstick in love with." —Darby Karchut, *Del Toro Moon* (Colorado Book Award Winner)

"A fun, thrilling read that will leave you wanting to spend a lot more time in the magical world of Willow Cove." —SpookyKidLit.com (starred review)

The Witches
of
Willow Cove

Josh Roberts

Owl Hollow Press

Owl Hollow Press, Springville, UT 84663

The Witches of Willow Cove

Library of Congress Cataloging-in-Publication Data
The Witches of Willow Cove / J. Roberts. — First edition.

Summary:
When seventh grader Abby Shepherd is just getting the hang of school, strange things start happening around her hometown of Willow Cove. It's not long before she discovers she is one of several teen witches, and her hometown just might have a few secrets in its history.

ISBN 978-1-945654-49-7 (paperback)
ISBN 978-1-945654-50-3 (e-book)
LCCN 2020935835

OWL HOLLOW PRESS

For Penelope, who told me I should write something like this.
As usual, you were right.

Part One

1

The House on Whispering Hill

A bby darted between the trees, hunched low to avoid being seen. Across the street, two boys in zombie costumes shuffled along the sidewalk, trading candy under the dim glow of the streetlights. Abby waited for them to disappear around the bend and then sprinted through the grass toward her best friend's house. A plastic skeleton rattled from the top of the doorframe as she slipped inside.

Mr. O'Reilly was seated at the kitchen table, elbow-deep in the candy bucket, and Abby rushed past him in a blur of pink sequins before he could remark on her costume. Upstairs, she tapped twice on Robby's door and nudged it open, revealing the familiar trail of comic books and pizza boxes all the way back to the window, where Robby's pet iguana Einstein lounged like a house cat on the windowsill. Robby sat at his desk, eyes trained on his computer screen.

"Promise you won't laugh," Abby said from the doorway.

Robby made a noncommittal noise as he brushed a few rusty brown curls from his forehead and adjusted the strap of his pointy purple hat, somehow looking less ridiculous as a freckle-faced wizard than Abby did in her Halloween costume.

"I ordered this monstrosity online," Abby said, clutching her dress as she inched inside. "I swear I clicked the warrior-princess one, Robby. *Warrior*-princess." She picked at the sequins along the hem, briefly considering plucking them all off before deciding it wouldn't make the costume any better. She pushed aside a pile of Spider-Man comics and plopped onto Robby's bed. "It wouldn't surprise me if Mom changed my order on purpose. She thinks trick-or-treating is for little kids. I bet she was trying to humiliate me into staying home."

"Just imagine if she knew what we're actually going to do tonight."

"The truth would only freak her out more."

Robby tapped at his keyboard. "You used to like playing princess."

"When I was six, maybe. Not thirteen."

"You're still twelve for another hour."

Abby rolled her eyes. "I already ate my birthday cake. It counts."

Einstein skittered onto the bed and nudged her like a puppy looking for attention. Abby scratched him under the chin, and he wagged his tail, gazing up at her with something like love in his eyes. Technically, he belonged to Robby's stepmother Tina, but he'd made Robby's bedroom his home long ago.

Satisfied, the iguana hopped onto Robby's bedside table and retreated to his window perch, toppling a steaming test tube in the process. Abby lunged and caught it right before it hit the ground, waving away a noxious green cloud.

"It's like a nerd exploded in here, Robby."

"A geek, technically. A nerd is—" But whatever he'd planned to say died on his lips as he swiveled to look at her. "Whoa."

"What? What is it?" Abby asked. "Omigod, is it worse than I thought?" She yanked her rhinestone tiara from her head and stared at it accusingly. Her cheeks burned with embarrassment, and she knew her fair skin must be nearly as red as her hair.

"No, no, it's just—" Robby sat up straighter. "You look really girly tonight."

Abby adjusted her glasses and studied her reflection in the mirror on the back of his bedroom door, frowning at what she saw there. "Don't get used to it. I still don't understand why we even need costumes. My mom's right about that. We *are* too old to dress up. And it's not like we're actually going trick-or-treating."

"We still need to get past my dad. Besides, once we're out there, it'll be worth it. Look at this." He rolled his chair away to give her a better view of the screen, where he'd been studying a satellite view of their small Massachusetts town, Willow Cove. He zoomed in on the rocky bluff along the coast. "Everyone thinks these images are updated randomly, but there's a pattern to it. I've been tracking it—I *knew* they'd refresh the street view today." He clicked the mouse again, switching views. "Check out the sign in front of Whispering Hill."

Abby leaned in closer. The sign read FOR SALE, and under that, SOLD. She shook her head. "How is that good news?" For weeks, they'd been talking about exploring the abandoned mental hospital at the top of Whispering Hill. Now, after sitting empty for decades, someone had bought the place? "What if the new owner catches us?"

"I think we'll be okay tonight. This might be our only chance to look around there, though."

"I just wish I wasn't dressed like a Disney princess."

"Yeah, about that…" Robby kicked open his closet door to reveal a long black robe and pointy witch's hat dangling from a hanger above his dirty laundry. An old broomstick leaned against the wall beside it. "Tina's stuck running pet séances and paw readings at the veterinary clinic tonight, but she made you a costume to go with mine. She said to tell you happy birthday."

Abby's eyes went wide. "Best stepmother ever!"

Fog billowed from the mouth of a giant papier-mâché cauldron on the front porch, twisting around Mr. O'Reilly as he waved goodbye to them. Abby and Robby had spent all week in his lab at school helping him prepare the dry ice, and she had to admit the effect was impressive. "Don't stay out too late," he reminded them. "It's still a school night."

Abby caught a glimpse of her mother silhouetted in the light of their kitchen window across the way, but it was too dark for her to spot them as they slipped into the woods. They padded down the old carriage road that ran almost the entire length of Willow Cove. The trail bisected the Hollows, where they lived, from the hilly area of town called the Heights. Muddy footprints and crisscross bike tracks marked the way, while jack-o'-lanterns flickered along both sides of the path, filling the night with an eerie orange glow.

Abby skirted a group of kindergartners and their parents before noticing Zeus Madison up ahead. Zeus was the only middle schooler to ever make the varsity football team, and he was already big enough to pass for a senior. Tonight, though, he looked like a giant pink bunny.

Abby called his name. He turned, his fluffy ears swaying in the night, and then hurried after his seven-year-old triplet sisters as they hopped along ahead of him, pink ribbons tied around their bunny tails. Abby ran to catch up, rising onto her tiptoes to touch his shoulder.

This time he stopped and shrugged a hello.

"What's wrong?" Abby asked.

"What isn't?" he replied miserably.

She stared at him, briefly mesmerized by the way the fluffy pink fur framed his dark brown face. He nodded in the direction of the triplets, who were now hopping in circles around them.

"Dad has half the police force out on patrol with him tonight, and Mom's sick with the flu, so I got stuck taking the girls out"— Robby caught up to them just as Zeus spread his hands to show off the full extent of his misfortune—"in this."

"Did you at least get anything good?" Robby asked.

Zeus opened his bag. Abby peered inside and wrinkled her nose. "Raisins?"

"Stay away from Mrs. Vickory's. She's got millions of them."

"You went all the way out there?"

Zeus nodded at the triplets. "They're making me take them to every house. Where are you guys headed?"

One of the triplets tugged on Zeus's tail, whining that he was taking too long. The other two had stopped hopping and looked ready to revolt, too.

"Whispering Hill," Abby said. She hadn't meant for it to sound braggy, but Zeus's eyes bulged anyway.

"You can't go there!" Zeus said.

"Why not?" asked Robby.

"Because—because—" A machete-wielding toddler in a hockey mask slipped around the group, trailed by his frantic mother. "Because it's haunted."

Abby shook her head. "It's not haunted."

"Is too." Zeus crossed his arms. "Why do you think they *call* it Whispering Hill? Ghosts from the mental hospital wandering around whispering to themselves—"

"Or it's just the wind coming in off the ocean," Abby countered.

Zeus narrowed his eyes. "Dad's always catching teenagers sneaking around over there, you know. Making out and stuff."

Abby wrinkled her nose. "Gross."

All three of Zeus's sisters began making loud kissing noises. "Oooo," said one of them, grinning and hopping from foot to foot. "Zeus is jealous…"

Zeus swatted at the triplets. "Am not."

Robby straightened his wizard's cap. "Anyway, we're just going up there to have a look around."

Zeus's sisters were tugging on his costume now. He scowled at them and sighed before turning back to Robby. "That's all you're going to do?"

"Scout's honor."

"You're not a scout!" Zeus yelled, but before he could say anything else the triplets dragged him back down the trail. Abby waved goodbye and sprinted ahead, already worried that they wouldn't have enough time to explore the old buildings before they had to turn back.

It took another half hour before they emerged onto the narrow dirt road at the foot of Whispering Hill. Thick vines choked the tall brick wall that stretched out from a sturdy gate. The moon had been full and bright when they'd left Robby's, but now it was just a narrow orange slit, like a cat's eye peering through the clouds.

Robby shined the light from his phone at a fallen placard resting on the ground near the real estate sign: OFFERED BY ELENA ROSENBERG, C.R.B. "Maybe we should have asked Zeus to come with us," he said, pocketing his phone and tugging at the rusty chain holding the gate shut. "I bet he could bring this whole thing down with one push."

"Not necessary." Abby hurled her broom and princess shoes over the wall and then scrambled after them, wishing Tina had thought to include a pair of black boots with the witch costume. Robby landed next to her as she was slipping the hideous pink shoes back on.

A ragged mist hung low over the ground on this side of the fence, smelling thickly of the sea. Waves crashed against the rocky coast somewhere just out of sight.

Robby sprinted up the twisting driveway, Abby just behind him. But when he reached the top of the hill, he stopped abruptly and she crashed into him as something in the distance made a loud, almost deafening, noise. *BOOM!*

"What was *that*?" he asked.

"Thunder?"

"It didn't sound like thunder." He listened, but the night had gone silent. "It sounded kind of like the front gate."

Fog rolled away from the hilltop, revealing twisted trees and overgrown shrubs choking the gray stone walls around the old hospital. Dozens of winged statues were perched along the windows and stairs leading to the entrance, giving the impression of slumbering watchdogs.

"Those are some creepy gargoyles," Abby said.

"Chimeras, technically. Gargoyles have waterspouts."

"Thanks, Wikipedia."

Robby shrugged. "They're also sometimes called grotesques."

He leapt back as headlights cut through the mist. Abby grabbed his arm and yanked him into the bushes as a black limousine came around the curve, pulling to a stop a few yards away. A tall shadowy man climbed from the driver's side and opened one of the rear doors. As he moved aside, a dark-haired woman in a red cloak emerged into the moonlight and appraised the building. She had pale, smooth skin, and looked young except for a streak of gray-white in her hair that caught the moonlight as she turned. She was probably in her late twenties, Abby thought. Definitely not any older than thirty.

"It's been a long time," the woman said in a vaguely British accent.

"Eight years," the driver replied.

"Nothing good has ever come from this place. We should tear it all down."

"As you say, Joanna."

Robby tensed. Abby glanced at him, and then moved to get a better look at the new arrivals.

"I suppose it will do for now, though," the woman continued. "You've made the necessary arrangements? I shouldn't think I'll need to—"

A twig snapped as Abby shifted her weight. Her breath caught in her throat. The woman's gaze darted to the bushes.

"What have we here?"

Abby swallowed. The woman crooked her head at them. "I'm in no mood for trespassers this evening." A long, narrow stick appeared in her left hand. She thrust it toward the house.

Leaves rustled in the trees edging the driveway, followed by a musky smell, and then the stairway was suddenly illuminated in a blurry red glow.

Abby squinted. "It's… It's the—"

Two dozen red eyes turned toward her.

"It's the chimeras," Robby finished. "But that's impossible. They can't—"

"They *are*, Robby!"

The winged monsters roared as one, the sound echoing everywhere, even inside Abby's head. When she covered her ears, the cry only grew louder. Sulfur burned her nostrils, and with a sound like shattering rocks, the chimeras broke free of their stone pedestals, swooping forward on unsteady wings.

Abby yanked on Robby's arm as she raced away. *Don't freak out!*

Her left foot caught a root and she went tumbling. Robby pulled her up, urging her on. Her ankle screamed as she kicked both shoes free and limped ahead.

Suddenly, the ground dropped away, waves shattering against the rocks below. Abby spun back around to find the chimeras bobbing before them like buoys on a choppy sea. The monstrous creatures were bigger than lions, and most of them had curved horns that glistened in the glow from their stone eyes. The nearest one bared a row of teeth the size of Abby's hands.

She swatted uselessly at them with her broom. "How is this

happening?" she yelled over the crashing of the ocean. The two of them were surrounded now on three sides with only the sheer cliff behind them.

Robby's face had gone ashen.

"We'll have to jump," Abby shouted.

"We're too high!"

She reached for his hand. "We'll be okay as long as we miss the rocks."

The chimeras parted as the woman marched toward them, her narrow stick casting an unsettling red glow.

"Abby," Robby whispered, "she has a lightsaber."

"No, I think it's—" The woman thrust the stick in their direction. "It's a wand."

Robby squeezed Abby's hand. "Definitely time to go."

Abby gripped the handle of the broom with one hand and wrapped her fingers around Robby's with the other. "Jump!" she yelled. She squeezed her eyes shut and screamed as salt air filled her lungs. The force of the wind spun her around, thrusting the broom between her legs as she tumbled. Somehow, Robby was behind her now—above her—grabbing at her broom, her elbow, her costume. Anything he could get his hands on.

Please let us hit the water, she thought. *Not the rocks!*

But they didn't hit the water.

Or the rocks.

Robby clutched at her back, behind her on the broom.

"Robby, are we...?"

"We are..."

"Flying!?" they said together.

The Witching Hour

A bby clutched the broom between her legs. Robby was squeezing her waist so tight, she found it hard to breathe. Somehow, they were hovering above the jagged rocks and crashing waves of the ocean.

"Are you doing this?" he shouted.

She could barely hear him over the wind. Putting all of her weight into her left shoulder, she sent the broomstick spinning back toward the cliff, eye-level with the chimeras. The woman was still standing among them, wand raised, waiting.

"The other way!" Robby screamed.

"I'm *trying*!"

Abby bent backward so sharply that her head collided with Robby's. The world lurched. *Concentrate on the broom*, she thought. *Figure the rest out later.* She jerked the broom forward and they soared away from the cliff into the night.

She screamed as they zoomed low over the patchwork fields of the old Jones farm and buzzed the top of the abandoned light-house along the coast before zipping toward the Heights. Finally, she wrestled the broomstick into submission near the center of town, called the Hex because of the tangle of streets that fed into it like a six-sided star. A few straggling trick-or-treaters wandered the sidewalks below, little more than dots. Abby urged the broom in the direction of the harbor before anyone looked up and spotted them. The longer she flew, the more confident she felt. After a while Robby's grip loosened until she could breathe without gasping. She glanced over her shoulder at him and saw that his grin matched her own.

They soared through the night, the rush of wind whipping Abby's hair behind her. Everything looked quiet and peaceful from this height—the salt marsh with its giant mounds of hay like tiny humps in the landscape, the glimmering yellow lights of the houses along the Heights, where the rich people lived. The middle school was dark, but there were still lights on at Tina's veterinary clinic. In the distance, Whispering Hill loomed menacingly over the rest of the town. Abby studied it for a moment, squinting, then turned the broom back toward the Hex and drifted to a rest above the town green.

She reached into her robe to check her phone, nearly slipping off the broom when she saw the time—and the half dozen missed calls from her mom.

Robby shifted behind her, checking his own phone. "We are so dead."

Abby kicked hard at the air, rocketing them back toward the Hollows and home. But now they were going too fast. The broom wobbled and bucked, and she started to slip. Her knuckles went white as she shifted, trying to regain her balance, but that only made her slide into Robby, who wrapped his arms around her just as they collided with the ground in a swirl of knees and elbows. The broom shot back into the night, sputtered, and plummeted into the treetops.

Abby rolled onto her back and groaned. "I think I broke something."

"What hurts?"

"Everything."

She climbed to her feet and then toppled forward, taking Robby down with her. A minute passed, then another, before she felt steady enough to stand.

Together, they hurried the last hundred yards through the woods before pausing at the edge of Robby's yard. He peered through the branches, his face going pale.

"Oh no. They're waiting for us."

"The chimeras?" Abby whispered, leaning to peer around him.

"Worse. Our parents."

Wisps of dry ice wafted out of the cauldron on Robby's porch, mingling with the fog rolling in off the ocean. A police cruiser was parked in the driveway, and from the bushes, Abby could see her mother pacing back and forth through the window. Mr. O'Reilly and Zeus's father, the chief of police, were crowded in the kitchen with her.

Abby tugged at the fabric of her witch's robes. "I'm supposed to be in that hideous princess costume. I can't just stroll in there dressed like this."

She scrambled up the maple tree by Robby's bedroom and crawled in through the unlocked window. Robby followed and then stood in the corner, eyes shut, while Abby changed. She'd only half zipped her dress when her mom's voice drifted up through the heating vent in the floor.

"But what if something happened to them?" her mother said.

"Let's not get carried away, Carolyn."

Abby stuffed the witch costume into her backpack and waved Robby over. "Come here. They're talking about us."

Robby dropped to his knees and pressed his ear to the metal

grate.

"Sometimes we catch kids sneaking around Whispering Hill," said Chief Madison. "I'll drive over there and have a look around."

"But why would they go all the way out there?" Abby's mother asked.

Abby locked eyes with Robby. "We can't let him go," she whispered. "What if that woman is still there?"

Robby swallowed hard. He nodded and started banging on the grate. Abby only had a second to adjust her tiara before the adults burst through the door.

"Kids?" said Mr. O'Reilly. "What are you doing up here?"

Abby's mom glanced at the open window. "They must have snuck back in. Where have you two been all night?"

"Nowhere," Abby protested. "We were just—"

"Abigail Elizabeth Shepherd." Her mother's face had gone red. "You should have been home an hour ago! You had us scared to death."

"We just lost track of time trick-or-treating." Abby caught Robby's eye. *And flying around town on a broomstick.* "I'm really sorry, Mom."

"Chief Madison has people out looking for you," Mr. O'Reilly said, his cheeks an unpleasant shade of scarlet. He adjusted his glasses. "I specifically reminded you that this is a school night."

"The important thing is that you kids are safe," said Chief Madison, squeezing into the room.

Abby's mother crossed her arms. "What were you doing all night?"

"I already told you. Trick-or-treating."

"Then where's your candy?"

"What?"

"If you were out all night trick-or-treating, where's the candy?"

"We ate it."

"And where are your shoes?"

Abby glanced at her bare feet. She shook her head.

"Home," her mother said. *"Now."*

3

Grounded

"I'm grounded?"

"Extremely," said Mr. O'Reilly. "For a week."

"But Dad—"

"Push it, and it'll be a month."

"But Dad—"

"That's enough, Robby."

"But you don't *understand*!"

Mr. O'Reilly stopped in the doorway. "What don't I understand, exactly?"

Robby opened his mouth to explain, but no words came out. He swallowed back a lump in his throat and shook his head miserably.

His father sighed. "That's what I thought," he said as he left.

Robby sank into his desk chair and powered up his computer. A minute later, the floor outside his door creaked. "Dad?" he called out.

But it was his stepmother Tina, still in her blue scrubs, who peeked through the crack in the doorway. "Mind if I come in?"

Einstein lifted his eyes lazily in her direction and wagged his tail as she closed the door behind her.

"I wish you'd been here earlier," Robby said. "I could have used some help with Dad."

"Someone was out tormenting stray cats all night. Probably Tommy Rexman, although I can't prove it. I spent most of my evening in surgery instead of paw reading." She removed her horned rim glasses and rubbed her temples, then replaced them and leveled her gaze at Robby. Curly gold hair framed her pink cheeks in disorderly ringlets. The effect usually made her look younger than she was, but tonight not even her makeup could conceal the purple bags under her eyes. "I promise I'll talk to your father in the morning. Right now, I want to talk to you."

"We just lost track of time, I swear."

She shook her head. "What were you thinking?"

"Did you come up here just to lecture me?" Robby snapped, though he knew his frustration was still mostly directed at his father. "You're usually on my side."

"I *want* to be on your side. But you scared me, too."

Robby let out a deep sigh. "Sorry," he grumbled.

"I'm just glad you're both safe." She reached across the desk and nudged him. "Did Abby like her costume, at least?"

He bobbed his chin. "Loved it. It was a little short, though."

"Well, you're both growing like weeds." Tina smiled uneasily. "Robby?"

"Yeah?"

"You're sure everything's... okay?"

Robby hesitated. "I'm sure," he finally said. Tina was great as far as adults went, but there were probably limits to what even she would believe.

"All right. Oh, one more thing." She held out her hand, though her face was all apologies. "Phone, tablet, smartwatch, all of it. Your dad forgot to take them."

"All of them?" he protested. "For how long?"

"I'll talk to him in the morning once he's cooled down."

After she disappeared downstairs, Robby swiveled back to

his computer and the satellite image of Whispering Hill he'd
pulled up. He stared at the screen for a long time and then rolled
the chair away from the desk, stopping at the edge of his bed. He
was tired, but there was one more thing he needed to do before
turning in for the night. He got up and dug through his closet until he uncovered the old cigar box he'd found in the attic a few
months earlier.

His mother's things.

Pictures. Letters. The police report from the night she'd disappeared near Whispering Hill.

He thumbed through them until he found a faded photo,
crinkled and smudged from being held too many times. It was his
favorite picture because he remembered the day it was taken—a
family picnic just after his mother had started teaching at the
middle school. There were other pictures, too, but most of those
felt like other people's memories. After a minute, he set aside the
photo and moved on to the letters. Nearly all were from his father
during their senior year together at Princeton, when she'd studied
abroad in England.

But there was *another* letter.

It was addressed to Emily Donovan, his mother's maiden
name, yet it had been postmarked just days before the accident:

Oxford University
United Kingdom

Dear Emily,

*It was lovely to hear from you again after all
these years, even if the circumstances are not
what either of us might have wished. You always were a shrewd girl, though. One of the
cleverest I ever taught. Perhaps our friendship blinded me to the danger of revealing so*

*much of myself to you, but it has never been
easy walking this path alone.*

*Should I have hidden more from you? How
could I have known you would end up in the
one place where you might someday discover
my true plans? You are the first to piece it all
together. I credit you for that. Not even your
new mentor understands the why of it as you
do. She clings always to names and dates,
small details that carry little meaning, while
the truth eludes her. It's different with you.
You are one of the few to ever truly know me.*

*So yes, I agree to see you again, my dear
friend, and Whispering Hill seems a fitting
place for our meeting. If our bond still holds
any meaning for you, I ask that you come
alone. Do not involve your new mentor or the
Council. Surely by now you understand they
have only ever sought to shelter themselves,
never to help those who truly need their pro-
tection.*

*Yours in friendship,
Joanna*

Robby read the letter three times before tucking it back into
the cigar box. Most of its meaning was still too cryptic, but one
piece had fallen into place tonight. The woman in the red cloak
was called Joanna, and in her own words, she'd admitted to being at Whispering Hill eight years ago. That couldn't be a
coincidence.

And if she could bring stone chimeras to life, what else

might she be capable of doing?

"I'm going to solve this, Mom. I promise."

Einstein nuzzled Robby's knee and peered up at him with pleading eyes. Robby made room in his lap and then stifled a yawn while the iguana got comfortable. A minute later they were both asleep, the cigar box still clutched in Robby's hands.

4

Partners

A bby's head pounded in rhythm to a mysterious symphony of buzzing and thumping. She squinted at her alarm clock and sank back under the covers. When the thumping grew louder, she lifted her head again and peered harder at the blurry numbers, nearly falling to the floor as they came into focus.

"Abby!" shrieked her mother from the hallway, thumping on the door again. "You'll be late for school!"

"I'm up!"

The thumping stopped. "Don't be long."

Abby reached for her buzzing alarm clock, accidentally knocking over all her birthday cards in the process. She swatted at it again until the clock went silent, then hastily rearranged the cards. There were a handful from her aunts and uncles and step-cousins, but nothing from her father. Last year, he'd sent a card but forgot to call. This year he hadn't even managed that.

Sitting up, she rubbed her eyes. The room swirled. Every-thing ached dully, as if she were just getting over a cold. Her princess costume lay in a heap on the floor next to her soccer cleats and a few of her favorite books. The witch costume poked out from her backpack, which leaned against the foot of her bed.

It wasn't a dream.

"Abby!" yelled her mother, this time from downstairs.

"I said I'm up!"

Light flooded the room as Abby pulled open the curtains. She scrunched her forehead and stared at her blurry reflection in the mirror. Nothing *seemed* any different.

But how do you explain last night?

"Abracadabra," she said experimentally.

Nothing.

"Hocus Pocus? Presto?"

Nothing and nothing.

"Expecto Patronum!"

Shrugging, she pulled her hair into a ponytail, threw on a pair of jeans and a comfortable sweater, and headed downstairs, her school bag slung over one shoulder. She was struggling to clasp her lucky pendant around her neck when she reached the kitchen and found her mother waiting there with her arms crossed. There were bags under her eyes and a few new gray hairs, which could only mean more bad news. Abby's mom always looked tired—she worked in social services by day and wrote romance novels whenever she had the energy at night—but Abby had never seen her look as defeated as she did that morning.

They stared at each other wordlessly. Finally, Abby couldn't take it anymore. "Sorry again about last night," she said. It was about the hundredth time she'd apologized, not that it appeared to be having much effect.

"I made you toast," her mother said, passing Abby a plate of crispy bread with a lump of hard butter on top. Abby was starving, so she accepted it gratefully.

"I didn't mean to worry you."

"You're already running late, Abby. We can talk about this after school."

"Can't we talk about it now?"

Mrs. Shepherd sighed and poured herself a cup of coffee. Probably not her first. "All right." She glanced down at her mug and wrinkled her nose, then topped it off and took a sip. "Where were you last night?"

Abby's heartbeat quickened. "Nowhere."

"In my experience…" her mother began. "When I was your age, I mean… boys and girls would go to Whispering Hill to hang out together. *Alone*, if you know what I mean. It's where I had my first kiss."

"Eww, Mom."

Mrs. Shepherd raised her hands. "I'm just saying, it's perfectly natural if you and Robby have feelings—"

"We're just friends."

"Then you *didn't* go to Whispering Hill together?"

Abby swallowed hard. She didn't want to lie, but who knew what might happen if she told the truth? What if her mother somehow found out about the woman in red and started asking even more questions? The less her mom knew, Abby decided, the safer she would be.

"Abby?"

"I already told you, we were trick-or-treating."

Her mother shook her head and sighed. "I know that's not true, sweetheart. I've just been on the phone with Chief Madison. Zeus says he ran into you and Robby as you were heading to the old hospital at Whispering Hill last night."

Abby put the plate of toast back on the counter. "Zeus told on us?"

"Abby." Mrs. Shepherd's eyes narrowed. "Missing curfew and trespassing are bad enough, but lying to me on top of it?" She exhaled. "If you think this kind of behavior is acceptable, maybe it's time for you and Robby to take a break."

"Mom, there's no reason to—"

"It wouldn't hurt for you to make some other friends, you

know. When I was your age, I had a whole group of friends I spent time with. Mostly girls."

"Please spare me any more stories from your youth."

Mrs. Shepherd closed her eyes and was silent for a moment. "I'm doing the best I can, Abby. You do understand that, right? I don't have anyone else to help me teach you how to behave or tell you when you've gone too far. Lying like this…"

"I'm running late," Abby snapped. She grabbed her jacket and school bag.

Her mother blocked the way. "Finish your breakfast. I'll drive you."

"I'd rather walk."

Abby skirted through the doorway before her mother could grab her keys. She barely registered the smashed pumpkins and stray candy wrappers littering the trail behind her house. It already felt like weeks since Halloween. *Maybe because I was only twelve last night.*

Not that being a teenager was off to a particularly good start.

"Do you know what time it is, Miss Shepherd?"

Abby bent over the office desk to meet the vice principal's eye. Ms. Bancroft's radish-shaped nose was known to change color with her mood, and this morning it raged an angry shade of purple. Abby tried not to take it as a bad sign. She glanced at the clock and said, "Eight thirty."

"Eight thirty-*three*," Ms. Bancroft corrected. "What time does school begin?"

"Eight o'clock," Abby mumbled.

"Speak up."

"Eight o'clock!" Abby repeated loudly into Ms. Bancroft's

left ear. The vice principal was practically deaf on one side, but Abby could never remember which.

"No need to shout, Miss Shepherd. Now, let's see. You'll need a hall pass."

"That's why I'm here."

Ms. Bancroft raised a wrinkled eyebrow. "Watch your tone, young lady."

"Sorry."

"What is the reason for your tardiness?"

Well, I was chased by terrifying monsters with creepy red eyes, escaped by flying away on a broomstick, and then got in trouble for lying to my mother about it. Now, my whole body hurts, I'm completely exhausted, and I'm questioning my sanity. How's your day going?

"I overslept."

Ms. Bancroft peered up at Abby. "The hormones, I expect."

"I really don't think that's it."

Ms. Bancroft's bony left hand shot toward a pile of yellow passes. "It will take you three minutes to reach the science laboratory. Don't dawdle." She peered over Abby's shoulder like an inquisitive troll. "And please show Rebecca the way."

Abby followed her gaze. "Who?"

A strikingly pretty girl with dark hair and light brown skin rose from a row of seats against the back wall. "She means me." The girl adjusted the collar of her pink cashmere turtleneck, took a breath, and smiled nervously at Abby. "I'm new. Do you have Mr. O'Reilly's science class now too?"

"Three minutes," Ms. Bancroft reminded them. "Off you go."

Abby waited until the vice principal turned away and then stuck out her tongue. "It's this way," she told the new girl. "Rebecca...?"

"Ruiz." The girl scooped up her backpack and followed Abby into the hallway. "People call me Becca. I just moved here."

"No talking in the halls," Ms. Bancroft shouted after them.

"She's half deaf and yet *that* she hears." Abby shook her head. "I'm Abby Shepherd. I'm not usually this late, but—" They turned the corner and nearly crashed into Olivia Edwards, an annoyingly popular cheerleader who used to make fun of Abby's red hair when they were in grade school. Olivia's best friend, Sarika Swann, was posing for a selfie with her hall pass while Olivia retrieved something from her locker.

As Abby and Becca approached, Olivia snapped the locker shut. "I heard the police were looking for you last night," she said in a tone that reminded Abby—once again—why they'd never gotten along.

"You *and* Robby O'Reilly," added Sarika, her olive-gold features creasing into a wicked smile. Sarika made it her business to know everything about everyone.

"The police?" Becca asked uncertainly.

Olivia appeared to notice her for the first time. She brushed a few stray curls of blond hair into place and narrowed her eyes. "Who are you?"

"Becca. I'm new."

"Well, it seems you've already fallen in with the wrong crowd."

Abby glanced at her hall pass. "We're going to be late."

"The police?" Becca repeated as they continued down the hall.

"Ignore them."

The girls walked the rest of the way in silence. Olivia and Sarika trailed behind, snickering just loud enough that Abby felt sure they were talking about her. When they reached the classroom, Abby spotted Robby working by himself at their usual lab bench near the front of the room. She waved and then handed her hall pass to his father, who was scrawling something on the whiteboard, his sleeves rolled up to his elbows and his hair sticking out in all directions.

"I overslept," she told him in a low whisper. "You know you're my favorite teacher."

"I appreciate that." Mr. O'Reilly held up a finger to Becca, who was waiting to speak with him. Olivia and Sarika slipped into the room as he pulled Abby aside. "Abby, you're not going to like this, but I need you to switch to a new lab partner today."

"What?" Abby blurted out.

"Shh. Abby, listen. When we're at school, I'm your teacher and you need to do as I—"

"But Mr. O'Reilly!"

"—as I ask of you." He glanced up at Becca, wiped his brow, and then turned back. "You're one of my top students, and I need you to help bring someone else up to speed on what we've been doing this trimester."

"Fine. Sorry." She'd been apologizing a lot lately. At least now she actually meant it. "Once I help Becca, can Robby and I go back to—"

"Not her," he said. It almost sounded like *he* was apologizing now. "She can partner with Robby."

"Then who?"

"Amethyst Jones," said Mr. O'Reilly, raising his voice over the din of the classroom, "could you please come here?"

A familiar, pale girl with shoulder-length purple hair drifted toward the front of the room, chewing a wad of gum the same color as her hair. Abby opened and closed her mouth. She and Amethyst had been friendly in grade school, but these days Amethyst wasn't anything like the shy girl who used to love kittens and ballet dancers. She'd pushed everyone away after her parents died the summer before fifth grade. Now she lived at her grandfather's farm on the outskirts of town and missed school a lot. Abby hadn't seen her in weeks.

Mr. O'Reilly cleared his throat. "Amethyst has been out sick. She thinks it would be helpful if you could catch her up."

"Me?"

"We have a *lot* of catching up to do," said Amethyst.

"Wonderful, wonderful," Mr. O'Reilly said absently. He'd already turned his attention to Becca. A few rows back, Tommy "T-Rex" Rexman took the opportunity to shoot a spitball at Daisy Green's head. It went wide, nearly hitting Daisy's twin sister instead. As Abby looked away, T-Rex was already bringing the straw back to his ruddy face for another shot.

"I hope you're better than me at potions," Amethyst whispered as they wandered to her lab bench. "Whatever I'm cooking in my beaker is turning green."

"Potions?" Abby asked, pulling out her notebook.

"Mostly I've been copying your boyfriend over there," Amethyst said.

Abby followed Amethyst's gaze toward Robby. He was staring at Becca with the kind of wide-eyed awe he usually reserved for new Star Wars movies. "He's not my boyfriend, he's my lab partner. At least he was. Why did you ask to be paired with me?"

"Because I know what you two were up to last night."

"Just because we went up to Whispering Hill doesn't mean—" Abby scowled. "You know what? Never mind. How did you even hear about that?"

"I didn't hear anything. I saw you. Flying."

Abby's mouth dropped open. She let out a quick breath. "Don't be ridiculous."

"Spare me. I know what you are because I'm one, too."

"One what?"

"A witch, obviously."

5

Strange Occurrences

"I'm not a witch."

"You definitely are," Amethyst said. "And you weren't exactly being subtle about it, either. I saw you fly right over my house. How else do you explain it?"

Abby hesitated. How could she be a witch and not even know it? That didn't seem like the kind of thing that just happened to you one day. "Maybe it was Robby controlling the broom?" she suggested. "Maybe he's secretly a wizard or something."

Amethyst put a finger to her lips. "Shh! Not so loud."

Abby looked around skeptically. The only people even remotely within earshot were T-Rex and his pasty-faced best friend, Joey Swett, and they both had the intellectual capacity of a tree stump. Besides, T-Rex was too busy ogling Becca like a caveman to be listening in on their conversation.

"And it's a warlock," Amethyst said.

"What?"

"The correct term. Warlock, not wizard."

"Is he?"

"No."

"How can you tell?"

"Oh, wow, you really *don't* know." Amethyst shook her head. "What a colossal waste of time this turned out to be."

Abby narrowed her eyes. "I think you're making this whole witch thing up."

"Do you? Then maybe you'll believe this." Amethyst wrinkled her forehead and whispered, "*Explaudo, phlegm.*" The air around her rippled like waves of heat on a summer day. A murmur spread across the classroom as the beakers of green goo at everyone's lab stations began to steam and bubble.

"What are you—"

Amethyst's lips curled into a wicked smile. She looked ready to say something when the first loud pop shook the classroom. At the back of the lab, Piper Finch screamed as her beaker erupted in a cloud of green slime. Lucinda Walker's beaker cracked, then burst. And then another explosion and another, up and down the laboratory, while kids yelled and laughed and dodged the gurgling goo. Mr. O'Reilly shouted something about safety goggles, but Abby was more focused on Amethyst.

"Stop it!" Abby whispered.

When Amethyst didn't respond, Abby punched her in the shoulder.

"Ow!" yelped Amethyst. The green goo slid back into the cracked beakers like a receding tide. "What did you do that for?!"

"That was—You shouldn't do—"

Amethyst frowned as she rubbed her shoulder and surveyed the classroom. Everyone was talking at once. Streaks of slime peppered the lab benches. A splotch of the green gunk dribbled off T-Rex's goggles and plopped to the floor, gummy and once again lifeless. "I only meant to blow up T-Rex's beaker," Amethyst said in a low voice. "I'm still getting the hang of things."

At the front of the room, Mr. O'Reilly was waving his arms and saying something about malfunctioning Bunsen burners, but no one seemed to be paying attention. All eyes had turned to Becca. Green slime oozed down her hair and neck, while a second trail zigzagged across her shirt.

"I—I think I need to go wash up," she said quietly, before darting out the door to a chorus of laughter. A moment later, Robby followed her.

Abby turned back to Amethyst. "Don't ever do that again."

"Does that mean you believe me now?"

"Unfortunately, yes."

Robby called out to Becca for the hundredth time. He'd wandered all the way to the other side of the school looking for her and was about to give up when he heard a soft whimper from one of the boys' bathrooms.

"Becca?" He nudged open the door and peered inside.

The whimpering stopped. "Go away."

Robby felt a lump form in his throat. "Becca, is that you?"

"I said go away. Please?"

"I will if you really want me to. It's just… this isn't the girls' bathroom."

A stall door cracked open. Becca let out a halting laugh as she brushed a strand of hair from her face. She'd tucked the rest behind her ears, and wet splotches on her shirt revealed where she'd scrubbed away slime. Robby looked closer, taking in the little details that he hadn't been able to get out of his mind since she'd walked into the science lab with Abby earlier that morning: the faint birthmark just below her lower lip, the freckles dusting each cheek, the Star of David pendant around her neck. Even sniffling and teary-eyed under the harsh glow of the bathroom lights, Becca was the prettiest girl he'd ever seen.

She wiped her eyes. "I'll go."

"Wait," he blurted, then froze. *Wait for what?* He had been so focused on finding her that he'd never considered what he'd say to her when he did. "Sorry I slimed you. Are you all right?"

She sniffled. "I think so."

"It's not toxic. The slime, I mean."

She swiped at her eye. "Well, that's one less thing to worry about." Then she tilted her head. "You came to check on me?"

"Yes. No. I mean—I just wanted to make sure you were okay."

Her expression softened into a half smile. "That was sweet of you."

"Really?"

"Really," she said. "It was so embarrassing."

"It could have happened to anyone."

"But did it have to happen on my first day here?" She shook her head. "Everyone laughed except you."

"I didn't think it was funny."

Becca leaned forward and pecked him on the cheek. The room seemed to swirl.

But before Robby had time to react, Becca retreated a step, looking mortified. "I'm so sorry, Robby. I didn't mean—I don't usually—I've never—" She took a deep breath. "I don't know why I did that."

"It's okay." Robby's face burned where her lips had brushed against his skin. He touched the spot with his fingertips, then dropped his hand to his side. "Don't worry about it."

Becca plucked at the wet streaks on her shirt. "The last few weeks have been very stressful for me, and then with today…" She raised her eyes to him. "I shouldn't have done that, though. Do you have a girlfriend who's going to totally hate me now?"

"No, I'm—uh, no."

"The girls in the hall said something about you and Abby hanging out last night."

Robby laughed. "She's my best friend. We always hang out."

"Oh." Becca fiddled with her pendant. "The way they were talking, it sounded like you two might be a thing."

"Not that kind of thing."

Becca wiped at her eyes again, then bit her lower lip. "I don't usually act like this around people I've just met, you know. Just so we're clear." The corners of her lips curled into a cautious smile. "You won't tell anyone about that kiss, will you?"

"It'll be our secret."

As they wandered down the hall, Becca asked, "Have you ever seen anything like that before? In the science lab, I mean."

"Dad's been asking for new lab equipment for years. It's always on the fritz."

"Mr. O'Reilly's your dad?"

"Yeah, he's…" Robby hesitated.

"I like him. I'm glad he paired us together."

The bell rang and Becca pulled out a sheet of paper from her pocket and scanned the contents. "It says I have study hall in the library now."

"Me too."

"Oh, good! Do you want to—I mean, maybe we could sit together?"

Robby couldn't think of anything he wanted more than to sit with her. But he *needed* to talk to Abby about what happened to them last night.

"You don't have to," Becca said quickly when he didn't respond.

"I want to. It's just that I need to talk to someone else… but only for today, I mean, about this one thing…" Everything was coming out wrong.

"Maybe we could hang out this weekend instead? I can already tell I'm way behind in science."

"You want to study with me?"

She slowed to a stop. "Only if you want to study with me."

Robby came to a stop, too, then turned to face her. "I would, but I'm grounded. Last night…"

"The police. I heard."

"It's not as bad as it sounds."

Her face brightened. "Your dad made us lab partners, though, right? He'd probably be okay with helping me get caught up, even if you're grounded."

"Yeah, he might—" Robby froze. His mouth dropped open. At the end of the hall, beyond Becca, stood the woman he'd seen at Whispering Hill. Today she was wearing a red skirt and a pale silk top, but the streak of gray in her hair was unmistakable. She met Robby's eye, returning his stare.

"But, if you don't want to…" Becca said, backing up a step, her smile gone. "I'm sorry, I think I misread—"

"What? No! I—" When he looked back over Becca's shoulder, the woman was gone.

"It's okay, Robby."

"I want to." He tore his eyes away from the empty spot at the end of the hallway. "I do."

Becca shook her head. "It's no big deal."

"But I really *do* want to. Sometimes kids hang out at a place called Hex-Mex on Saturday nights. It's downtown. We could meet there around seven if Dad lets me."

"You're sure?"

"I mean, we are lab partners."

Becca allowed herself another hesitant smile. "Maybe it would help if I asked him?"

"It definitely would."

She broke into a full-fledged grin. "Then that's what I'll do. But first, could you show me how to get to the library?"

6

An Unexpected Development

When class ended, Abby shoved her lab book into her backpack and hurried after Amethyst. "You can't just leave," she said, grabbing Amethyst by the shoulder before she could reach the door. "We need to talk."

Amethyst stepped aside to let T-Rex pass. "We already talked. We're all done now."

Abby scooted in front of her. "Can you show me how to do things like that?"

"Do I look like Obi-Wan Kenobi? I'm not here to teach you anything."

"Then why *are* you here?" Abby demanded. Amethyst tried to elbow her way out the door, but Abby dropped her bag, blocking the path. "You skip school for a month and then you just show up today—"

"Because I thought *you* might be able explain what's going on. I mean, you actually flew. I'm stuck learning everything from a book."

"There's a book?"

Amethyst leaned in. "Tons of 'em."

"Where do you get the books?"

Amethyst shook her head. "Bye, Abby."

"You can't just tell me I'm a witch and then walk away!"

"Watch me."

Abby cut in front of Amethyst again. "Do you still live at the farm?"

Amethyst sighed. "Yes."

"Will you be around tomorrow?"

Amethyst blew a bubble the size of a beach ball. "Maybe."

"All right then." Abby stepped to the side. "See you tomorrow."

Amethyst rolled her eyes. Abby watched her disappear down the corridor before scooping up her bag and starting toward study hall. She marched past the crowded tables near the front of the library and sank down into one of the reading chairs nestled in the stacks, dropping her bag onto the next seat to save Robby's place. She was still thinking about everything Amethyst had said when he arrived a few minutes later.

"Our parents suck," she said as he plopped down next to her.

"They do," he agreed. "Mine especially. I'm grounded."

"Zeus told his dad that we went to Whispering Hill last night, and now my mom thinks we were, I don't know, kissing or whatever." Abby wrinkled her nose. "Apparently *she* used to go there to make out."

"There must not have been as many homicidal statues back then."

Abby started to laugh, but her stomach clenched when she noticed a red smudge on Robby's cheek. "Is that lipstick?"

"No," he said a second too late, then rubbed at the spot on his cheek.

Abby blinked. "Robby, you can tell me."

He fidgeted with the hem of his shirt, then leaned in close, his voice dropping to a whisper as he reached into his backpack and pulled out an old wooden cigar box. "There is something I need to talk to you about, actually. Something important." He took a deep breath. "I don't think my mom's disappearance was an accident."

"Your… mom?" Abby adjusted her glasses. Something about the tone of his voice sent alarm bells ringing in her head. Robby almost never talked about his mom anymore.

He opened the cigar box and handed her a yellowed envelope. "It's a letter from someone agreeing to meet her at Whispering Hill right before she vanished."

"She didn't just *vanish*, Robby. Her car was totaled."

"They never found her body."

Abby bit her lower lip to keep from saying something that might upset him. She carefully opened the envelope and drew out the letter.

"It wasn't an accident," Robby insisted when she'd finished reading. "Someone destroyed my mom's car. Someone with a connection to Whispering Hill." He pointed to the bottom of the page. "Look at the signature. It's the same name as the woman from last night. And she said she'd been there eight years ago."

"Has your dad seen this?"

"I don't know. Maybe." Robby pressed his lips together. "I doubt it, though. When I found the cigar box, it was in with all of Mom's old books. I think he stuffed all her things together to get them out of the way. He was a wreck after she… after it happened."

"It could all just be a coincidence. And the person who wrote the letter seems to have really liked your mom. Don't you think you're making kind of a big leap?"

"Abby, that woman tried to *kill us*. And I saw her again. Just now. In the hallway—"

Abby jumped as something hard thumped into the back of her chair. She twisted to see T-Rex's meaty face grinning at her through a gap in the bookshelf. He disappeared for a second, and then reappeared in front of her. Joey Swett emerged on the other side of the stacks, pinning Abby and Robby between them.

"What's this about?" Abby asked, leaping to her feet.

Robby shook his head as he stood. "No idea."

Joey gripped her by the arm and yanked her away from their table. She thrashed and kicked at him, but he was stronger, and she hadn't expected him to grab her. His breath reeked like skunk as he leaned in. "T-Rex wants to have a talk with Robby about his new lab partner."

"Stop it, Joey."

Joey's grip tightened. His hands were cool and clammy around her wrists. Thin beads of sweat glistened above his lip under the fluorescent glow of the overhead lights.

"You're hurting me!"

Robby glared at Joey. "Leave her alone."

T-Rex pushed Robby against one of the bookshelves, then jammed his forearm under Robby's chin to pin him there. "You should take your own advice. Leave the new girl alone."

"What did you say?"

"You heard me. Just because your dad made you lab partners doesn't mean—"

"Do you... even... know her name?" Robby said, struggling under T-Rex's weight.

T-Rex's eyes narrowed. "I'll find out."

"Are you *kidding* me?" Abby demanded. She tried to twist free again, but Joey curled his arm around her throat and hauled her back another step. "You can't just call dibs on girls!"

T-Rex smirked at her. "Wanna bet?"

Robby wriggled free of T-Rex's grip and backed up a step, smoothing his collar as he stood to his full height. "Something tells me you're not her type, anyway."

It was probably the bravest thing Abby had ever heard her best friend say. Also, the stupidest. T-Rex shoved him into the bookcase again, this time harder. Robby grunted in surprise and wobbled as he tried to keep upright.

Abby tried to imagine what Amethyst would do. Cast some

kind of spell? But how? She tried to channel the sensation she'd felt when she was flying the night before, but it was like grasping for a word she couldn't quite remember.

Instead, she slammed the heel of her left sneaker into Joey's shin with all the force of eight years of soccer practices behind it. He stumbled back. When T-Rex's eyes flicked in her direction, Robby punched him in the face, knocking the bully off-balance. T-Rex's lower lip was already swelling by the time he hit the floor.

Robby gaped at his hand. His knuckles were bleeding.

"I can't believe you just did that!" Abby said, rushing to his side.

Robby flexed his fingers. He looked like he couldn't believe what he'd just done, either.

Olivia Edwards squeezed into the narrow space between the shelves, followed by Sarika Swann and a bunch of other classmates. Sarika snapped a picture of T-Rex sprawled on the floor. Ms. Bancroft, the vice principal, elbowed her way to the front of the crowd, the tip of her nose a dark shade of crimson. "You," she said, pointing at T-Rex, "to the nurse's office. Immediately. Joey, go with him."

T-Rex glared at Robby and whispered something under his breath as he pushed his way to his feet and out of the room.

Robby shoved his bloody hand inside his pocket. "We were just sitting here when they came up and—"

"My office. Now."

"But *he* pushed me!"

"Now, young man."

Sarika thrust her phone in front of the vice principal's face. "Robby punched him. I have it all right here."

"But I didn't start it!" Robby protested.

As Abby tried to follow, Ms. Bancroft turned back with a sharp glare. "I'll speak with you separately."

"But Ms. Bancroft!"

The vice principal glanced at her watch and then returned her gaze to Abby. "We can have that discussion after school unless you quiet down right now, Miss Shepherd."

Abby stared helplessly as Robby gathered up his things and followed Ms. Bancroft out of the stacks. She caught a glimpse of Becca standing beside Olivia and Sarika, a strange expression on her face as she watched Robby leaving the library.

7

A Mystery at Mrs. Vickory's

"**O**uch!" Robby grimaced, flexing his fingers, then raised his hand to show Tina. "Do you think I broke anything?"

"Can you move your fingers?" she asked without taking her eyes off the road. It had been Tina, not his father, who'd finally come to get him after an hour and a half in Ms. Bancroft's office. Most of the kids passing the big fishbowl window had gawked and laughed. Becca came by twice—once with Olivia and Sarika, who snapped a picture of him sitting there, and later on her way to another class.

He wiggled his fingers. "Yeah, I can move them. But they hurt."

"Then they're not broken."

"Do I need a tetanus shot or anything?" he asked. "Rabies? I cut my hand on his teeth."

Tina put on her turn signal and pulled over to the side of the road. She was chuckling as she turned to face him.

"What?" he asked.

"Give me your hand." Her fingers were soft and sure as she pulled at the tender skin. "That boy has sharp teeth. No wonder they call him T-Rex."

"Do I need to see a doctor?"

"I am a doctor."

"You're a veterinarian."

"It's basically the same thing. You'll be fine. You had a tetanus shot. Let's just hope you didn't break any of that boy's teeth. I don't think your father wants to pay for Tommy Rexman's dental work."

"I don't think he'll be happy no matter what I do."

Tina raised her right eyebrow conspiratorially. "Can you keep a secret?"

"Sure."

"Your dad's proud of you."

"He is not."

Tina touched Robby's hand again. "You shouldn't have punched Tommy Rexman. Obviously, we don't condone that. But if anyone ever had it coming, it was that boy… and from what I hear, *he* started it. You were sticking up for yourself. Believe me, your father knows that."

"If you say so," Robby muttered.

"I do." Tina held his gaze. "That doesn't explain why you're suddenly getting into fights and skipping curfew, though."

When Robby didn't say anything, she flashed the turn signal again and pulled back onto the road.

Finally, he said, "Can I ask you a question?"

"Anything at all. You know that."

"How do you know if you like someone? I mean, *like-like* them."

The corners of Tina's mouth turned up. "Is all this about a girl?"

"Maybe."

"I never meant to fall in love with your father, you know. That wasn't part of the plan. But knowing how I felt about him was the easy part. It was harder to put myself out there. I'm sure

it was the same for him. He'll always love your mother, and I—
Well, I'm a bit older than your dad." She laughed. "You'll always find reasons *not* to take that leap if you look for them. Do
you know if this girl likes you?"

Robby's cheeks burned. "I think so."

"Then what's the problem?"

"Apparently T-Rex is interested in her, too."

"And suddenly it all makes sense." Tina was still chuckling
as she pulled into the driveway. "Now I'm having my own flash-
backs to middle school."

"I'm supposed to study with her tomorrow night. I thought it
might be okay with Dad because it's school-related, but that was
before I got into a fight."

"How about this," Tina said. "Promise not to get into any
more trouble?"

Robby met her eyes and nodded.

"All right." She cut the engine. "I'll see what I can do about
your study date."

Robby pulled the hood of his sweatshirt over his head as he left
his house the next morning. A stiff breeze bent the trees that
lined the muddy path through the woods, carrying with it the
scent of the ocean. He'd just reached the point where the Hollows trail intersected with the steep climb to the Heights when a
twig snapped nearby. He stopped and peered into the bushes, half
expecting T-Rex to jump out for round two.

"Psssst."

Robby's breath misted as he squinted into the shadows, and
then Zeus's dark face materialized through the branches of a
weeping hemlock. Robby let out a deep breath. "Why are you

hiding in there?"

"Pretend you can't see me," Zeus whispered. "Act casual and come in here."

"What's going on?"

"Just do it, Robby."

Robby scurried under a low branch before stumbling into a small shadowy grove at the foot of the hill. A football helmet and a bag full of shoulder and knee pads lay beside a rock.

Zeus craned his head over Robby's shoulder, scanning the trail again as if he were expecting someone else. "Where's Abby?"

"I haven't talked to her today."

Zeus rubbed his temples. "I just assumed she'd be with you. She's always with you." He turned his gaze back to the trail, then shook his head.

"Why all the secrecy?" Robby asked.

"I'll get in trouble if anyone sees us talking. Dad says you're a bad influence."

"Me?"

"Breaking curfew. Picking fights."

"I didn't start that fight. How did you hear about it, anyway?"

"Sarika sent a picture of T-Rex's bloody lip to the whole class."

Robby sighed. "I'm really dead now."

"What was he so mad about, anyway?"

"It's stupid."

"What was it?"

"Did you meet the new girl yet?" Robby flexed his fingers. His hand still hurt.

Zeus tilted his head. "Does he think you like her?"

"I *do* like her. At least, I think I do. We're supposed to meet up tonight, actually. Tina got my dad to relax my punishment as long as I go check on Mrs. Vickory. She wasn't at school yesterday and Tina wants to make sure her cat's okay."

Zeus frowned. "Mrs. Vickory is the worst. She gave me a bad grade on a test last week because she doesn't like my handwriting."

"My dad says she was mean back when he had her for history. And that was thirty years ago." Robby glanced at Zeus's football equipment. "Shouldn't you be at practice?"

"I'm thinking of skipping." He shrugged. "I don't really like football."

"But you're so good at it."

"That doesn't mean I enjoy it. No one on the team even talks to me."

"*Someone* must talk to you."

"Coach does. But he mostly yells."

"You don't have any friends on the team?"

Zeus mumbled something under his breath.

"What?"

Zeus swallowed and kicked at the pile of leaves at his feet. "I said sometimes it feels like I don't have any friends, *period.*" He plunged his hands into his pockets, no longer meeting Robby's eyes. "That's why I come here. It's easier to forget how lonely I am when I'm exploring the old caves, I guess."

Robby followed Zeus's gaze to a thin, dark gap splitting the bedrock of the hill. He felt the color rising in his cheeks and neck. Zeus didn't have *any* friends? That couldn't be possible. Robby stared down at his hands, his mouth going dry. Finally, he said, "You have friends."

"Name one."

"*We're* friends."

"We used to be friends. Now we're just… friendly."

"That's not—"

"When was the last time we hung out?"

Robby scrunched his nose. "I don't remember."

"Yeah, because it was like two years ago."

"Because you're always busy with football!" Robby said defensively.

"You still hang out with Abby all the time, and she plays soccer year-round. Indoor and outdoor, practices twice a week…"

"But she's my neighbor."

"We all used to hang out when we were little, though," Zeus continued. "You, me, Abby—the Three Musketeers. All for one and one for all. Now it's like I'm invisible to everyone." He sighed, then added in a soft voice: "Especially Abby."

"You're not invisible. I just never knew you even wanted to—hold on. What do you mean, *especially* Abby?"

"It doesn't matter."

"Zeus."

"Robby." Zeus plucked a tiny branch from the hemlock and started peeling away the needles. "You went to Whispering Hill together. I know it wasn't just to look around. Nobody goes there just to look around."

"Is that why you told your dad you'd seen us?"

"I didn't tell." Zeus's shoulders drooped. "Fine, maybe I did. But you were out really late. Dad asked if I'd seen you and it just kind of came out."

"I talked Abby into going with me, but not for *that* reason."

Zeus's expression softened. "Swear?"

"Swear. You know you could have told me you like her."

"I get all tongue-tied around her these days. She probably thinks I'm an idiot. And it's not like I have a chance anyway." He kicked a few pebbles. "I should probably get to practice. Someone will tell my dad if I skip."

"Wait! Let's hang out sometime." Robby considered the terms of his punishment and shook his head. "When I'm not grounded anymore, I mean."

Zeus grinned, then tilted his head toward the shadowy opening. "How about now? I know a shortcut to Mrs. Vickory's house. It's on the way to practice."

The light from Zeus's phone made the ice along the narrow cave walls glint like diamonds. Robby hugged his arms to his chest, sometimes hunching, sometimes squeezing through tight spaces, as they traveled through the twists and turns. Zeus pointed out where the passage split off into two paths, one leading toward the old lighthouse and the other to the center of town.

"I knew there were supposed to be caves in the Hollows," Robby said, breathing into his hands for warmth, "but nothing like this." Most caves formed in limestone, not the kind of granite found in the northeast. These tunnels were more like jagged fissures in the bedrock, though, pushed and prodded and shaped by the weight of a million tons of loose dirt and rocks. Even if they'd originally formed from some kind of erosive process, something about the scale of them made Robby wonder if they were entirely natural. Shaking his head, he said to Zeus, "How did you find all these tunnels?"

"Like I said, I get lonely." Zeus adjusted his equipment bag and then pointed the light toward a small gap up ahead. "This is the way out."

They clambered through a small opening of sharp, toothy rocks at the base of the hill behind Mrs. Vickory's house on the outskirts of town. Robby hadn't been out this way much—there weren't many other houses around—but he couldn't believe he'd never noticed the cave. It was well hidden, though. Even now as he peered back through a patch of scraggly trees casting shadows at odd, windblown angles, he had to squint to find the opening he'd just come from.

He pushed past a brittle pine tree and stopped. Mrs. Vickory's old Victorian had always reminded him of its owner—stern and gray, with two small murky windows cut into the slate roof like vacant eyes. But today, shattered glass littered the yard, and the back door hung crookedly from its bottom hinge. A wrought iron weather vane jutted out of the ground not far from the door, as if it had popped from the top of the house like a cork before crashing back to earth. The smell of ozone grew stronger as they approached the porch, like the air after a lightning strike. Robby couldn't help thinking about the police report from his mother's accident. The first responders had called it a "spontaneous atmospheric abnormality."

Zeus fumbled for his phone.

"I'm going inside," Robby said, brushing past.

"What? No, bad idea. This looks dangerous. I should call my dad."

"Mrs. Vickory might still be in there." Robby shouted her name as he reached the porch and pulled on the back door. It fell to the ground with a thud. He peered into the darkness. "Is anyone here? Mrs. Vickory? Hello?"

There was no answer. Robby inched into the kitchen and cracked the shutters to let in more light. The contents of the refrigerator had spilled onto the linoleum floor. A toaster, smashed to bits, added to the mess. The house groaned as Zeus stepped inside. "What do you think could have caused this?" he asked.

"Spontaneous atmospheric abnormality," Robby said under his breath.

Hazy black dust shimmered in the sunlight cutting through the kitchen window. Robby's throat felt itchy just looking at it. He covered his nose and mouth with the collar of his shirt and then flicked the light switch. Nothing happened.

In the living room, Mrs. Vickory's ancient television lay shattered. A toppled bookcase spilling dozens of blackened books across the floor barred the way upstairs. Here, too, everything was coated in black dust.

"Better make that call to your dad now," Robby said. The

tickle in the back of his throat grew stronger. He pulled his shirt tighter over his face as he kicked a few books aside, then tried to shove the bookcase with the other arm.

"Robby…"

"I'm just going to have a quick look upstairs."

"No, Robby, I think—" Zeus coughed. "I think I found something." He knelt beside a couch that looked as if it had been blown halfway across the room. In one hand, he held an old book, blackened around the edges. With the other, he pointed at the floor, where scorch marks stretched across the hardwood in a way that vaguely suggested arms and legs flung out at wild angles.

Robby took in the source of the black dust—a thick pile of ashes near the middle of the scorched area. He crossed the room and knelt beside Zeus to get a better look. "You don't think it's…" he began, but before he could finish the question, he sneezed, and ash flew everywhere.

Then something upstairs moved.

Zeus started violently and tugged at Robby's shirt. "We need to go. Now."

"There could be someone up there."

"That's what I'm afraid of!"

Robby returned to the bookcase. It wasn't just leaning against the doorway, like he'd thought before. It was lodged in the frame. "Hey, come give me a hand."

"Are you crazy?" Zeus stole another glance at his phone, then looked up at Robby, eyes wide. "The police—"

"—might get here too late if someone needs help up there."

With both of them pushing, the bookcase moved more easily. Robby took a deep breath through his shirt and climbed into the darkness toward the second floor, Zeus following close behind. They felt their way along the walls until they reached an upstairs window. Robby cracked the shutters to let in more light, revealing a long narrow hallway with three doors, all firmly shut.

He carefully opened each one and peered inside.

Bookcases lined the walls of the first room. A few books had fallen onto a worn leather chair near the door and a few more were scattered across the hardwood floor. A bathroom and a bedroom accounted for the other doors. They, too, were empty.

"Satisfied?" Zeus asked.

Robby shook his head. Something about the second floor seemed off. He retraced his steps to be sure he hadn't missed another stairway. If the back steps were on that end, and the carriage road was over there, then the attic should be right about… "Here," he said, stepping back into the library and scanning the ceiling. The faint outline of a hatch caught his eye. He scraped the leather chair into the middle of the room and rested a foot on each armrest for balance.

"For the record, I've got a bad feeling about this," Zeus said, even as he helped steady the chair.

Robby traced the outline of the hatch until he found a nook big enough to curl his fingers inside. He pulled, and a built-in ladder sprang free from the overhead door, nearly beheading Zeus, who dived away at the last moment as the ladder's legs came to rest on the floor.

Robby got down from the chair and climbed the ladder, cautiously sticking his head through the hatch. Light from two small windows bathed the attic in a soft glow. Dusty books and stacks of yellowed newspapers lined the walls. The faint outline of a painted white hexagram was scrawled across the floor. Robby scrambled up the rest of the way to get a closer look.

"What is this place?" he whispered as Zeus joined him. Portraits of middle school-aged kids covered nearly every spare inch of wall space above the newspaper piles. Newer photos, still shiny, had been tacked to the far wall. "That's our class."

Zeus squinted. "Not the whole class."

"Just the girls," Robby realized. He fought back another sneeze and then unpinned a photo of Abby that had been circled in red ink. Five other photos had been circled, too. He pocketed Abby's picture before turning back to Zeus. "Now you should *definitely* call the police."

But another photo caught his eye. He wiped away the grime to make sure his mind wasn't playing tricks on him. Two women smiled out of the shot. One looked like a younger Mrs. Vickory.

The other was his mother.

THUMP!

Robby jumped. Books and newspapers tumbled to the floor. He quickly stuffed the picture of his mother and Mrs. Vickory into his back pocket next to Abby's before turning to see if Zeus was okay.

"It's coming from over there!" yelled Zeus, backpedaling toward the ladder. "We need to get out of here, *right now*."

Robby scanned the room again. Back near the windows he saw another door. As Zeus protested, Robby turned the handle. Two small yellow eyes stared back at him from the darkness. Robby sneezed.

"What do you see?" Zeus whispered.

"Achilles."

"Bless you."

"No, that's his name. Achilles. He's Mrs. Vickory's cat. He's—" The animal croaked weakly and ducked back a step. One of his ears looked singed around the edges. "I think he might be hurt. We'd better bring him to Tina." Robby scooped Achilles inside his jacket. "We can call your dad on the way."

8

The Witch Doctor

R obby had never seen Tina's clinic so busy. Pets of all stripes mewed, barked, and cawed as he and Zeus pushed their way through the midmorning rush to the front desk. He placed his jacket on the counter in front of Piper Finch, an owlish girl with dark skin and springy black curls. Piper was the same age as Robby and Zeus, and usually volunteered in the back room with Tina, but today it looked like she'd been pressed into emergency duty out front.

Two older women manned the phones and computers on either side of Piper. Robby buried his face in the crook of his elbow and stifled a sneeze.

"Do you have an appointment?" Piper asked.

"I need to see Tina."

Piper looked up and adjusted her glasses, which made her already big eyes look like two white eggs. She brushed a puff of hair from her face and smiled. "Hi, Robby!"

"Uh, hi."

Piper blinked at him.

"I need to see—"

"I heard what you did to T-Rex," she said. "Did it feel good? I bet it felt amazing."

"It kind of hurt, actually. He's got a hard head. Empty, but hard."

She giggled. "You're funny." She reached below the counter, retrieved her asthma inhaler, and took a big puff. "And brave."

"Is Tina free?" he asked.

Piper's hands flipped absently through the pages of the schedule book, but her eyes never left Robby's. "She might be able to see you in"—she glanced at the clock—"an hour, maybe?"

"She's my stepmother, Piper. I don't need an appointment."

"You do today." She shrugged. "We're shorthanded. That's why I'm stuck working the front desk, which I'm definitely *not* supposed to do. Something about child labor laws?"

"Piper, I need to see her now."

"Maybe in half an hour?"

Robby adjusted his jacket until two fluffy black ears poked out. Achilles let loose a weak meow, more like a croak.

Piper glanced at the cat's singed ear, then again at Robby, who sneezed.

Achilles scooted into Piper's arms. "Are you all right?"

"We're fine."

"I meant the cat. What happened?"

Robby and Zeus exchanged a glance. "Are you asking us or the cat?" Robby said, raising an eyebrow.

"You."

"The police are involved," Zeus said.

Piper seemed to notice him for the first time. "Wait, where's Abby?"

Zeus tossed his hands in the air. "See? Invisible!"

"I haven't seen her today," Robby said.

"She was supposed to be here an hour ago so I could help with the séance."

"Séance?" asked Zeus.

"It attracts a lot of tourists from Salem," Robby explained. "Piper, please. I need to talk to Tina now." His eyes were welling up again. Another sneeze was imminent.

She studied him for another second and then nodded. "Tina should be finishing up with Mrs. Fickles soon."

Robby and Zeus followed Piper to the back area where a few of the clinic's exam rooms had been set aside for pet séances and paw readings. She took Achilles into one of the rooms and closed the door behind her.

Zeus's phone vibrated. He mouthed "my dad" as he hunched away to take the call.

Robby picked up a dog biscuit from a bowl sitting next to the door. It was flat and thin, like a tarot card, and it had a gibbous moon etched into one side and Roman numerals on the other. Tina baked them at home on weekends.

As he twirled the biscuit between his fingers, his mind wandered to the photo of his mother and Mrs. Vickory. They'd both been history teachers at the middle school, and now Mrs. Vickory had disappeared, just like his mom. A line from the mysterious letter nagged at him. *Not even your new mentor understands the why of it as you do.* Could Mrs. Vickory have been his mom's mentor?

The door creaked open again, and Piper stuck her head into the hallway. "Just another minute."

"We need to give an official statement later," Zeus told Robby as soon as he finished his call. "Dad says we shouldn't have gone inside Mrs. Vickory's house, but he's glad we rescued the cat. And that we found that room."

"What room?" asked Piper.

Robby and Zeus exchanged a glance. "Forget about it." Robby remembered Piper's picture had been pasted on Mrs. Vickory's wall. It had been circled, too.

Piper moved aside as an elderly woman and her cockapoo stepped into the hallway followed by Tina. For a split second,

Robby thought he read panic on her face. She scribbled a few words onto a slip of paper and handed it to Piper. "Please see them out."

Piper frowned. "Can't I stay?"

"Another time, I promise."

"But you promised *today*!"

"I know, Piper. I'm sorry. Next time, for sure."

Tina motioned Robby and Zeus into the examination room and closed the door. It took a moment for Robby's eyes to adjust to the dim glow of the candles, which provided the only light. Tina retrieved Achilles from a couch against the far wall. He'd been lounging there patiently. Robby sneezed, covered his face with his shirt, and then quickly pulled it away. The fabric was black with ash.

"Please sit," Tina told them, motioning to the puffy red cushions that circled a small table on which a crystal ball rested. She clapped her hands, and overhead lights flickered to life. Then she blew out the candles, cleared a spot on the table for Achilles, and sat. In the light, Robby could see how Achilles had gotten his name; he was all black except for one white spot just behind his back left paw—his Achilles' heel.

"What happened?" Tina asked the cat. Achilles mewed excitedly. Tina nodded, inspecting his singed ear.

Zeus elbowed Robby. "Is this normal?"

"Normal for Tina."

"The good news is Achilles will be fine." Tina stroked the cat under the chin. "Now let's hear your version, boys."

"I went to check on Mrs. Vickory like you asked—"

"The whole house looked—"

"One at a time. Robby, you first."

"It looked like there'd been a struggle. Maybe even an explosion. Black dust was everywhere." He held up his hand to show off his darkened fingertips. "We found Achilles upstairs."

"There's a secret room in the attic," Zeus added. "Pictures of girls hanging everywhere."

"Headshots," Robby said. "Yearbook photos, I think. Thousands of them, including girls from our class at school."

Tina glanced at Achilles, who bobbed his head before turning his attention to cleaning his tail. "Did it look as if anyone else had been in that room recently?" Tina asked the boys. "Anyone who didn't belong there, I mean."

"It wasn't disturbed like the rest of the house."

"Well, that's one piece of good news, anyway."

"You don't seem surprised," Robby said.

"Not entirely." Tina leaned back on her cushion and surveyed Robby behind her horned rim glasses. "Was Abby with you? She's supposed to be helping out today. When she didn't come in this morning, I wondered if she'd gone looking for you instead. It's been so busy I haven't had a chance to call."

"Abby and I don't do everything together."

Tina lowered her glasses and focused her gaze on Robby. "Well, you were together on Halloween, and I'm beginning to think you haven't told me everything that happened that night."

Zeus shifted in his seat and shot Robby an *I-told-you-so* glare.

"What does any of that have to do with Mrs. Vickory or her cat?"

Tina bit her lip. "It might be best if we continued this conversation alone."

"Zeus can stay."

She considered them both before nodding. "Not a word of this to anyone, then."

"Scout's honor," said Zeus.

"All right, Robby, this is very important. I need to know if you saw anything unusual on Halloween. Anything you didn't want to tell me about before. Maybe something you didn't think I'd believe?"

Robby gulped. "I may have… omitted certain details."

Tina smiled gently. "Which details, exactly?" She reached across the table and placed a hand on his. "I'll believe you."

Robby blinked. "Okay, it's not like—" He glanced at Zeus. "Abby and I did go to Whispering Hill. We didn't *do* anything! But we saw this woman who… sent statues chasing after us. And then we sort of escaped when Abby flew us away on the broomstick you left with her costume."

Zeus laughed, but the sound died in his throat when Tina didn't join in. She'd gone very pale. "Wait, Abby can fly?" he asked.

"Tell me about the woman," said Tina.

Robby closed his eyes. "Dark hair with a streak of gray. Pale skin. About your height. She wore a—"

"—red cloak," finished Tina.

"You know her?"

"This is important. Did she see Abby's face?"

"It was pretty dark, and we were hiding in the bushes, but maybe? It's possible. And then yesterday…"

"There's more?" Tina asked.

"I thought I saw the woman at school. I could have imagined it. It was only for a second, and then she was gone. Tina, who is she?"

Tina pursed her lips. "You need to go home right now. You too, Zeus. Under no circumstances are you to go looking for Abby, do you understand?"

They nodded, although Robby definitely did not understand.

"And Robby? Take Achilles with you. Keep him close. Don't argue," she added when he opened his mouth to protest. "I know you're allergic. It's just for a few hours. I'll explain everything when I get back."

"Back from where? Is Abby in danger?"

"It's nothing to worry about," Tina said, suddenly all practiced cheerfulness. She grabbed her car keys and coat. "Everything's fine, Robby. Everything's just fine."

9

Amethyst's Tale

A bby rapped her knuckles against Amethyst's front door.
No one answered. She glanced at the bike she'd ridden to
Amethyst's propped against the side of a dilapidated
barn, and then at the clock on her phone. She was supposed to be
at the veterinary clinic, so this would have to be a quick visit—
assuming Amethyst was even home.

She knocked again, louder this time.

There was a noise on the other side of the door. Abby peered
in through a dirty window and found two big eyes and a wet
snout pressed up against the glass. Then another pair of eyes appeared, these decidedly more human, and the door clicked open.

"Stay, Spooks, *stay*!" commanded Amethyst as something
small and furry rocketed through the open door and raced down
the front steps. It scurried toward the barn, disappearing inside a
small hole in the side wall.

"That's a raccoon!" Abby said, more to herself than Amethyst.

"His name is Spooks." Amethyst craned her neck over Abby's shoulder. She kept the door opened a crack. "He's excited
we have company, even though I told him you're not staying."

Abby looked from Amethyst to the barn and back again. "You live with a rodent?"

"He's not a rodent! He's a Procyon."

"A what?"

"A nocturnal mammal, just like me. He's usually better behaved than this. I think he's showing off for you."

Abby tried to peek into the house. "Are there any more in there?"

"No, it's just me and Spooks."

"Your grandfather lets you have a raccoon?"

"I said it's just me and Spooks. My grandfather died two months ago."

Abby gaped at her. She listened for another voice inside the house, any kind of movement, some sign that Amethyst was messing with her. "Who takes care of you?" she finally asked.

Amethyst snorted. "I do."

"Does anyone know?" Abby took a tentative step toward the doorway. "My mom works in social services—"

"Another reason you won't be coming inside."

"—and I literally cannot stand to be in her presence at the moment. The last thing I want is to have a conversation with her about your grandfather. Or why I came here."

"Why *did* you come? I said not to."

"And I said we need to talk."

"I don't have anything else to say."

Abby shoved her foot into the doorframe just as Amethyst tried to shut it. "Then I'll do the talking," she said as she swung her backpack off her shoulder and propped it against her hip to unzip it. Amethyst watched with practiced indifference as Abby lifted out a list of names she'd spent all night assembling and thrust it at her. Amethyst eyed the crumpled piece of paper as if she'd just been handed an unexpected homework assignment.

"What's this?"

"A list of potentials."

"Potential what?"

"Witches. People like us. I don't think we're the only girls in this town who have powers."

Amethyst passed the list back to Abby. "Something in the water?"

"The blood, actually. At least that's my theory." Abby returned the list to her backpack and retrieved the spiral-bound notebook she used for history class. "Last night, I started thinking about what you and I have in common that would make us both, you know... witches." Her voice trembled as she spoke the last word aloud. She hoped Amethyst didn't notice. "Then I remembered the genealogy project we did for Mrs. Vickory in September." She pointed to the family tree she'd sketched in her notebook. "You and I share the *same* ancestor. And we're not the only ones. Maybe it doesn't mean anything, but what if it does?"

Amethyst stared at Abby for a long time without saying anything.

Abby stuffed the notebook back in her school bag and waited. If Amethyst were still even a little like the girl Abby remembered from grade school, she wouldn't be able to resist a puzzle like this.

Finally, Amethyst stepped back and cracked open the door. "Are you coming in or not?"

Inside, cobwebs stretched across the ceiling while a breeze whistled through the cracks in the walls. "Home sweet home," Amethyst said as she led Abby up the steep stairs to the second floor. Another set of stairs brought them to a door with a handmade sign that read ABANDON HOPE ALL YE WHO ENTER in purple glitter glue.

"You really live here all alone?"

"I'm *not* alone. I have Spooks. He's an orphan, too."

Abby hesitated. "How did your grandfather die?"

"Natural causes. I would never hurt him. I loved my grandfather. I just don't need some nosy adults coming here and telling me what I can and can't do. Spooks and I are fine by ourselves." The tone of her voice practically dared Abby to disagree.

"But where did you bury the—never mind," Abby said when Amethyst scowled. "How do you afford to eat, though? Pay the bills?"

"My grandfather's Social Security check is deposited into an account in both our names. I get by."

Amethyst's bedroom door creaked open. Her long black skirt swirled up dust as she led Abby inside. The grime on the windows didn't let in much light, and every bulb in the room was either broken or caked with cobwebs, but a circle of candles gave off enough light to see by.

An unmade twin bed and a beat-up dresser with a cloudy mirror was shoved against one wall next to a stepladder that led to a rooftop widow's walk. Abby's eyes were drawn to a framed picture of Amethyst's parents and a much younger Amethyst smiling back. It must have been taken after one of her dance recitals. She looked like any other girl back then, with her hair in a bun and a pink tutu around her waist. The only similarity between that Amethyst and the one Abby saw before her now were the eyes, which had always been large and curious.

Amethyst plopped to the floor inside the circle of candles. She elbowed a Ouija board out of the way to make room for Abby. In the dim candlelight, it felt like the middle of the night. Abby pushed her notebook and the list of names across the floor toward Amethyst. Last night she'd felt confident she had worked out the possible connection in her head, but now that she found herself face to face with Amethyst's skeptical expression, a sliver of doubt crept in.

"Our common ancestor's name was Victoria Snow," she said, clearing her throat. "She was born in 1691, a year before the Salem Witch Trials. She was an orphan, so I have no idea who her parents were. That's as far back as I can trace our bloodline. You, me, and about a third of the other kids in our grade are related to her."

Amethyst studied the list. "And you think this is the connection between us?"

"Can you think of anything else we have in common?"

Amethyst laughed. "Point taken." She blew a huge bubble of purple gum, eyes closed in concentration. When it popped, she chewed for another moment and said, "If you're right then I think we can cross off a few of the people on here right now." She whispered something and a pen materialized in her hand. She scratched out three names. "When's Lucinda Walker's birthday?"

"Last month," Abby said. "Why?"

Amethyst scratched out Lucinda's name. "Not a witch."

"How do you know?"

"You turned thirteen on Halloween. I got my powers on my thirteenth birthday, too. I fell from the loft in my barn and thought I was going to break my arm. Instead, I levitated. It's like someone flipped a switch on my birthday and the electricity suddenly came on. I felt that same spark in you the second you walked into the science lab yesterday. But I didn't get that from any of the other girls who've already turned thirteen."

"What spark?"

"You really haven't noticed it?"

Abby shook her head. Amethyst looked disappointed, but she positioned herself so their knees touched. She took both of Abby's hands and leaned forward until their foreheads nearly touched, too. "How about now?"

"Nope," Abby said. "Sorry."

"Concentrate."

Abby closed her eyes. Amethyst's palms were clammy and a little rough. Her knees were like pinpricks of pressure where they met Abby's. Candlewax and burning wicks mingled with the scent of sweat between them, and Abby drifted forward, as if in a trance, until their foreheads met, skin to skin. Amethyst seemed to pulse with life, as if there were somehow *more* to her.

Abby opened her eyes and blinked. Even with the connection broken, she still sensed something had changed. Amethyst's whole body crackled with a kind of purple energy brighter than her hair. The air around her body swelled and subsided in subtle waves, just as it had for a moment in the science lab when she'd made the beakers explode.

"I feel it," Abby whispered. She exhaled deeply. "How?"

Amethyst released Abby's hands. "It's strongest right after you use magic. It starts to fade the longer you go without casting a spell—or riding a broom."

"Like magic residue?"

Amethyst shrugged. "That's my guess."

Abby glanced down at her list again. "There are still a lot of names on here." She borrowed the pen from Amethyst and crossed out the other girls who'd already turned thirteen, then scanned the rest of the list. "Brittany Jennings, Sarika Swann, Shameka Rossi, Ursula Clayton, Olivia Edwards, Daisy and Delphinium Green—wow, those last three all have the same birthday. We're going to be busy that day."

"Doing what?"

"Finding out if they're like us."

Amethyst wrinkled her nose. "I'll admit you're not so bad. I don't actually hate that you came here today. But I don't want anything to do with Sarika Swann or Olivia Edwards even if they *are* like us."

"I'm not exactly the president of their fan club, either. But Sarika's birthday is on Monday. Wouldn't you rather know if she suddenly gets superpowers?"

Amethyst sat, thinking. Finally, she nodded. "I guess."

"Good." Abby bumped Amethyst's knees again, now grinning. "Because I need someone to show me how to do magic. Help me, Obi-Wan Kenobi."

"The first rule," Amethyst said, the barn doors groaning in protest as she pulled them open, "is you have to promise not to tell anyone you came here." Late morning sun filled the building, illuminating a few dozen hay bales stacked in an open semicircle near the entrance. The smells of mud and hay mingled with something that might have been wet paint.

Amethyst took the ladder to the loft two rungs at a time. Abby followed until Amethyst stopped near the top, turned to look at her, and held up one hand. "Not a single word. I don't want anyone figuring out I live alone, and I especially don't want anyone knowing I'm a witch. If you're ever found out, they better not be able to trace it back to me. Promise?"

"Promise," Abby said.

"That includes Robby."

Abby hesitated.

Amethyst narrowed her eyes. "Promise, Abby."

"Fine," Abby said. "I promise."

They found Spooks asleep in the loft. He looked up at them lazily, deemed Abby to be no threat, and lowered his eyelids again. Up close, Abby could see how he'd gotten his name. His face and neck were stark white except for two black patches around his eyes that made it look like someone had poked holes in a sheet, like a ghost.

Amethyst crouched to give him a little scratch, then snapped her fingers. *"Incendere!"* The floor below flickered to life with six tiny flames. In the glow, Abby could see that Amethyst had painted a red hexagram on the ground. One thick candle lit each point.

"Apparently, my mom was into this stuff, too," Amethyst explained. "The hexagram was already there. I just added a fresh coat of paint."

"What's it for?"

"No idea. It looks cool, though." She pointed to a stack of old leather-bound books inside the hexagram. "Those were Mom's, too. I've been doing some reading—that's where I learned most of what I know, which isn't much. You wouldn't believe how many things the books get wrong. The only way to know what's real and what's not is trial and error, so this is where I practice. Want to see something awesome?"

Before Abby could respond, Amethyst yelled, *"Leviosa!"* and she let herself fall backward off the edge of the loft. Abby reached out to grab her, but Amethyst floated away with her arms outstretched and face lit with a satisfied smile. She lay flat on her back six feet above the hexagram like someone relaxing on a pool float, her skirt drooping beneath her like a loose curtain. Abby fought the urge to clap.

"Now you try it."

Abby poked her foot over the edge of the loft and prodded at the air. It all seemed too simple. How could just saying a word make the impossible happen? "Were you speaking Latin?" she asked.

Amethyst nodded. "It means *levitate.* All you have to do is say and think it at the same time. The rest just sort of happens."

Like flying, Abby thought. *I can do this. I've already done it.*

She took a tentative step off the loft, and then pulled back. On Whispering Hill, she'd just reacted, but it was different now that there weren't any monsters chasing her.

"Try it," Amethyst urged.

Abby backed up a step, then another. She sprinted forward

and leapt. Amethyst yelled something, but Abby couldn't make out what. She had just enough time to realize she was falling before she hit the ground, tumbling hard into the hay bales. She rolled onto her back and let out a deep breath.

"You forgot to think about levitating," Amethyst scolded.

Abby sat up, wiggling her fingers and toes. Everything still worked, even if her limbs were screaming. "Someday, we'll laugh about this," she said hopefully.

"I'm already laughing. Try it again."

Abby planted herself in the center of the hexagram and clenched her hands into fists.

"*Leviosa*," she said.

Nothing.

"You've got to picture it," Amethyst urged. "The word itself doesn't matter that much. It's the *idea* of the word and the connection you make in your head between the word and the deed— the visualization of it. You can do it."

Abby closed her eyes and pictured herself hovering above the floor. In her mind's eye she floated face-to-face with Amethyst, wobbling unsteadily in the flickering candlelight.

"That's it," said Amethyst. "Keep going."

The air squished and buckled beneath her. And then it expanded, as if inflating below her. She felt like she was balancing on stilts made of Jell-O. Her eyes snapped open. Amethyst's face was right in front of hers, grinning like a kid on Christmas. Abby took a tentative step with her arms outstretched. The invisible Jell-O stilts moved with her.

Amethyst grabbed Abby's hand. "*Descende*," she whispered, and the pair twirled to the ground like ballerinas until their toes touched the floor. Amethyst curtsied. "All the spells in the books are written in Latin. I think it's supposed to be the common language of magic, but other languages work, too. I tried it with Pig Latin. Same result."

"Is there anything we *can't* do?"

"Oh, sure. Once you master the basics, you realize all the stuff that's still out of reach. Like we can't change our appearance—that's called metamorphic transmogrification, and it's really advanced. I think we'd need a wand for starters, and the books don't talk much about how to get one."

"Well, what do the books talk about then?" Abby peered at the hardbound volumes stacked against one of the hay bales.

"Secrecy. They're all very clear on that point. We don't tell people what we can do."

"Why not?"

"Do the witch trials ring a bell?"

Abby shivered. "People wouldn't—"

"Yes, they would. Do you have any idea how many people still have to hide who they really are? I mean normal people, not even witches. Society hasn't evolved much since the Puritans when you consider it."

"I guess I hadn't thought of it that way."

"You should read this one first," Amethyst said, floating one of the books into Abby's hands. In gilded cursive, the spine read *Principles of Spellcasting.*

Abby's eyes bulged when she saw the author's name. "Agnes F. Vickory. Amethyst, what if that's *our* Mrs. Vickory?"

Amethyst snorted. "That old crone?"

"Well, we should at least ask her. Imagine if there were a real witch to help us figure things out." *One who isn't out to kill us*, Abby added to herself, thinking about the woman from Whispering Hill. "We can check with her on Monday."

"I won't be there on Monday. I only came back to school yesterday to talk to you. I haven't been in much since my grandfather died."

"Doesn't the school ever call?"

Amethyst shrugged. "You think I can't fool Ms. Bancroft?"

"Well, you should come Monday."

They sat next to each other inside the hexagram. Amethyst

watched while Abby flipped through the book, but after a while she picked up another volume. "Here's something you could try," Amethyst said, pointing at a page in a book called *Eighteen Essential Enchantments*. "It's a memory charm."

"Why would I need that?"

Amethyst shrugged. "Make your mom forget she's mad at you?"

"No power in the universe is strong enough to do that."

After a while, Amethyst finally let out a giant yawn, stretching her arms into the air. Abby was feeling stiff, too. She shifted, stretching her neck from side to side. "This is pretty impressive."

"What is?"

"Levitating, lighting candles—you."

Amethyst's cheeks flushed. "I turned thirteen first, that's all. I got a head start. And it's easier to practice when you never go to school." She bowed her head. "You're the one who can already fly."

"I haven't tried it since that first time." Then, tentatively, Abby added, "We could practice some of this together after school next week if you want."

"I guess that would be all right."

If her stomach hadn't let out a very loud rumble, Abby wouldn't have noticed the day slipping away. She checked her phone again, but the battery had died. "I should have been at the veterinary clinic hours ago. I volunteer there sometimes."

Amethyst looked at her sideways. "You haven't changed at all since we were little."

"Have too."

"Not too much, I hope." Amethyst cleared her throat. "Which one are you reading now?"

Abby tilted the book in Amethyst's direction—*Crowley's Compendium of Creepy Creatures*.

"Oh, yeah, *that* one. Don't read it before bed. It'll give you nightmares." She whistled until Spooks appeared, scurrying down the ladder and into her lap. She scratched his chin. "Lunch time. Which reminds me, you'll get hungry after spellcasting. Like, ravenous. And your whole body will hurt. Most mornings I wake up feeling like I have the flu."

"I didn't feel so great after I flew, now that you mentioned it," Abby said. "I thought it might be because I crashed." She leaned in, drawing her eyebrows together. "You're sure you're okay out here?"

"Why wouldn't I be?"

"You don't get lonely?"

"Because it's just me and Spooks?"

"Yeah, there's that. And…"

"And because I don't have any friends at school?"

"I wasn't going to say that."

"Then what were you going to say?"

"I don't know. You act like you don't *want* any friends at school."

"Everyone wants friends. I'm just not going to change who I am to get them. This is me. This is what I look like. This is how I dress. Take it or leave it."

"You make it sound so simple."

Amethyst laughed. "It is simple, Abby."

"My mom would freak if I had purple hair or dressed like you."

"Score another point for me, then," said Amethyst, but this time her smile looked more forced.

"Speaking of, I really should go. My mom will be furious if she finds out I ditched the clinic. Mind if I borrow this one?" She held up a thin Latin dictionary called *Words for Witches*. Amethyst nodded, so Abby stuffed it into her backpack along with *Whither, Witchcraft?* and *Witches, Witchcraft, and You*. She looked up at Amethyst. "You're wrong, by the way."

"About what?"

"About not having any friends at school."

"Yeah?"

"See you Monday?"

"Monday," Amethyst repeated, as if it were the sweetest word in the English language.

10

Hex-Mex

There was frost on the car when Robby climbed in later that evening. As his father scraped ice from the windshield, Robby squinted into the mirror above his seat, smoothing his hair in the dim light. His rusty curls stuck out at wild angles, but at least his eyes had stopped swelling now that he'd stowed Mrs. Vickory's cat in the attic with a blanket and a bowl of dry food.

His father tapped on the steering wheel as he drove toward Hex-Mex. Robby would have preferred going with Tina, but she still wasn't home from wherever she'd raced off to after leaving the clinic. He fidgeted with the zipper on his backpack in silence as his dad pulled up to the curb.

The more Robby replayed his conversation with Becca, the more he worried she might have changed her mind. She'd barely met anyone at school when she'd suggested they study together. Since then, he'd managed to get into a fight *and* sent home from school. He wouldn't blame her if she decided not to come.

Mr. O'Reilly shifted the car into park, and Robby made a show of searching his bag for the pencil and notebook he knew were already there. "Thanks for the ride," he finally said, scooting out.

His father leaned toward the passenger side. "See you at nine-thirty."

"Hex-Mex closes at ten."

"All right." His father's face softened into a smile. "Ten it is. And Robby?"

"Yeah?"

"Relax, buddy."

Am I that obvious?

A wart-nosed witch in a crooked sombrero grinned down from the sign above the door. Robby pushed his way inside, elbowing through a group of girls and heading toward the back of the café, where Becca was sitting on a couch next to Olivia and Sarika. T-Rex hovered nearby, laughing at his own joke. Becca wilted to one side as T-Rex leaned in to whisper something in her ear.

"Robby, thank God!" she said when their eyes met. She leapt up and crossed the distance between them so fast that T-Rex found himself sputtering to an empty seat. A murmur swept through the café as guests looked up from their drinks.

The room grew quiet as T-Rex approached Robby and Becca.

Instinctively, Robby closed his hand into a fist. It screamed painfully back at him.

"I thought I told you—" T-Rex began.

Becca straightened to her full height. "I heard about what you told him." She stood on her tiptoes and poked T-Rex in the chest. "I barely know you, and I can already tell you're the most vile excuse for a human being I've ever met in my life."

Joey materialized at T-Rex's side. "You just need more time to appreciate his charms."

"I've had more than enough of his charms." Becca grabbed Robby's hand. "I saved you a seat."

As Becca led Robby through the crowd, T-Rex slammed the

door on his way out of the restaurant. "That boy has been my shadow since the minute he got back from the nurse's office yesterday," she said. "He's in *all* my classes. I couldn't believe it when he showed up here, too. I've tried ignoring him, humoring him, reasoning with him. Everything except... *telling him off*."

They settled onto the couch next to Olivia Edwards, who rolled her eyes at Robby and then returned her attention to her phone. Becca slid close enough that their legs touched. She pulled out her science textbook, laying it half on her own lap, half on Robby's.

"So, I was going over the assigned chapter before you got here, and it turns out I'm not as far behind as I—" A scrap of paper fell to the floor as she flipped through the book's pages. Robby scooped it up just as Becca tried to yank it away. "Oh no," she said, her face suddenly flushed.

"What's this?" Robby asked.

Becca buried her face in her hands. "I didn't realize that was still in there."

Robby blinked as he took in a perfect likeness of his face. "You drew this?"

"You weren't supposed to see it."

"It's really good."

Becca hesitated. "I sketched it after you left school yesterday."

"Why?"

Olivia groaned and clicked off her phone. "I thought you were supposed to be smart. She thinks you're cute. Don't ask me why." Then she stood and marched off like she couldn't get away from them fast enough.

Becca's face was frozen in a half smile.

"You think I'm cute?"

She winced. "Sorry."

"I think you're cute, too. I mean, actually you're"—he swallowed— "you're really pretty."

She tilted her head. "Am not."

"You'll just have to take my word for it." He grinned. "So, what do we do now?"

Becca sank back into the couch and let out a deep breath. "We could get to know each other?"

"Mom moved her real estate business to Massachusetts a few years ago," Becca explained. "I was living with my dad in Wisconsin until last week."

"Why the change?"

"He started a new job in September and had to move for work, and Mom finally won custody." Becca shrugged. "And voilà, here I am. This is my third school this year."

"How do you like it so far?"

Becca smiled. "It's definitely been the most eventful."

She turned so they were facing each other. Robby counted the freckles on her cheeks and studied the tiny birthmark just beneath her bottom lip. His heart racing, he trailed his fingers across the fabric of the couch between them, only stopping once his hand found hers. He caught her gaze. She smiled and squeezed his hand in return.

A blinding flash lit the room, and Robby's eyes shot open as Sarika whipped her phone back into her purse, grinning at them like a paparazzo. "It's too dark in here without the flash," she said. "As you were."

"What are you *doing*?" Robby and Becca asked at the same time.

"Spreading the news, obviously."

Sarika drifted back into the crowd before Robby could think of a response. Becca fumbled for her books, avoiding eye con-

tact. Then Robby heard his dad calling his name over the din of
the room and glanced at the clock—just 9:30.

"We agreed on ten!" he pointed out as his father made his
way over, but his anger died as he saw his father's face. His eyes
were wet and red-rimmed. His skin had lost all its color.

"What's wrong, Dad?"

"It's Tina."

Robby sat up. Becca reached for his hand, wrapping her fingers around his.

"I found her car. The police, they didn't—" His father
stopped and took a deep breath. "She's missing. Her car is totaled and she's missing." He didn't have to say the rest. They
both knew it.

Just like Mom.

11

Secrets and Lies

Early Sunday morning, Abby was holding her soccer ball in one hand and Amethyst's Latin dictionary in the other as she squinted at the writing in the dim light. "*Verto*, soccer ball." Her whole body shook from the force of her concentration, and then there it was—a small tug of friction as the ball started to rotate in her palm. It got easier every time she tried the spell.

She knew it wouldn't be fair to use magic in a soccer game, but she couldn't help thinking about the bend she could put on her corner kick. She was fantasizing about scoring the winning goal as the sun peeked through her window and the smell of coffee wafted up from the kitchen. She floated the ball back to the corner, stopping it above her cleats and shin guards, where it hovered like a small moon.

Witchcraft, she thought. *Flying brooms and magic spells, just like in the stories.* None of it felt quite real just yet, but the proof was right there in front of her, suspended a few inches above her soccer gear.

At least she wasn't alone. That was the thing she kept coming back to—the relief over finding someone else like her. Amethyst had already gone through the confusion of discovering she was a witch and come out the other side.

And somehow Amethyst had managed it all by herself.

Voices from downstairs shook Abby from her thoughts. It was too early for her mother to be expecting anyone, not that she would have mentioned it to Abby, anyway. Not since the blow up yesterday after Abby had arrived late to the veterinary clinic and found it already closed for the afternoon. She'd been hungry, so she'd ridden her bike to Hex-Mex and then, with nowhere else to go, she'd wandered around a few shops. How was she supposed to know Tina would call her mother looking for her?

So now she was in trouble again. And just as Amethyst had warned, she was starving again, too. So hungry she felt sick to her stomach—not to mention achy all over. That settled it. She dropped the soccer ball to the floor, clicked open her door, and peered into the hallway.

"Oh no," Abby heard her mother cry from somewhere downstairs. "Last night?"

Abby moved to the top of the stairs. In the kitchen, the visitor seemed to be doing most of the talking. She heard her name, and then recognized the voice—Mr. O'Reilly. Before she could decide whether or not to go downstairs to see what was going on, Robby appeared in the hallway looking tired and rumpled, as if he'd slept in his clothes.

She retreated a few steps as he climbed the stairs, holding her door open for him. "I didn't think my mom would let you come over here again."

He sank onto her bed. Up close, she could see he'd been crying. "Robby, are you okay?"

He shook his head. "Tina's gone."

"What? Where did she—"

"She left the clinic looking for you yesterday after…" He sniffled and then cleared his throat. "Something happened at Mrs. Vickory's house. I found her cat alone and was bringing him to Tina. She asked me about Halloween, and I told her about us going to Whispering Hill and the woman in red, the chimeras and the flying—all of it. And she *believed* me. Then, she looked really worried and said she had to find you right away. That was the last time I saw her. But Dad found her car late last night." He swallowed. "Where were you?"

Amethyst's voice came to her unbidden. *Promise you won't tell.*

"I went—" She hesitated. It was Robby. What would be the harm?

Promise, Abby.

"—to Hex-Mex," she said, wincing a little bit. "Then I did go to the clinic, only the place was already locked up for the day. Why was she looking for me?"

Robby's jaw was set in a way that told her he didn't entirely believe her. He pulled a crumpled photograph from his back pocket and held it up for her to see.

"That's me," Abby said. Someone had circled her face in red ink. "Where'd you find that?"

"Mrs. Vickory's."

"Why would she have a picture of me?"

"I don't know, but Tina didn't seem surprised by that, either. There's something weird going on. Even weirder than what happened on Halloween." He dropped the photo on her bedside table. "Where were you really yesterday?"

"I told you."

"Hex-Mex doesn't open till lunchtime. Where were you before that?"

Wouldn't you like to know? It was an angry thought. A stupid one. But the one thing Abby knew for certain was that whatever had happened to Tina had nothing to do with Amethyst Jones. If she mentioned she'd gone to Amethyst's farm, even without saying why, how long would it take before Robby suspected the truth about Amethyst, too? He was too smart not to piece it together.

"It's nothing you need to worry about." She thought of all the times Tina had cheered at her soccer games or shown Abby something interesting at the veterinary clinic. Tina was like a cool aunt, sometimes even like a second mother. "I promise you it's not about Tina, though. You have to trust me on that."

Robby sniffled. "It's just like what happened to my mom."

"What is?"

"Mrs. Vickory's house. And Tina's car, too, from the way my dad described it. Both were just… obliterated. I think it's that woman from Whispering Hill." He wiped his eyes. "Joanna. Re-member the letter to my mom? You get why I need to know where you went? If you saw her—"

"I didn't. I swear I didn't."

"Then why won't you tell me the truth? You usually tell me everything."

Abby's phone buzzed on the bedside table. Her stupid phone—if she'd only had enough battery, all of the confusion yesterday could have been avoided. Tina might not have even left the clinic. She scooped it up and glanced at the screen as she dropped onto the bed next to Robby.

Sarika had texted her a picture.

Abby jumped back to her feet, gaping at her best friend, then back at her phone, then back at Robby. "You told me you were grounded."

"I am."

"Not last night." Her face was burning. She turned the phone to face Robby, revealing the picture of him sitting on a couch next to Becca, practically attached at the hip. "You used to tell *me* everything, too."

"We were just studying!"

"Doesn't look that way. Are you guys, like, *together* now?"

"I don't know. I—" He scowled. "Why should you care?"

Abby crinkled her nose. "I don't care like that. You're such a hypocrite, though. 'Where were you, Abby?' We're supposed to be best friends, but you kept all the stuff about your mom a secret from me. Don't you think you should have told me about that before we went to Whispering Hill? And now this?"

"I just wanted to be sure first."

"Is that what happened with Becca, too? You wanted to be sure before you told me you had a girlfriend?"

"She's not my girlfriend!"

Abby stared out her bedroom window, feeling guilty for accusing Robby of anything when Tina was missing. Across the way, a dark-haired girl was standing on Robby's front steps, ringing the doorbell. "Tell that to her."

"What are you talking about?"

"Better go say hello before she leaves."

Robby climbed to his feet and leaned over her shoulder to look outside. Becca was staring down at her phone. "She must have come to see how I'm doing." He took a deep breath. "We were together when my dad told me about Tina."

"You better go," Abby said.

"Abby, please."

"I'll yell down and tell her you're coming."

He grabbed the photo of Abby and stuffed it back into his pocket. "See you at school, then."

"Wait, you're *actually* leaving? I was just being—" She sighed. "Stay, Robby. We have a lot to talk about."

"Are you going to tell me where you went yesterday?"

Abby closed her eyes and took a deep breath. "I would, but I made a promise," she finally said. "It's not—It's got nothing to do with—"

"Didn't think so."

He slammed the door and stomped his way down the stairs. Abby dropped back onto her bed, feeling sick to her stomach again, certain that this time it was more than just the side effects of spellcasting. How was it possible that she knew how to do magic, and yet she'd never felt more powerless?

12

The Serpent and the Swann

"But you didn't tell him," Amethyst said, leaning against Abby's locker on Monday morning, a concerned look on her face. Around them, students rushed to grab their books and bags before the first bell.

"I promised you I wouldn't. Just like I promised you I wouldn't tell my mom you live alone in a condemned hovel, even though I should."

"You definitely shouldn't," Amethyst warned.

"Robby already knows I can fly, though. Why can't I tell him everything else? The rest is just details."

Amethyst leaned closer until their eyes were inches apart. "He knows that you flew on Halloween. He doesn't know how or why. And he doesn't know anything about *me*, which is how I prefer to keep it."

"My best friend hates me now."

Amethyst snorted. "He will never hate you."

Abby had a clear view of Robby's locker from where she stood. It was currently attracting a crowd. "He's been keeping secrets, too," she said, more to herself than to Amethyst. "He told me he was grounded this weekend, not hanging out at Hex-Mex with Becca Ruiz."

"Maybe he was afraid you'd be upset?" Amethyst suggested.

Abby scowled. "Whose side are you on? Besides, he should know I don't care who he likes."

"I don't care either. I'm only here today because you talked me into scoping out potential witches—like her." Amethyst nodded in the direction of Sarika, who'd joined the gaggle of students near Robby's locker, holding up her phone like a reporter as she pushed her way to the center of the action.

"I take it all back," Abby said. "I don't want to know if she's like us. I have too much to think about today, anyway."

"I haven't felt any sparks yet," said Amethyst hopefully. "That's a good sign."

When the bell rang, Abby grabbed her gym bag, and then she and Amethyst hurried to the girls' changing room, already late for class.

"Sarika better show up," Amethyst said. "This will be my first gym class all year, and I'm not doing it for my health."

"Don't you get in trouble for skipping?"

"I don't skip, technically. And when I do come to school, I forge a note from my grandfather."

By the time Abby and Amethyst made it to the locker room, most of the class had already changed and left for the gymnasium. Olivia and Sarika were reapplying their makeup in the mirrors above the sinks, while Piper Finch was putting off facing Mr. Rexman as long as possible.

Olivia frowned as Abby and Amethyst dropped their bags onto the changing bench. "Amethyst Jones. Is this a joke?"

"The circus must be in town," said Sarika, letting out a cackle. "Any comment on Robby's new girlfriend, Abby?"

"Ignore her," said Amethyst.

Olivia wrinkled her nose. "Are you two friends now?"

Amethyst turned her back to them. She pulled on her gym shirt and inspected herself in the mirror. "Don't let them bother you."

"They used to just ignore me." Abby hopped into her gym shorts. "That was better."

"What's *better* is getting even." Amethyst arched an eyebrow, muttered something under her breath, and flicked her wrist in the direction of the sinks. There was a loud banging as the fixtures popped free of the plumbing, and water spewed toward the ceiling like geysers. Olivia and Sarika shrieked, pointing fingers at each other as water dripped from their chins and pooled around their feet. Amethyst grabbed Abby's hand and pulled her from the changing room.

"Still no spark," Abby said. "Maybe Sarika's not like us."

Piper stood at the top of the stairs, walking toward class as slowly as humanly possible. Abby held the door as Piper and Amethyst wandered into the gymnasium just before the second bell. Most of the kids were already stretching at center court, but T-Rex and a few other boys were chatting under the basketball hoop, sniggering in the direction of the Green twins, Daisy and Delphinium. For maybe the first time in her life, Abby was glad that she and Robby weren't in the same class.

Mr. Rexman patrolled the cavernous room, whistle between his lips and tight black shorts pulled up over his belly button. He looked a bit like a rabid terrier—doughy face, saggy eyes, stocky legs. He was red-faced and foaming at the mouth, and class hadn't even started yet.

"You girls," he said, pointing in Abby's direction. He spit out his whistle when he saw Amethyst next to her. "Go limber up. Fitness test today."

Piper sighed as they joined their classmates. "Why does he torture us?" She took a long drag from her inhaler.

"How hard can it be?" asked Amethyst.

"Spoken like someone who never goes to gym class," said Piper as she bent to touch her toes. "I swear he doesn't even recognize asthma as a legitimate medical condition."

The shrill ring of Mr. Rexman's whistle cut short their conversation. "Line 'em up!" he yelled. "Boys over here, girls over there. We'll alternate rows. Alphabetical by first name. Abby, Amethyst"—he glanced at his clipboard—"Becca. One, two, three, you get the idea. Everyone else behind them. Move it, people!"

"But my full name is Rebecca!" protested Becca from among a gaggle of girls, a hint of panic in her voice.

Abby hadn't noticed that Becca was in the class. When Becca spotted Abby, her expression changed to a friendly smile. She waved hello with a tentative wiggle of the fingers. Abby wanted to be annoyed, but she couldn't think of any fair reason. She waved back.

"Come *on*, Abby." Amethyst tugged on her hand so hard that she had to spin around to avoid being pulled off her feet.

"We'll do the rope climb today," Mr. Rexman called, to a wave of moans. "You first, Abby. Up you go." He gave her a reassuring smile and a hard pat on the back.

Abby wrapped her legs around the rope and scurried to the top like she was climbing one of the trees behind her house, then scuttled back down. A few girls near the back of the line clapped. Becca smiled encouragingly. Abby gave a theatrical bow and stepped aside for Amethyst to take her turn.

Mr. Rexman scribbled something on his clipboard. "Next."

To nearly everyone's surprise, Amethyst touched the ceiling, too. "I was all set to secretly levitate if I needed to," she told Abby as they made their way to the back of the line.

"You're a real farm girl," Abby said. "Very sturdy."

Amethyst stuck out her tongue.

More than half the class had climbed by the time Olivia and Sarika appeared in the doorway looking as if they'd tumbled out of a washing machine. Olivia glared at Amethyst and Abby, and for a second Abby wondered if she somehow knew why the sinks had exploded. Just as quickly, she dismissed the idea. Olivia scowled at everyone all the time.

Mr. Rexman scrutinized Olivia and Sarika. "You're late."

"You're going to need to call a plumber," Olivia snapped.

"Front of the line, both of you." The girls approached the rope like prisoners marching toward their execution.

"Sarika fell off and broke her arm last year," Abby whispered to Amethyst. "Actually, that gives me an idea…"

Sarika took the rope between her hands and knees. She stopped after just a few segments, but Mr. Rexman blew his whistle until she began to scurry up again. When she reached the halfway point, Abby leaned in close to Amethyst. "Make sure no one's watching me, okay? I think I know how to find out if she's a witch." She focused on the rope and whispered, "*Funis… ambulare… serpens…*"

Amethyst repeated the words, trying to make sense of the Latin. The rope began to snake back and forth in increasingly wider arcs, swinging like a slow pendulum. Sarika gripped the rope like a vise as it picked up speed.

"*This* is your plan?" Amethyst demanded.

"It's more like improv," Abby admitted before resuming her chant. She thought if she could shake Sarika free, the adrenaline rush of the fall might produce something similar to what she and Amethyst had experienced on their birthdays. The rope continued to pick up speed, sending kids scrambling out of the way.

Sarika's grip loosened, and then she slipped and fell to the floor with an audible crunch, half on the safety mat and half off. As she tried to lift herself up, her arm gave way. "I broke it *again*?!" she screeched. She raised her other arm at Mr. Rexman. "I am *so* suing this school!"

"I can't believe I just did that," Abby said, cringing. She rushed to Sarika's side and tried to help her up. "Amethyst, help me."

But Amethyst didn't move. "Abby," she whispered, "we have another problem."

The entire gymnasium erupted in screams. Abby spun
around and nearly shrieked herself. A giant snake was dangling
from the ceiling, wriggling where the rope should have been. It
looked like a python from a monster movie.

"Omigod," Abby said, scrambling back as Mr. Rexman blew
his whistle at the snake. "Amethyst, what did I do?"

"Transmogrification," Amethyst whispered.

"What?"

"Transmogrification. You just turned one thing into something else. I bet you pictured a snake when you said *serpens…*
poor choice of words."

"How do I turn it back?"

"I don't know! You shouldn't have been able to do it in the
first place. That's *really* advanced magic!"

The snake continued to writhe, hissing and snapping whenever it swung close to one of the students. There was a loud,
ominous creak, and then the snake dropped to the floor with a
thud and slithered toward the crowd, baring fangs the size of
meat cleavers.

"Make it stop!" Abby yelled.

"*You* make it stop!"

Suddenly, the gym went silent. Piper was inching toward the
snake, both arms out, palms up. The snake hissed at her. She took
a deep breath from her inhaler and continued forward as the
snake flicked its tongue, tasting the air between them. Carefully,
Piper knelt and waited for it to slither to her. Then she leaned
closer until they were eye to eye in the center of the gym.

"Piper, careful," Abby warned.

Piper whispered soothingly to the snake. With one hand, she
brushed it gently between the eyes. The air around her sizzled
with electricity. Abby exchanged a glance with Amethyst, who
nodded. She'd felt it, too. The spark.

As Piper shifted to sit cross-legged, the class formed a semicircle around her and her new reptile friend. The snake laid its

head in her lap, close enough that it could have swallowed her whole. Piper whispered so softly that Abby couldn't make out the words, but her tone reminded Abby of the way Tina would soothe injured animals in the clinic. And just when Abby thought she couldn't hold her breath any longer, the snake's scales grew coarse and fibrous, flickering twice between green and yellow, before it turned back into a rope.

Piper let out a deep breath.

"How did you do that?" Abby asked.

"It didn't really want to be a snake," Piper said. "It *liked* being a rope. Somehow it just… turned itself back."

A dozen voices started yelling at once. "But it was—"

"Did you see—"

Abby gaped at Amethyst. "So much for our secret."

"Cover your ears," Amethyst warned.

"My ears?"

"Just do it. You too, Piper."

Amethyst mouthed a few words Abby couldn't make out. A heartbeat later, Sarika's tremulous voice broke through the silence. "I—I—broke it *again*?!" Sarika cradled her arm. "I am *so* suing this school!"

Mr. Rexman blew his whistle, shrilly tweeting until the room went quiet. Bits of the ceiling littered the floor. The rope lay in a pile near Piper's feet. Mr. Rexman moved to Sarika's side to check her arm, then called for someone to get the school nurse. The rest of the class filed into the hallway toward the boys' and girls' locker rooms.

"That was amazing!" Amethyst told Piper as they fell in step behind the other girls. "How long have you been able to do that?"

"Do what?" asked Piper, blinking. Her eyes were as wide as soccer balls. She touched her head. "Did something hit me? I can't remember anything. Sarika was climbing and then the ceiling caved in. My grandmother has dementia. Is this how dementia starts?"

"I told you to cover your ears," Amethyst said, annoyed. "I used a memory charm."

"A what?"

"Piper, when did you turn thirteen?" Abby asked gently.

"This morning." Piper rubbed her head again. "Is this early-onset Alzheimer's? Is that a thing? Can it start in middle school?"

Amethyst turned to Abby. "Why isn't she on our list?"

"What list?" said Piper.

"We made a list of people who share the same ancestor as us," Abby explained. "Remember the genealogy unit from Mrs. Vickory's class in September?"

"I had mono in September," Piper said.

Abby slapped her forehead. "That's right, you missed the whole unit." She ran her fingers through her hair, thinking hard. "Piper, how long has your family lived in Willow Cove?"

"On my mom's side, forever. My dad's from Kenya, though. It's a sweet story. They met in the Peace Corps."

"You don't have dementia," Amethyst interrupted. "You're a witch."

"Don't be mean." Piper sniffled. "Why is everyone always so mean to me?"

"We're witches. And so are you, I think. I accidentally turned the climbing rope into a giant snake. You must have convinced it to change back."

"I did?" Piper rubbed her temples. "There was a snake?"

"You're a witch," Amethyst repeated. She put her arm around Piper's shoulders and tried to explain quietly as they ducked into a corner of the locker room. Piper listened wide-eyed, shaking her head now and then. Abby listened for a while and then decided Amethyst had the situation handled. The locker room had emptied by the time she retrieved her clothes.

She liked the idea of Piper being a witch. Now that she

thought about it, Piper had always had a way with animals that seemed a bit supernatural. Even Tina said so.

When the bell rang, students swarmed the halls. Lost in her thoughts, Abby walked toward her history class accompanied by Amethyst and Piper. She came to an abrupt halt when she reached the doorway.

Waiting at the front of the room was the woman from Whispering Hill.

13

Miss Winters

"Ow!" said Amethyst, crashing into Abby. When Abby didn't move, Amethyst tried to push past, but Abby grabbed both sides of the door frame to block the way. "Let's skip class today."

"Not that I have anything against it on moral grounds," said Amethyst, "but why?"

Abby dragged her a few feet into the hallway. Piper followed them. "We can't go in there."

"You can and you *will*," a chilling voice commanded.

All three girls turned. The woman from Whispering Hill stood in the doorway with her arms crossed and a humorless smile on her face. The air rippled around her like heat coming off the tarmac on a summer's day. She wore a tweed skirt and tight black turtleneck that accentuated her figure. The telltale streak of gray in her hair added an air of maturity to her otherwise youthful appearance.

"Abigail Shepherd, Amethyst Jones, and Piper Finch?" she asked.

Amethyst and Piper nodded. Abby just stared.

"Please come in and take a seat."

Amethyst and Piper shuffled into the classroom. When Abby still didn't move, the woman raised an eyebrow. "Come along, Miss Shepherd. I don't bite."

Abby took an empty seat at the front of the classroom next to Amethyst and pretended to riffle through her school bag as she took in the room. Robby was sitting next to Becca. He caught Abby's eye, then looked away.

"Everything all right?" Amethyst whispered.

Abby shook her head. If the woman hadn't recognized her and Robby, she didn't see any reason to give her a reminder.

"You may call me Miss Winters," the woman said in the same vaguely British accent Abby recalled from Halloween. "I'll be your substitute until a full-time replacement can be found for Mrs. Vickory. Would one of you be kind enough to tell me where you left off?"

Several of Abby's classmates raised their hands. Margery Chen thrust her hand so high she looked as if she might levitate clear out of her seat. As Miss Winters's gaze passed over Robby, he stared straight ahead. If she recognized him, she gave no indication of it. Finally, she called on Olivia.

"Chapter six. Origins of the witch hysteria in Puritan New England," Olivia told her.

A pout settled across Miss Winters's face. "Of course. And tell me, dear, what have you learned so far?"

Olivia trailed a finger down the page and began to read. "'In February of 1692, two young girls in Salem Village became afflicted with unnatural fits—'"

Miss Winters walked to the front of the room and scrawled the year 1692 on the whiteboard. "Continue," she urged Olivia. "What kind of fits?"

"S-screaming, throwing things, crawling under the furniture," Olivia said, eyes trained now on Miss Winters instead of her book. "Making weird noises. That kind of thing."

"Naturally," said Miss Winters. "And then?"

Olivia cleared her throat and returned to the textbook. "'Other young women began to exhibit similar behavior. Soon, three villagers named Sarah Good, Sarah Osborne, and a slave from Barbados called Tituba were accused of using witchcraft on the young girls.'"

Miss Winters held up a hand. "When was this?"

Olivia glanced down at her book again, but Margery spoke up first. "March 1, 1692," she said, reading from her own textbook.

"Thank you. Please, keep reading, Margery."

Margery squinted at the page. "'In June 1692, Salem convened a special court to judge the accused, which numbered in the dozens. The first to be tried for witchcraft was Bridget Bishop, who was known to the villagers for her dubious moral character. She was found guilty and executed by hanging on June 10.'"

"Interesting," Miss Winters murmured, almost as if speaking to herself, "but far from complete."

She turned her back to the class, writing with vigorous strokes on the whiteboard, then turned to face them again. The number 1692 had been crossed out. A new number, 1691, stood out starkly behind her. "What does your book say about the events of 1691?"

Margery stared blankly at the book in front of her. No one else raised a hand to help. Abby glanced at Amethyst, whose eyes narrowed as if she were having the same thought. Their common ancestor, Victoria Snow, had been born in 1691.

Miss Winters surveyed the class, her gaze lingering a second too long on Abby. She crossed the room and lifted Abby's book from her desk, then thumbed through the pages, frowning. "Just as I feared. If this book is to be believed, not a single thing of interest happened in 1691. And *that* is the very problem we must correct. History is more than the accumulation of names and dates. It is a story—yours and mine. Behind every rote fact are real people like you and me whose names may not be in the history books, but whose stories are no less important." She allowed her words to sink in. "Now, as to what your book has taught you, I'm afraid it's all wrong."

Margery looked up. "W-wrong?"

"Quite." Miss Winters dropped Abby's textbook into the trash bin. "Consider, for example, the origins of the witch hysteria. It didn't start with a couple of preteen girls writhing in the dirt and foaming at the mouth. It didn't even start in Salem." She laughed. "History begins at home, boys and girls, and as this town is your home, I cannot have you spending another minute in this classroom *reading* about your history when you should be outside discovering it for yourselves. Living history is all around you, so we are taking a field trip, right now."

Everyone looked around, confused. Near the front of the room, T-Rex laughed and then fell silent when Miss Winters caught his eye.

"*Now*, all of you," she said to the class. "Follow me."

"Don't we need a permission slip?" asked Piper.

Miss Winters opened the door and marched out of the classroom. Abby fished her textbook out of the trash, stuffed it back into her bag, and hurried to catch up with Robby as the class scrambled into the hallway. He was ahead with Becca, though, and walking so quickly that she got the message—he still didn't want to talk to her. She fell in step with Amethyst and Piper instead.

A stiff breeze assaulted her as the class headed toward the athletic fields, which sat behind the school. The day was gray and misty and smelled thickly of the nearby marshes, and Miss Winters hadn't waited for anyone to grab their coats. Abby wrapped her arms around herself while Amethyst continued to fill in details for Piper, whispering softly for privacy. Lost in thought, Abby didn't realize Amethyst had asked her a question until she felt someone punch her arm.

"Ow!"

"Next time answer me."

"I'm sorry. What did you say?"

"I said Miss Winters is practically nuclear with magical energy. Do you see how the air ripples around her? She's definitely a witch."

Abby watched Miss Winters lead the class across the fields with Pied Piper–like determination. "I know."

"Wait, another witch?" said Piper.

"Yeah, but not a good one," Abby said. "She nearly killed me on Halloween."

Amethyst's eyes bulged. "You didn't think that was worth mentioning? You show up at my house demanding answers—"

"I know."

"—and you didn't think to mention—"

"I *know*," Abby repeated. "I was just waiting for the right moment."

"Any moment would have been fine!" Amethyst yelled. A few people turned to look. She lowered her voice. "I can't believe I was almost starting to trust you."

"Amethyst—"

"You know the worst part?" Her nostrils flared. "I *knew* I shouldn't—"

"You *should*, though," Abby said. "You can, I mean. I didn't tell anyone about you, did I? Even when it would have been so much easier if I'd just told Robby everything. I'm sorry I didn't mention Miss Winters, but it's not about trust. I just didn't know… what to say."

They followed their classmates in a silence interrupted only by the howling wind. Piper stared straight ahead as they walked, determinedly not picking a side. Finally, Amethyst let out a deep breath. "I guess you've had a lot on your mind."

"I still should have told you."

Amethyst gave her a sidelong glance. "Lesson learned?"

"Lesson learned. No more secrets."

"All right." Amethyst almost smiled. "So, another witch. That could be good?"

"Except for the part where she tried to kill me. And Robby thinks—" Abby took a deep breath and searched for him up ahead. The class had stretched out like an accordion. Robby and Becca were just tiny figures in the distance. "He thinks she might be responsible for a lot of the disappearances around here. Mrs. Vickory, his mother all those years ago, his stepmother…"

"Something happened to Tina?" whispered Piper, taking a gulp from her inhaler.

"Tina vanished," Abby confirmed. Her stomach twisted at the thought. "That's all I know right now."

"We don't know that Miss Winters had anything to do with it, though," Amethyst protested. "And she isn't trying to kill anyone now, so that's progress."

The three girls joined a few other stragglers near the middle of the softball diamond, which abutted the rain-soaked soccer and lacrosse fields like a patchwork quilt. Rolling hills and an open meadow stretched beyond. Behind them, the brick-and-ivy walls of the middle school were just a tiny smudge on the horizon. Wherever Miss Winters was leading them, it wasn't on school grounds.

"'Now is the winter of our discontent,'" moaned Daisy Green, a tall chestnut-haired girl with rosy cheeks and a smattering of freckles on her fair face. She'd spent the summer at a theater camp in London and had come back quoting Shakespeare and sporting a fairly convincing English accent. Today, she looked like a Renaissance Faire princess in a paper-thin beige dress with an emerald sash around her waist. Her teeth chattered as she hugged herself against the cold.

"It's not even winter yet," said Daisy's fraternal twin, Delphinium, called Delphi by her friends. Taking two steps to every one of her sister's just to keep up, she wiped her thick-rimmed glasses on her sleeve, then tucked them back onto her face. Delphi was the shorter of the two, with shoulder-length dark hair in a bob cut and plump red cheeks that stood out against her otherwise light coloring.

"'Barren winter, with his wrathful nipping cold—'"

Amethyst eyed the twins dubiously. "What's that all about?"

Abby shook her head. "You get used to it eventually."

"I should have worn my cloak," Daisy complained as Abby, Amethyst, and Piper fell in step with her and Delphi.

"And your galoshes," Delphi added, pointing to her own bright yellow rubber boots. "I told her to wear them. Honestly, she doesn't even read our horoscope. It was all right there. Mercury's in retrograde."

"Know-it-all," Amethyst muttered to Abby under her breath. "I hate people like her."

"In fairness, you kind of hate everyone," Abby replied.

"Not everyone. I can almost tolerate you."

At the top of a hill, Miss Winters announced they'd arrived at their destination. A few students cheered. Most just shivered. Robby and Becca were huddled together beneath one of the six weeping willows dotting the hilltop. Abby waved, trying to get Robby's attention, but he never looked her way. Miss Winters spread her arms wide, gesturing to the drooping branches. Her cheeks looked like two red apples on her porcelain face, but she seemed to be enjoying the brisk weather. "Who can tell me how this place came to be called Willow Hill?" she asked.

"The willow trees," said T-Rex, looking proud of himself.

"There *are* willow trees here," Miss Winters agreed, "but they were planted much later. This is a fascinating example of etymology." When most of the class stared blankly at her, she clarified: "Etymology. The study of the origin of words.

"The meadow we just crossed, this hill, this whole town, was once the playground of six girls—Catherine, Mary, Rose, Emily, Anne, and Susanna. The Winslow sisters. Their farmhouse was right about… *there*." She pointed to a vague mound near the foot of the hill. "Willow Hill was an apple orchard in those days, and somewhere near *this* very spot"—she smacked the tree nearest to T-Rex and Joey, who jumped in surprise—"is where the sisters' unfortunate fate was sealed, though no one could have predicted it at the time."

Miss Winters walked a few steps and patted the gnarled bark of another of the old willows. "History is a story without beginning or end, but it does have moments one can point to in hindsight and say, 'That was when it all changed.' For the six Winslow sisters, that moment was a cold January day in 1691, here atop what was once called *Winslow* Hill."

She surveyed the class. "Your book speaks of Salem as if it were some distant remnant of the past, but Salem is all around you. This right here—*this* is Salem." She planted a foot into the soft, wet grass. "Or it was, long ago. Salem once stretched up and down the coast, and went inland for miles too. And the witch scare started right here—not with the fitful outbursts of two young girls, but with a betrayal that no book ever mentions."

Branches swayed as a gust of wind whistled past. A few students raised their hands, and Miss Winters surveyed the class before her eyes settled on Delphi. "Yes, Miss Green?"

"It's just…" Delphi shrugged. "I've lived here all my life, and I've never heard anything about Willow Hill being connected to the witch trials. Or about any Winslow sisters."

"All your life?" said Miss Winters. "All twelve years of it?"

"Almost thirteen."

"I'm sure you've heard the stories of ghostly voices atop Whispering Hill, though. Cries in the night, whispers of evil deeds long past?"

Delphi nodded.

"People will tell you the voices belong to patients of the old mental hospital. Perhaps some of them do. But the pain stretches back much further. The whispers belong to the six Winslow sisters, hanged for witchcraft on Whispering Hill long before your textbook would have you believe the hysteria even began. The records may be gone, but the ghosts remain."

T-Rex snickered at the mention of ghost stories. Abby snuck a glance at Robby. This time, she caught him looking back.

"But why did they—" Delphi began.

"The lesson," Miss Winters cut in, "is that history cannot be taught entirely from a book or a classroom. History is all around you, in this town even more than most. You have simply to look at the ground beneath your feet to find it." Her gaze settled on Abby, Amethyst, and Piper, huddled together beneath one of the willows. "Or perhaps the blood running through your veins."

Delphi nodded. The rest of the class did, too, all of them a little spellbound. Abby snuck a sideways glance at Amethyst, whose expression was clouded with a mixture of apprehension and awe.

"The bloodline," Abby whispered.

Amethyst nodded her head almost imperceptibly.

"Now, back to school, all of you," Miss Winters was saying. "I won't have you late for your next class on my first day."

As the students filed down the hill, Miss Winters called, "Miss Shepherd, Miss Jones, Miss Finch, walk with me."

Abby, Amethyst, and Piper fell cautiously into step with her while the rest of the class sprinted ahead.

"I haven't told that story in a very long time," Miss Winters said. "Do you girls believe in witchcraft?"

"Yes," Amethyst said.

"Kind of?" replied Piper.

"And you, Miss Shepherd?"

In that instant, Abby knew beyond any doubt that Miss Winters remembered her perfectly from Halloween. "I have for a few days now," she replied carefully.

"Then we are halfway there already."

"You scared me," Abby said, shivering as she remembered

the chimeras and the glowing red wandlight. "I could have died falling off that cliff."

"And I'm very sorry for that. You startled me as well. I… overreacted." Miss Winters's expression softened. "This town is often unkind to people like us. I let my fear get the better of me. Of course, I quickly saw that you could handle the broom in your hands better than most. And look at what you've learned because of it—you flew!"

"You can fly?" whispered Piper, her owlish eyes wide with wonder.

"It takes some girls years to master the skill," Miss Winters continued. "To say nothing of the transmogrification you performed in the gymnasium this morning." She held up a hand in anticipation of Abby's next question. "I could sense the pattern on you the moment you walked into my classroom. You're special, Abby, and it's good you've learned that so early. You'll push yourself harder. But it also means you need guidance before you harm yourself or someone close to you. I have so much to teach you. To teach *each* of you."

"You—want to teach us?" Amethyst asked breathlessly, the longing clear in her voice.

Miss Winters smiled. "Why else do you think I've come?"

14

Shadows of the Past

Robby drifted back toward the school, Becca at his side. Every time he looked over his shoulder, Abby seemed farther away. He was still angry with her, but he was worried, too. He couldn't understand why Miss Winters would pose as their new history teacher.

Becca slowed to match his pace. She'd spent half of Sunday at his house keeping him company while his father made one frantic phone call after another. She squeezed his hand now with a comforting familiarity. "You look like a candle in the wind with your hair whipping around like that," she told him.

"A candle?"

She wrapped her fingers tighter around his. "It's cute."

"You might be the only one who thinks so."

"Maybe I'm just the only one who's told you."

T-Rex had been lingering ahead of them. Without warning, he spun around and shoved Robby to the soggy ground, toppling Becca at the same time. Then he loomed over them both, his hand clenched into a fist.

"TOMMY REXMAN!" Becca yelled as she climbed to her feet and wiped mud from her knees.

T-Rex grunted. Robby barely dodged a kick to the groin.

"You are such a *brute*," Becca yelled. "Leave him alone."

"*Leave him alone*," T-Rex mimicked.

Robby scrambled to his feet, stepping in front of Becca. "How's your bloody lip today?" he asked.

"Still good enough to kiss with," T-Rex said, puckering in Becca's direction.

"Not in a million years," she said.

T-Rex glanced back toward Willow Hill, then wagged his finger at Robby. "You won't always have a girl around to save you," he spat before stomping away.

"I *hate* him," Becca said as she wrung muddy water from her shirt. "Are you all right?"

"I'm fine. You?"

"This shirt's ruined and my dignity is bruised, but otherwise I'm okay." She frowned in T-Rex's direction. "Has he always been like that?"

"This seems worse than normal. Even for him."

"Normal?" interrupted Olivia. Robby hadn't heard her approaching. "Hello, *nothing's* normal anymore. Exploding sinks in the locker room? Oozing green slime in the science lab? And someone like her getting together with... *you*? Everything is the opposite of normal."

Becca gripped Robby's hand again. "Just go away, Olivia."

Olivia snickered and then sprinted to catch up with T-Rex.

"What's her problem?" Becca asked.

"I think she assumed you'd want to be friends with her."

Becca rolled her eyes. "Does it seem like she and I have a lot in common?"

"No. She's kind of mean, but—"

"Kind of?" Becca laughed. "There are girls like her at every school. I can't stand the way she..." Becca shook her head. "Never mind."

"Tell me."

"Just the way she talks about people, like everyone's inferior. It doesn't matter, though. I'm more concerned about you."

"Me?"

"I'm not blind. Something happened between you and Abby."

"Why would you say that?"

Becca smiled weakly. "You wouldn't even make eye contact with her in class today. I may be new here, but even I know that's not normal."

"We had a fight."

After a long pause, Becca said, "I bet I know why. You guys were a thing. Then I came along."

"It's not like that."

"Then what happened?"

Robby shrugged. "She's keeping a secret from me."

"Isn't she allowed to have secrets?"

"Not this kind."

"We all hide parts of ourselves, though, don't you think? I'm a half-Jewish Latinx girl from Wisconsin. And I'm kind of a geek, too. But I don't go around advertising that."

"I like geeks."

"So do I." She laughed, then leaned into his shoulder. "That's why I like hanging out with you."

Miss Winters strode past them alongside Abby, Piper, and Amethyst. Robby waved to Abby with his free hand, realizing mid-wave that Abby and the other girls were walking *with* their new teacher, hanging on her every word.

His mouth fell open even as Abby waved back, barely more than a flick of her wrist, then marched after Miss Winters without so much as a backward glance.

When the bell rang at the end of the day, Robby lingered at Becca's locker while most of the school rushed toward the doors. On
the other side of the hallway, Piper and Amethyst crowded
around Abby's locker, talking quickly and peering down the corridor toward Miss Winters's classroom. Fighting indecision,
Robby glanced in their direction and then back at Becca as she
shuffled through items in her locker.

He couldn't understand why Abby would go anywhere near
Miss Winters after what had happened at Whispering Hill, especially after what he'd told her about his mother and Tina. But he
remembered that Piper's and Amethyst's pictures had been circled on the wall at Mrs. Vickory's house, too. The more he
thought about it, the more Miss Winters's interest in all three of
them made sense.

Becca threw herself against her locker door to slam it shut.
"Two days at this school and my locker is already a disaster."

"Hmm," Robby said absently. His eyes were back on Abby's
locker. He'd decided to talk to her—to all three girls—but as he
took a step in their direction, Miss Winters rounded the corner
and led them to her classroom.

Becca snapped her fingers. Robby shook his head. "Sorry.
Just distracted."

Becca's phone buzzed. She smiled apologetically before
checking her messages. "My mom's waiting outside. I should
go." But she didn't make any effort to leave. They stood together
until her phone buzzed a second time. "She's not a patient woman, my mother." Becca tucked her phone back into her pocket.
"Want to come over?"

Robby leaned back against the lockers. The overhead lights
flickered, casting shadows on the spot where Abby had been
moments earlier. "I can't today. Dad wants me to go straight
home. Tomorrow?"

Becca tried to hide her disappointment with an unconvincing
smile, but her eyes were on Abby's locker too. "Sure," she said.

She waved goodbye as she disappeared through the door.

Robby considered spying on the girls and Miss Winters before thinking better of it. Still, he felt like he needed to do *something*. He pulled up the internet on his phone, which his father had returned to him after Tina went missing, and made a few half-hearted searches, hoping to find some hidden meaning in the story Miss Winters had told them earlier. But it soon became clear that no one else had ever heard of Catherine Winslow or her sisters. Robby was still scrolling through the useless results when Zeus rounded the corner carrying his football equipment.

"I think Abby's avoiding me," Zeus said.

Robby pocketed his phone and looked up. "Why do you say that?"

"She sped up when she saw me earlier. *Sped up,* Robby! Do you think she's still mad I told on you guys the other night?"

"Maybe." Robby shook his head. "For what it's worth, she's not speaking to me, either."

"What did you do?"

"Nothing."

Zeus's eyes narrowed. "What did you *do*?"

"We're just fighting. Forget about it." He eyed Zeus's football bag. "What would happen if you skipped practice today?"

"Why?"

"Abby might be in danger."

Zeus dropped his bag to the floor. "How can I help?"

The town archives were housed at the Willow Cove Historical Society, one of the many ramshackle old buildings near the school. It was a quick walk, but Robby couldn't help looking over his shoulder as they slipped inside.

"She's your *history teacher*?" Zeus blurted.

"Not so loud." They tiptoed past the old lady at the front desk, who was snoring in rhythm with the tinkling bells above the doorway. Robby peered into the archive room and signaled for Zeus to follow. He closed the door behind them, then whispered, "Technically, Miss Winters is a substitute."

"And she's definitely the woman with the chinchillas?"

"Chimeras," Robby corrected. "Yeah. Definitely."

He flicked on the lights, casting a soft yellow glow over a labyrinthine collection of shelves that stretched into darkness. The room smelled of mildew and old leather. Robby eyed the stacks of rare journals, property records, and other materials. There had to be a thousand volumes in the rare books area alone, maybe twice that.

Zeus lifted a hardcover from the nearest shelf and began flipping through the pages. "What are we looking for?" he whispered.

"Any references to Willow Hill, the Winslow sisters, or ghosts at the site of the state mental hospital." Robby considered for a moment and then added, "Anything to do with the local witch hysteria, period. See if you can find something about Willow Cove being part of Salem. Put all the interesting books aside. We can compare notes later."

Leaving Zeus to his task, Robby wandered to the back, deciding to work from the opposite end. He was sure the historical society had to have some kind of order to their collection, but he couldn't make sense of the system.

He started a pile and got to work.

"Robby," whispered Zeus an hour later.

"What?"

"Robby," Zeus repeated, through gritted teeth.

Robby replaced the book he'd been skimming and walked to the front of the archives. Zeus had an enormous book in his hand. He wasn't alone.

Miss Winters surveyed them both. "What are you boys doing here?"

"Research," Robby said quickly. "You?"

"Same." She smiled pleasantly. "Find anything interesting?"

"W-we—" Zeus stammered. "We were just leaving."

Miss Winters eyed the book tucked under Zeus's left arm. She extended her hand. "May I?"

Her eyes betrayed surprise as she studied the dust jacket. "*A Secret History of Witchcraft and Warlockery in the Massachusetts Bay Colony, Volume One,* by Agnes F. Vickory," she read. "Your former history teacher? Fascinating choice, Mr.—?"

"Madison," said Zeus. "Zeus—I mean, Zachary Madison."

"The sheriff's boy."

Zeus nodded.

"I was inspired by your class," Robby said.

Miss Winters turned, her eyes narrowing as she took him in. "I recognize you. Robert O'Reilly, isn't it?"

"Robby," he corrected. "Robby Donovan O'Reilly."

There it was—a subtle flicker of recognition at the mention of his mom's maiden name. Miss Winters nodded, her face again unreadable.

"I appreciate your enthusiasm," Miss Winters said, her voice softer, "but remember what I told you earlier—*living history*, not books. I'll hold onto this one, so you don't forget. Now, off you go before I decide to wake up the nice old lady at the front desk and tell her two kids have been rifling through the rare books collection."

Robby locked eyes with Miss Winters. "I'm not afraid of you."

She held his gaze as the corners of her lips curved into a smile. "Young man, I'm not afraid of you, either."

The boys didn't say a word until they reached the hidden grove near Zeus's house.

"Did you see the look on her face when she saw that book? Zeus, we *must* have been onto something! If only she hadn't taken—"

"She didn't."

"Didn't what?"

"She didn't take it." Carefully, Zeus lifted his sweater to reveal a bunch of yellowed pages poking out from under his belt. "Not all of it, anyway. I tore out as much as I could when I saw her coming."

Robby leaned forward. "You tore out the pages?"

"You'll be glad I did. You're not going to believe what's in here."

Robby leaned against the granite wall as he scanned the pages. By the time he reached the end, his knees buckled. "That's her." He looked at Zeus for confirmation and then back at the tattered page in his hand, a reproduction of a sketch that looked just like Miss Winters, right down to the streak of gray.

"Look what it says under the picture," Zeus urged. "Her name and the year it was drawn."

Robby glanced down again.

"Joanna Greylocke. 1691."

15

Sign of the Witch

The lighthouse loomed over the rocky headland like a tilting giant, its gray granite exterior more like that of a stony medieval tower than a traditional lighthouse. Abby eyed the structure doubtfully. In grade school, she'd learned it was built out of local granite blocks with the hope it would stand the tide of centuries. Up close, it now looked as if one good push would send the whole thing tumbling into the ocean.

"What do you think?"

Abby turned her attention back to Amethyst and Piper. "Sorry, I wasn't listening." She'd been doing that a lot lately: getting lost in her own head. She still wasn't certain she'd made the right choice by agreeing to let Miss Winters teach them. They'd been having lessons for a week now, though, and Abby had to admit that Miss Winters hadn't given her even the slightest cause for suspicion. If she were being honest, she actually looked forward to the lessons. And it didn't hurt that her mother seemed enthusiastic about her doing extra credit with girls from school. It gave Abby more cover than she could have hoped for, especially with how things had been going with her mom since Halloween.

And yet...

For every spell she learned, every incantation memorized, every potion brewed, part of her still wondered if Miss Winters *could* be responsible for Tina's, Mrs. Vickory's, and Robby's mom's disappearances. Worse, she worried about what Robby might do to try to prove their new teacher's guilt. If there was one thing Abby had learned in her week of lessons, it was that Miss Winters was not someone Robby should cross. Abby didn't think anyone would stand a chance against a witch as powerful as Miss Winters, but she and her friends might have better luck with their abilities than Robby ever would on his own.

"I asked if you think they'll come?" Amethyst said.

Abby nodded. "Definitely. Delphi is crazy about her grades."

"What about Daisy?"

"She usually goes along with whatever her sister wants. If Miss Winters told them this was part of their local history project, they'll come. Now, let's try the door."

A hexagram was carved into the rotted wood planks. Abby's fingertips tingled as she traced it, as if she were awakening the building from a long sleep. "*Reclude*," she said, picturing the door opening. She'd advanced to the point where she didn't have to speak the words aloud for her spells to work, but Amethyst and Piper weren't there yet, and she didn't want to show off. The hexagram pulsed—first the outer circle and then each interior line until the entire pattern bathed the night with a scarlet glow. The door creaked open as if Abby had turned the handle and pushed it herself.

Inside, the air reeked like the mud flats at low tide. Abby clawed aside a cobweb as she pushed her way into the room, stepping around a pile of desiccated crab shells. A fluffy seagull chick cawed in protest, and Piper darted toward it, cooing.

"Why does Miss Winters want Daisy and Delphi to come here of all places?" asked Amethyst.

"Because it's out of the way? Because no one will notice if

something goes wrong? Because there's more room here than at school?"

"Whispering Hill is pretty out of the way," Amethyst pointed out. "Why not have us meet them there if that's where Miss Winters actually lives?" She poked at the shells with the toe of her shoe. "I'm tired of practicing in broom closets, but this isn't exactly an upgrade. Where is she, anyway? I thought she'd want to be here to observe us."

"She says she's got something else to do first. Something delicate."

"*Delicate?*"

"Her word, not mine."

"So mysterious," said Amethyst. It sounded like a compliment coming from her.

"Over here, you guys!" called Piper, hunched on her hands and knees opposite the gull chick. It made a cawing noise that sounded like a cat vomiting. Piper cawed back, a pretty good imitation, then stood up and brushed herself off. "The stairs are this way. He says the old harbor light still works."

"Who says?" asked Amethyst.

"Flapper—that's his name. I mean, in Seagull it's closer to, 'I flap above the sea in search of the choicest tasty mollusks,' but it's Flapper for short. Anyway, he lives here. His mother abandoned him, that's why he's still so small. Poor thing can barely fly at all." The gull chick flapped its fluffy wings and bobbed unsteadily on spindly legs before floating up to Piper's shoulder and pecking at something in her hair. She giggled. "It's okay, I'm your mommy now."

"That is *so* unsanitary," Amethyst complained under her breath.

Abby raised an eyebrow. "That from the girl who sleeps with a raccoon?"

Amethyst stuck out her tongue.

"Let's check out the top floor," Piper suggested. "Maybe

we'll be able to see Daisy and Delphi coming."

Abby waited until Piper and Amethyst had started up the steps, and then thought, *Claudere.* The outside door swung shut and clicked locked again.

The stairs spiraled along the sides of the lighthouse before ending five floors up at a door so thick with grime that at first Abby thought they'd reached a dead end. She pried it open and stepped onto the platform just below the beacon light. A short, rusted railing wobbled in the wind. The gallery's narrow wooden planks creaked with each step but seemed solid enough to hold their weight.

Resting her hands on the railing, Abby leaned over for a better look. The lighthouse sat at the end of a long, bare strip of land that jutted into the ocean like a crooked arm. She could see Daisy Green stepping gingerly toward the lighthouse, arguing with Delphi, who trailed a few steps behind. Daisy stopped to smooth her skirt and inspect her shoes for seaweed, then adjusted her woolen hat and resumed walking.

"What are they saying?" asked Piper.

Amethyst tilted her head in the twins' direction. "Let's listen."

"We can't eavesdrop," said Piper.

"The government does it all the time. It's practically a constitutional right."

"I don't think that's in the Constitution," said Piper, glancing at Abby for support.

Abby thought it would be okay just this once. "*Audire*," she whispered.

Voices reached them as if through speakers.

"'All the voyage of our life is bound in shallows and in miseries,'" complained Daisy.

"Enough with the Shakespeare!" Delphi wiped her cheeks and then pulled off her glasses to clean them. "Miss Winters's instructions were very clear. We need to go inside and have a look around. How else are we going to write the essay? I'm not getting a bad grade because you're chicken."

"I'm not chicken."

"And anyway, I have it on good authority—"

"Our horoscope is *not* good authority."

"—that this is a very important night for us. Something big is going to happen."

"Good big or bad big?"

"A little of both, if I read the stars right."

"A few stars line up and suddenly you're all gung-ho for creeping into an old lighthouse just because our new history teacher tells us to. We should be home eating our birthday cake."

"You have to admit something is up around here. This whole town is acting weird, *including* Miss Winters. And Mercury is still in retrograde, so—"

"I don't even know what that means," complained Daisy. "You know who hangs around spooky old lighthouses? Deranged lunatic serial killers with meat hooks for hands, that's who."

"You watch too many movies, Daze."

"We watch the same movies, and you said yourself to expect something good *and* bad. My money's on a meat hook killer. If he goes for you first, I'm running. Sorry. Save yourself. Anyway, here we are. What do you make of that?"

That was the hexagram carved into the lighthouse door. The twins stood in the shadows, hands on their hips.

Moment of truth, Abby thought.

"Seems like a warning," said Delphi. "Keep out."

"'Is this a dagger which I see before me?'"

"What?"

"It's from *Macbeth*. God, how are you even my twin? Never mind." Daisy prodded the hexagram experimentally with her left mitten. Nothing happened. She took off her mitten and tried again with her bare fingers. The hexagram flared red and the lighthouse door creaked open.

"Well, that answers that," said Amethyst.

"Welcome to our little coven," Abby said.

Daisy rubbed her temples as if she had the world's worst migraine. She leaned against the rounded wall of the lighthouse's first floor near one of the broken windows. Her hair whipped in the breeze.

Delphi grinned from ear to ear. "I knew it, Daze. I totally knew it!"

Daisy frowned. "You didn't know *this*."

"Actually, I did! I just didn't think you'd believe me. But it was all there in the stars. I'd have had to be blind not to see it. Which one of you is in charge?"

"None of us," said Abby. "We have a teacher."

"Miss Winters," said Delphi. "Knew it."

Daisy looked queasy. "Why isn't she here, then?"

"I'm here now," said a voice from across the room.

They turned to see Miss Winters watching them from the open doorway. She removed the hood of her cloak, batted a stray lock of hair from her eyes, and smiled encouragingly at Daisy and Delphi. "Congratulations, girls. I have high hopes for both of you."

Delphi grinned.

"You passed the test," Miss Winters explained. "The sign of the witch has been used for centuries to identify those with the sixth sense."

"I'm sorry... the *sixth* sense?" said Daisy.

"The spark that makes you different. The ability to sense magic in others is its most basic manifestation. It's there in the shadow that dances in the corner of your eye, in the whisper only you can hear." Miss Winters stepped into the lighthouse. The door creaked behind her. A tiny wisp of electricity crackled from her fingertips as she froze it in place, half open to the night.

"So cool," said Delphi.

Miss Winters reached into her cloak and produced the thin willow switch she used as a wand. She fashioned a flickering numeral six in the air, which splintered into six equal parts, and then three, and then two, each time quickly reunifying into its original shape. "Mathematicians show the number six as a spiral without line or angle. Who can tell me why?"

Abby shifted from foot to foot. This was all new.

"The spiral is the shape of a fetus in gestation," Miss Winters said. The flickering numeral shifted into the form of an unborn child: head bowed, knees clutched to its chest. The image faded until only a wisp of smoke remained. "The ancients chose the number six to represent the fertility and fruitfulness of the fairer sex—of us. Of you. And again, we must ask, why six?

"We see. We taste. We hear and smell and touch," she continued. "With these five senses we observe the natural world. Yet as witches we know there is more because we witness the supernatural all around us. We harness it every time we cast a spell. And this is where the power of six reveals itself: our *inner* sight. The mind's eye allows us to perceive the strands of magic and bend them to our will. Only when you harness all six of your senses can you transcend the natural world with any great effect. The rest is just parlor tricks."

She strode to the center of the room and surveyed each of the girls. "Take a moment to search for the spark of power that connects you to one another. Close your eyes, empty your minds, ignore everything but what your senses tell you."

It reminded Abby of what she and Amethyst had done that first day at the farmhouse, when Abby hadn't initially been able to sense the magical spark that Amethyst had so easily detected in her. She squeezed her eyes shut and allowed the cold ocean breeze to sweep over her. Her skin prickled with goosebumps. The air tasted of salt water and winter. She focused on every sound—the way the wind whistled through the broken windows, the rustle of footsteps, the subtle twitch of Flapper's wings. Every shallow gasp from her friends, each raspy inhalation. The ocean waves crashing against the headland rocks beyond.

She opened her eyes.

Amethyst blazed in a kaleidoscope of purples. Daisy and Delphi shimmered in pale pinks. The air around Piper flickered fast and frenetic, like the frightened heartbeat of a cornered animal.

"I—I see something!" cried Delphi. She covered her mouth with a hand to stifle the gasp. "Abby, you're—you're—"

"On fire," said Amethyst, grinning.

Daisy and Piper glanced at Abby with wide eyes. Abby held her hands out before her, opening and closing her fists until she saw it, too—flames. She jumped and shook her hands reflexively.

How?

"We alone can see the patterns in nature," Miss Winters said once they had all quieted. A gray, ghostly light churned around her like waves crashing against the rocky coast, as cold and deep and unknowable as the roiling sea. She raised her wand and brought it down in short, sharp strokes. The night rippled with phosphorous scars.

"This is how spells are made: by observing the patterns in nature and then knitting them into something new. We combine the strands of our five senses and bend them to our will until we have created a *new* shape. Any witch can cast a spell that has already been stitched together, but only six witches working together can assemble a new pattern. Observe these six equilateral triangles." She sent tiny shockwaves to each point of the hexagram on the half-open door. "Together, they form a whole that's greater than the sum of their parts. But remove just one and the pattern cannot hold. It takes the six senses working in concert to harness the supernatural, much as it takes six triangles to form a hexagram. This is why your coven must be six girls. No more, no less."

Piper frowned. "But there are only five of us."

"Oh, no," said Amethyst.

Abby felt it, too. Another spark nearby, prickly like a thorn bush. She shot a glance at Amethyst, who returned her look of alarm. There was only one name left on their list of potential witches.

"What?" said Daisy, catching their silent exchange. *"What?"*

"You six need each other," said Miss Winters with a note of apology. "You may come in now, dear."

Abby's stomach tightened. The sixth girl appeared in the doorway, a wicked grin splitting her too-pretty face. She must have come straight from cheerleading practice because she still wore her orange-and-black miniskirt. The air crackled around her like electrified barbed wire.

Olivia Edwards stepped inside the lighthouse and closed the door behind her. "It's like I landed on the Island of Misfit Toys," she said.

Piper took a long drag from her inhaler.

Delphi dropped her head into her hands.

Daisy gawked at Olivia, mouth open, then turned back to her twin. "I would have preferred the meat hook killer."

Part Two

16

The Hollows

"Red—no, pink!" said Robby, scrunching his nose, trying to read Becca's mind. They were sitting across from each other on the soft pink carpet of her bedroom floor, their knees touching, asking questions and trying to guess each other's favorite things. He snuck another peek in her direction, his mind made up now. "*Definitely* pink."

"How'd you guess?" she said, laughing as she nudged him with her foot. She wore a pink zip-up sweatshirt over a pink T-shirt. Ankle-high running socks, also pink, peeked out from the hem of her blue jeans.

Robby nudged her back—mostly because he liked the way it felt when they touched. He liked Becca, period. With Tina still missing and his friendship with Abby still strained, hanging out with Becca was the only time over the past few weeks when he didn't feel like his whole life had been turned upside down.

"My turn," he said. "Favorite memory?"

Becca touched her silver necklace, considering. "Summer before third grade. We visited my grandparents in Venezuela for the first time—my dad's side of the family. I had more aunts and uncles and cousins to play with than I could count. I don't think

I've ever been happier. Now it's just me and Mom, and I'm not even sure she wants me here." Her face brightened with forced cheeriness. "My turn again?"

"Your turn," he agreed. "Sorry, hold on." His phone buzzed in his pocket. He saw it was Zeus and left the text unread.

"Who was that?"

"Zeus."

"Knew it." Her smile had faded, though. She twirled a long lock of hair, then looked up, her forehead furrowed in concentration like she was trying to solve a particularly difficult riddle. "His dad is the police chief, right?"

Robby nodded.

"Does he—has Zeus told you anything about the investigation? Into your stepmom's disappearance, I mean."

"The police don't really have any leads," Robby said.

Becca bit her lower lip, considering. "What about you guys?"

"What do you mean?"

"Any leads? You and Zeus?"

"Why would you think we—"

"Because you two sneak around a lot," Becca said, meeting his gaze, determination in her eyes. "I thought maybe *that's* what you guys are always up to."

Robby's cheeks flushed. "We don't sneak around."

"Whispering in the hallway," Becca said, ticking off a list with her fingers. "Slamming your laptop shut as soon as I sit down near you in study hall, disappearing after school…"

"I don't do any of that."

"You do *all* of it, Robby. Like that time you told me you had to go straight home from school—I saw you hanging out with Zeus ten minutes later when my mom was driving me home. What was that all about?"

"I… don't remember."

"Yeah, okay," Becca said, throwing up her hands. "I may

not know everything that's going on, but I know when someone's not being totally honest with me." She shook her head.
"It's hard enough dealing with a new town, new school—trying
to make new friends—without also having to worry that some of
those friends are keeping a big secret from me. I know things are
weird with your stepmom missing, so I've been willing to cut
you some slack. Because I really *like* you."

"I like you, too."

Becca let out a deep breath. "Then tell me what's going on."

*You'd think I'm insane. And if I told you, I might be putting
you in danger.*

Robby's eyes drifted to his backpack. He thought of the yellowed pages tucked inside and the portrait of Miss Winters from
more than three hundred years earlier. He thought of all the photos he'd seen at Mrs. Vickory's house—of Abby and the other
girls who'd all started taking extra lessons with Miss Winters after school.

It was all connected. But how?

Miss Winters wasn't the young woman she appeared to be,
that much he knew for sure. The pages inside his backpack were
the first piece of the puzzle he'd need to solve if he hoped to un-
cover her past and stop whatever scheme she was planning in the
present. And if he was lucky, he'd be able to track down Tina
and his mother, too.

If they were even still alive.

His phone buzzed again. He blinked, startled out of his
thoughts.

"Go ahead," Becca said, trying very hard not to sound sul-
len. "It might be important."

Robby glanced at the screen.

Miss Winters.

The Hollows.

Come right now.

Becca placed a warm hand on his. "What is it? You're white

as a sheet."

"Nothing, but I—" He blinked. "I have to go."

"I thought you were staying for dinner? My mom made matzo ball soup."

"I know, I'm sorry. It's an emergency."

Becca pulled back her hand. "I thought you said it was nothing."

"I meant nothing to do with… what we were talking about before."

Becca's gaze darted to Robby's phone. He clicked the screen dark and climbed to his feet, stomach tightening. Smells wafted up from the kitchen, and Becca's mother appeared at the bottom of the stairs, smiling and waving an oversized oven mitt in their direction before skirting back into the kitchen.

"Call you tomorrow?" Robby said hopefully.

Becca stared past his shoulder without making eye contact. "If you want."

Robby found Zeus near the darkened gap in the bedrock of the hidden grove, still in his full practice pads and football uniform. Zeus removed his helmet and looked around nervously.

"Are you alone?"

Robby thought of the look on Becca's face as he'd left her house. He'd never felt *more* alone. She'd been watching from her bedroom window, dropping the curtains when he started down the path from the Heights to the Hollows. He'd almost gone back—to apologize, to tell her the truth, to find some way to make her understand. Only the urgency of Zeus's message had kept him from turning around.

"What happened?" Robby asked.

"I took the shortcut home after practice like I always do," Zeus said. "That's when I saw Miss Winters. In the tunnels. She was *right there*." He thrust a finger at the narrow cave opening. "You've got to see this."

They crawled through the crevice that had once taken them all the way to Mrs. Vickory's house. Around the first bend, Zeus directed his phone's flashlight toward the rough wall.

Robby squinted into the light. "I don't see anything."

"Exactly," said Zeus. "Now, watch this."

He handed Robby his phone and motioned for him to shine it on the cave wall. Zeus thrust his hand toward the granite embankment. The air shuddered as his hand passed *through* the wall up to his elbow.

Robby gaped. "No way."

"It's like you've been saying all along. Magic." Zeus pulled his hand back from the wall and inspected his fingers for damage. "She went right through. She hasn't come out."

"Did she see you?"

"No. I'd already turned off my flashlight because I could see the way out. And I wasn't about to follow her."

"I am," Robby said, tossing his backpack to Zeus. "Hold this for me?"

Zeus tossed it back to him. "I wasn't about to follow her *alone*. That's why I texted you. Safety in numbers."

"Somehow, I doubt that. Let's go."

Robby pushed the toe of his shoe into the wall. It felt like sticking his foot into a bowl of Jell-O. He wriggled his toes inside his shoe to make sure they still worked before pushing through to the other side. He came out gasping. Zeus stumbled through after him.

Robby plunged one hand back the way he'd come to make sure he still could, and then waved the light of his phone around the space to get a better look. The farther they went down the tunnel, the slicker the walls became. The air smelled more of the sea than earth. He wondered if it came out near the water.

As they walked, the tunnel narrowed to a small opening. Robby squeezed through on his hands and knees, emerging into a wider, roughly rectangular chamber. Salt water dripped from the ceiling to the slippery cave floor. Here, there was no question the chamber had been carved from the granite bedrock by something other than nature.

"What is this place?" Robby wondered. His voice echoed dully back at him. He scanned the walls for another passage. "Where did she go?"

"Robby," called Zeus in a slightly panicked voice. "I'm stuck."

Robby shined his phone back toward the wall. Zeus's head and shoulders poked through the gap, but the rest of his body remained on the other side. Robby gave Zeus a strong tug, and he tumbled forward, crushing Robby beneath him, both of them panting for breath.

"Now I know why you made varsity," Robby said. He climbed unsteadily to his feet and scraped his head against a protruding rock. His ears rang dully and everything around him seemed a little blurry at the edges.

"What the heck is that?" whispered Zeus in an awe-filled voice.

Robby rubbed his head. "A big rock."

"No, not that." Zeus fumbled for his phone and pointed the flashlight toward the far end of the chamber. A perfect hexagram shimmered back at them from some kind of raised altar carved into the bedrock. "I meant, what is *that*?"

17

Needles

"I hate her," Abby said.

She held her lunch tray between clenched fingers as Amethyst suppressed a yawn, blinking at her in the fluorescent lights of the cafeteria while students shuffled between tables toward their usual seats.

"Who?"

"Who do you *think*?"

Amethyst plucked raccoon hair from her shirt. "I don't know. Becca?"

"No, I don't mind Becca."

"Olivia Edwards, then."

"*Yes*, Olivia Edwards. I hate her."

Abby placed her lunch tray on their table, eying the grayish turkey breast suspiciously. The school had been serving turkey in one form or another since last week. Thanksgiving was still more than a week away, but Abby didn't think she'd be able to stomach any more turkey by the time it finally arrived, no matter how hungry she got from spellcasting.

Daisy, Delphi, and Piper joined them a few minutes later. "The malodorous toad has a new boyfriend," Daisy said, her eyes flickering in the direction of the double doors where T-Rex and Olivia were holding hands and making eyes at each other. "I can't believe we have to spend time with her. Everything would be better if it were just the five of us."

"Miss Winters said there needs to be six," said Delphi.

"I only see five of us at this table right now," Piper said between bites of turkey. "Olivia's never going to be one of us."

"Maybe things will get better," Delphi suggested, without much conviction.

After a week, Abby couldn't imagine their situation being any worse. She'd never liked Olivia, but until recently, they'd more or less kept out of each other's way. Now, Olivia was proving to be as good at mastering spells as she was at hurling insults at everyone in their coven.

"Looks like T-Rex decided to let Joey have a go at the new girl," said Delphi. Abby followed her gaze to another table where Becca sat by herself while Joey loomed over her with a steaming plate of turkey and stuffing. She was bent over a notepad drawing something in colored pencil. Her lunch sat uneaten next to her books.

"Why isn't Becca sitting with Robby?" Abby wondered aloud.

Amethyst pointed to another table in the far corner of the cafeteria where Robby sat by himself. "Go ask him."

"What? No, I can't."

"If you don't, I will, if only so I don't have to watch you pining anymore."

"I don't *pine*," protested Abby. "I just miss hanging out with him."

Amethyst shoved Abby toward Robby's table. She touched a finger to her lucky pendant, then screwed up her courage and walked the rest of the way.

Robby sat up, surprised, as she slipped into the chair beside him. His expression hovered somewhere between curious and perplexed, so she gave him her most disarming grin. "How's it going?"

His face relaxed into a half smile. "I've been better."

"Me too."

"Dad's doing all right," he finally said. "All things considered, I mean. It's hard with Tina gone."

"I miss her too. I'm sorry she… that she was looking for me when it happened."

Robby opened his mouth to say something, but then he appeared to think better of it.

"How about you? Is everything okay between you and…?" She glanced in Becca's direction. Joey had finally given up and stalked back to his own table. Becca was watching them from across the cafeteria.

Abby looked away, feeling flushed. "Not that I care about— I mean, I *care*, obviously…" She didn't know whether she was saying too much or not enough. "I just want you to be happy."

"I'd be happier if we were still friends."

Abby's stomach fluttered. "We are friends. We'll always be friends."

"Then why are you avoiding me? Why are you…" Robby's voice faded as he peered over her shoulder at Becca. "Keeping secrets?" he finished under his breath.

Because I'm trying to protect you, Abby thought. *Because if Miss Winters is really as bad as you think, I don't want you to risk your life snooping around when I can do it for you.* But she knew that argument wouldn't sway him. He wouldn't want to be protected. "I'm trying to learn about myself, Robby. About what I can do."

"Like flying?"

Abby met his gaze. "Miss Winters is the only one who can teach me."

A flicker of movement passed between the tables behind Robby, and then Olivia was disentangling herself from T-Rex's grip and sneering down at them.

"Romeo and Juliet together again," she said gleefully, loud enough for half the cafeteria to hear. Behind her, Becca's chair scraped away from her table. She scooped up her books and tromped away.

"Robby," Abby pleaded. She reached for his hand, grateful that he didn't pull back. "That's not what this is about. I don't— I'm not—"

The tips of his ears burned red. His jaw was set as he glanced at where Becca had been sitting and then back to Abby. He gave Abby's hand a squeeze. "Just promise you'll be careful around Miss Winters. You can't trust her. I know you don't believe me, but she's not what she seems." Then he collected his backpack and tray and followed Becca out of the cafeteria.

Olivia snickered and waltzed away with T-Rex in the other direction.

"I hate her," Abby said. Her hands curled into fists. Phosphorous wisps glowed white-hot from her fingertips as she retreated to her own table.

That night, Abby made her way to the lighthouse for their evening lesson with the moon as her companion. Snow had been piling up all afternoon, but by sunset it had given way to a steady drizzle of freezing rain. She found her friends huddled outside the lighthouse door, staring longingly at the guttering candlelight inside. Olivia stood away from the group with a look on her face like she might catch something if she got too close to the others. Abby scowled at her before joining her friends.

"What's going on in there?" she asked.

"No idea," said Delphi, breathing through the folds of her

knitted scarf. "We're not allowed in just yet."

"You didn't see the answer in the stars?" Amethyst asked, raising an eyebrow.

Delphi pulled her scarf down long enough to say, "There *aren't* any stars tonight."

"S-s-so cold," Piper chattered. Flapper, whom she'd adopted, pecked at the rain in her hair from atop her left shoulder.

"You could have him take a look," Abby said. Flapper squawked in response before shifting to Piper's other shoulder. He'd tripled in size since they'd found him.

"I think he's too fat to fly now," whispered Amethyst.

Olivia planted herself in front of the door and crossed her arms as if she'd been anointed Miss Winters's personal bodyguard. "No one's going to take a look," she said. "Miss Winters values her privacy."

"There's a fine line between privacy and secrets," Abby said, her conversation with Robby about their teacher still fresh in her mind. "It won't hurt to have a look inside." If Miss Winters was up to something, it would be better to find out sooner rather than later.

She eyed the windows, then cast a simple levitation spell.

"Get down from there," snapped Olivia.

As she tried to grab Abby's ankles, Amethyst moved to block her. Olivia stepped around, but Daisy and Delphi raced to bar her way.

"Miss Winters values initiative, too," Abby called down to Olivia as she steadied herself against a rotting sill about nine feet above the ground. At first, she could only make out a few familiar shapes inside—broken furniture, an iron cauldron shoved up against the far wall. Then she saw Miss Winters kneeling at the center of the room inside the painted hexagram they used during lessons. She had her back to Abby and was chanting.

"What's she doing?" shouted Amethyst.

Inside the lighthouse, the air began to swirl so fast it became a blur. Abby strained for a better look, but her glasses were too wet to see clearly.

"Abby!" yelled someone from below. She ignored it.

The blur around Miss Winters spiraled even faster. Hazy faces appeared at each point of the hexagram, wavering and twisting like reflections in a funhouse mirror. They vanished just as quickly, but short, gnarled sticks lay where they'd been—one at each of the hexagram's six points.

What just happened?

A sharp pain struck Abby between the shoulders without warning, breaking her concentration. She lost her grip on the sill, and the world whistled by until she hit the ground, gasping. Everything wobbled as she tried to sit up. She raised her hands to her mouth, and they came away speckled with blood.

Olivia towered over her victoriously, but Amethyst and Delphi shoved her aside, together pulling Abby to her feet just as the lighthouse door opened and Miss Winters appeared in the entryway. Olivia darted inside before Abby could think of an explanation.

"I tried to stop Olivia from firing that spell at you," Amethyst whispered. "She was too fast. You okay?"

Abby squeezed her friend's hand. Now that she tried to put weight on her feet, her whole body hurt, but it was normal pain—the achiness she'd come to expect after casting a levitation spell, the sharp twinges after falling from a great height. Still, her balance felt off. More than that, her *mind* felt off, like she'd been stuck on a carnival tilt-a-whirl since breakfast.

The other girls buzzed excitedly as they filed inside and took their usual spots inside the hexagram.

Amethyst held back, her gaze lingering on the window. "What did you see?" she asked.

Abby shook her head. She felt like she had cotton balls between her ears. It was hard to focus. From inside the hexagram, Daisy said something about wands. Abby barely heard her.

"I'm not sure," Abby told Amethyst, closing her eyes. She thought she remembered faces, almost like ghosts, but then the image vanished, and she couldn't find it again. She blinked as she stepped inside the hexagram. "I… can't remember."

Olivia's attack spell must have included the raw ingredients of a memory charm, because Abby had been having trouble remembering anything more than fuzzy fragments of the evening. She fingered her new wand absently, a gift from Miss Winters, as she walked home with Amethyst, shaking her head in frustration. "I remember Miss Winters saying something about a needle. It's all muddled, though."

"Definitely a memory charm," Amethyst told her.

The wand in Abby's left hand was a knobby willow stick, nine inches long and thin as a pencil, but it thrummed like it had a life of its own. "Until now, you have been painting without a brush," Miss Winters had told them. That much Abby remembered. "Your efforts have been colorful, but messy. Magic requires precision to bend it to your will. Your wand is that focusing instrument."

"Miss Winters said the more complicated the spell, the more precision you need," Amethyst explained. "Without it, we use too much of our own energy. That's why we're so hungry and ache so badly post-spellcasting. Think of the wand like a needle and think of the magical strands you want to knit together as your yarn. Cast on, like this." Amethyst stopped walking and placed one hand on Abby's right shoulder. Her fingers closed over Abby's wand hand and moved it in a circle.

"Magic is the act of knitting the ordinary threads of the natural world into something extraordinary. That's what Miss

Winters said." Amethyst guided Abby's hand in the opposite pattern. "Cast off when you've finished the spell." She lowered Abby's wand hand to her side.

They stopped at the intersection where the old carriage road split, one way leading toward Abby's house and the other in the direction of Amethyst's. Abby thought she saw movement in the woods just beyond and squinted through the light rain for a closer look. Olivia was glaring at her from behind a thick tree, holding a finger to her lips. She'd sprinted out of the lighthouse as soon as their lesson ended, but hiding in the woods was strange, even for her.

What is she up to?

Abby turned to Amethyst. "See you tomorrow, okay?"

Amethyst nodded encouragingly. "You'll get this whole wand thing in no time. We can go over it again tomorrow if you want."

Once Amethyst had disappeared from view, Olivia emerged from the bushes and approached Abby, her boots flicking mud onto Abby's pants as they squished into the damp ground in front of her.

"What were you doing in there?" Abby asked.

Olivia whistled. A moment later, T-Rex, Joey, and Sarika stepped onto the path behind her, shivering in the cold. T-Rex flicked a pocket lighter on and off without looking at it, the light of the small flame not reaching his eyes.

"Are you out of your mind?" Abby shouted. She considered hiding her wand, but then thought of a better use for it.

"Ow!" shrieked Olivia, batting at Abby's arm.

Abby poked her a second time before slipping the wand into her back pocket. T-Rex howled with laughter.

"How much do they know?" Abby demanded. "If Miss Winters finds out—"

"She won't."

"This is beyond stupid, even for you."

"I know what I'm doing. Just like I know I'm a better witch than you."

T-Rex snorted. Sarika held up her phone with her non-broken arm to snap a picture.

"Oh, for heaven's sake," Olivia muttered, pointing her wand at each of her friends. They blinked in confusion. "It's not like I ever let them *remember* anything. They wait outside when I'm training and then I wipe their memories before we do anything else." She pulled the phone from Sarika's fingers, deleted a few photos, and then handed it back to her. "It beats only having you freaks to talk to about this stuff."

"What just happened?" Sarika asked. "Is that Abby Shepherd? What are we doing here?"

"What *are* you doing here?" Abby demanded.

Olivia leaned in so close that only Abby could hear her. "We need to talk."

"About what?"

"When I tell you not to do something, like peeking through the lighthouse windows, you're going to start listening to me. Got it?"

Abby crossed her arms. Her back still throbbed from the fall, and she bit back a groan from the sudden movement. "You blindsided me tonight. I'd like to see you try something like that when it's a fair fight."

"Would you really?"

Abby didn't like the self-satisfied tone of Olivia's voice. She felt as if she'd walked into some kind of trap—as if Olivia had been hoping she'd react this way.

"Amethyst says you can fly," Olivia said, grinning.

"Yeah, I've flown," Abby replied, though she hadn't had any luck with it since that first time—she had bruises all over her body from her failed attempts. Still, she wasn't about to admit that to Olivia. "But I'm not going to teach you."

"I don't need your help. I want to race you."

Abby shook her head. "Race?"

"You heard me. Meet me at the lighthouse at midnight on Thanksgiving."

"You expect me to just sneak out of my house in the middle of the night?"

"Assuming you're not too scared." Olivia nudged Abby in the shoulder. "I'll bring my broom. You bring yours. We'll see if you can keep up."

18

The Secret History

On Thanksgiving Day, Robby climbed the ladder to the attic and dropped a handful of fresh kibbles into Achilles's food bowl. He'd never intended to keep Mrs. Vickory's cat at the house for long, but he'd promised Tina he'd look after him until she got home. Now even the thought of sending Achilles to live somewhere else felt like an admission that Tina would never return.

He placed a fresh cup of water next to the food dish and knelt to give the cat a scratch under the chin. Already, Robby's eyes were watering, and his lungs felt thick and heavy from being so close. He crossed the narrow space and cracked open the attic window for some fresh air. Outside, yesterday's storm had coated the last stubborn leaves of fall with ice, and the pine trees at the edge of his yard glittered white like a Victorian Christmas tableau. The wind that whistled through the woods beyond sounded haunted and forlorn, more like a dreary midwinter day than the last week of November. But the longer he listened, caught up in his thoughts about Tina and Achilles, the more he became aware of another sound.

Laughter?

He craned his neck to get a better look at Abby's backyard. There, Abby and Amethyst Jones were putting the finishing touches on a snowman with scraggly tree branches for arms and a purple wool hat that looked too small for its round head. Amethyst stepped back, inspecting their work, and tipped her hat at the snowman.

The snowman tipped its hat in return.

Robby gasped, then ducked out of sight before the two girls saw him. Through the ice-speckled glass, the snowman rolled into view and across Abby's backyard before vanishing into the darkened woods. Abby followed it to the edge of her yard, guiding it with what looked like a willow switch in her left hand. The tip of it glowed a stark blue that made the air around it sparkle with energy.

A wand, Robby thought. *Abby is using a wand.*

Flying on the broomstick on Halloween hadn't been a fluke. Abby could do magic… and so could at least one of her new friends. If they all could, it would mean that Mrs. Vickory had somehow picked the only six girls out of everyone in their grade that had the same potential. And now they were all spending extra time with Miss Winters—even Olivia Edwards, who pretended not to have anything to do with Abby and her friends but still followed Miss Winters around with unconcealed devotion.

Abby was smarter than Olivia, though. She wouldn't just blindly follow Miss Winters, especially not after what had happened on Halloween or after what Robby had told her about his mother and Tina. So why *would* she expose herself to Miss Winters like this? And why would she continue to avoid him?

We are friends, she'd told him that day in the cafeteria. *We'll always be friends.*

"But friends tell each other things," he said aloud. "Friends let each other help…"

Was Abby keeping secrets and keeping her distance to protect him from Miss Winters?

Was he doing the same thing to Becca?

Fighting back a sneeze, he knelt to give Achilles another scratch under the chin. Then, his mind made up, he pulled his phone from his back pocket and began to type.

The sound of a smoke detector reached him in the attic a few minutes later. He rounded off Achilles's food bowl with a few more kibbles and followed the alarm to the kitchen, where he found his father slumped on the floor in front of the stove with his head buried in two blackened mitts, smoke streaming from the oven.

Robby waved at the smoke detector, then stood on a chair and yanked out the batteries. The contents of the oven looked more like a charcoal briquette than anything fit for human consumption. Robby took in the limp green beans smoldering on the stovetop next to a viscous goo that might have once been mashed potatoes.

"Behold our Thanksgiving feast," his dad said, looking up. Something black smudged his cheeks. "How about Chinese?"

"You go. I'll take care of the mess."

Robby had nearly finished scraping the potatoes into the trash when Zeus appeared in the window above the sink, marching from the woods like a yeti tromping through the snow.

"What happened in here?" Zeus asked, holding his nose as he let himself in.

"Dad burned the Thanksgiving dinner. Cooking was… *is* Tina's thing." He dumped the remains of the turkey into the trash. "You look happy. Did you guys win the game?"

Zeus beamed. "We got slaughtered. But the season is finally

over!" He grabbed a wooden spoon and scraped the green beans into the garbage while Robby dealt with something that looked vaguely like cranberry sauce. "In other news," Zeus said, "I staked out the hexagram again last night. No change, no sign of Miss Winters. All I got was a minor case of frostbite. Are you having better luck?"

Robby tried a fragment of cornbread and then dropped the entire loaf into the garbage. He shook his head. "I've been reading up on hexagrams. They're associated with witchcraft, conjuring spirits, that kind of thing… but it's pretty much been a dead end for me, too."

Zeus leaned against the refrigerator, wrinkling his nose. "I don't like it."

"Like what?"

"Conjuring spirits. I know you said Abby can… do things. Flying and stuff." He raised a hand to stop Robby from interrupting. "But I'm just saying, even if she can take care of herself, that sounds seriously dangerous. I wish we could actually *do* something to help her."

"We are doing something."

"Robby, I've never studied harder in my life than I have with those pages from the *Secret History*, but we're not any closer to stopping—"

"Miss Winters came to Willow Cove for a reason. Everything she's doing, everything she's done so far has been planned for hundreds of years. We need to figure out what she wants and why. *Then* maybe we can stop her."

Zeus frowned. "At least in football you get to hit people."

"Your football team just got slaughtered, remember? This is smarter."

"I can't just sit around and wait, though. Everything we try just leads to more dead ends."

"I've been thinking about that, too." Robby closed the oven door and tossed his dad's now-melted mitts into the trash along with the rest of the Thanksgiving feast. "We need help. Someone who might see things differently than us."

Zeus peeked out the kitchen window, where Mr. O'Reilly was still sitting in the car, resting his head on the steering wheel. "Your dad?"

"No, I think it's time to tell Becca the truth."

"Not about Abby."

"I told *you*, didn't I?"

"That's different." Zeus crossed his arms. "You know how I feel about Abby. We have to protect her secret."

"I know that, but I can't keep lying to Becca about the rest of it."

"I still don't think it's a good idea. If Miss Winters is dangerous—"

"What about Miss Winters?" asked Becca. She was standing in the doorway, and she didn't look happy.

Robby and Zeus exchanged a look.

"You got my text." Robby smiled at her. She didn't smile back. "I wasn't sure if you'd come."

"I almost couldn't. Mom's driving me to the airport in ten minutes. Second Thanksgiving."

"Second Thanksgiving?" Zeus asked.

"You get two of everything when your parents are divorced. What's so important, Robby?"

He led her and Zeus upstairs, then closed the door to his room. He'd cleaned up and cleared a spot on the bed, but Becca remained standing, arms crossed. Zeus settled there instead.

"I know you think I've been acting weird," Robby began.

"I don't just *think* it."

"All right." He took a deep breath. "It's because I didn't want to get you involved in something dangerous."

"What are you talking about?"

"Miss Winters is a witch."

An angry laugh escaped Becca's lips. "*That's* why you

wanted me to come over? Goodbye, Robby."

"She did something to Tina!"

Becca shook her head. "Our history teacher attacked your stepmother?"

"And that's not all. She also—"

"You know what I hate?" Her voice was chilly as she took a step toward the door. "Being lied to. All this sneaking around, and that's the best you came up with?"

Zeus shot off the bed to block her way. "Hear him out."

Becca threw her hands in the air. "Not you, too?"

"He's telling the truth."

"What if I can prove it?" Robby asked.

Becca checked her phone. "Two minutes. My dad will flip if I miss my flight."

Robby opened his backpack. He nudged Einstein off his desk before placing the yellowed stack of papers where the iguana had been. "This was written by Mrs. Vickory—our old history teacher. It's the only copy we can find. It might be the only one that still exists. Listen to this part." He flipped to the second to last page. "'Joanna Greylocke, an orphan and distant relation to the Winslows of Salem, is believed to have crossed the Atlantic and become a ward of William Winslow at age thirteen.'"

Becca rubbed the back of her neck, looking more irritated than interested. Robby hurtled forward anyway. "'There are two references to a *Joanna Winslow* in legal documents from Salem and Boston, roughly corresponding to the period in question. Few details are known of her early life or what became of her after the trial and subsequent conviction of William Winslow's six daughters for practicing witchcraft. There is no evidence to suggest she remained with the Winslow family during its precipitous decline and ultimate ruin. The last reference to either a Joanna Greylocke or Joanna Winslow comes in 1691 from the pages of a diary purported to belong to the young woman.'" Robby looked up at Becca. "Then there's a footnote describing the diary. 'Bound journal with cherrywood cover. Carved with her initials. From the author's personal collection.'"

"Okay," said Becca. "What's your point?"

"Miss Winters told us there was no mention of the six Winslow sisters in the history books, but she was wrong. Mrs. Vickory knew all about them."

"You think Miss Winters attacked *her*, too? Why? So she could steal her job?"

"Not Miss Winters—*Joanna Greylocke*. That's her real name." He held out the final page. "Look."

Becca took the yellowed sheet. Her eyes narrowed as she studied the portrait. "You think this is Miss Winters?"

"It is her," Zeus cut in. He dragged a finger across the yellowed page. "Right down to the streak in her hair."

"She practically told us her first day in class," Robby said. "'Living history,' remember? She was talking about herself. *She's* the living history."

"The resemblance..." Becca whispered, shaking her head.

"It's not just a resemblance. It's the same person. Joanna Greylocke is Joanna Winslow. Joanna Winslow is Miss Winters. Who knows how many other names she's used over the past three hundred years? That's *her*, Becca."

"I can think of a half dozen other explanations better than yours," Becca replied, but she sounded less sure than she had earlier.

"Miss Winters tried to kill me. I was at Whispering Hill on Halloween, and she..." Robby trailed off, wondering how he could explain without giving away Abby's role in the story.

Becca's face had lost a little of its color. "Whispering Hill?"

"That's where Miss Winters lives."

Becca's phone buzzed. She swallowed, then let out a wobbly sigh. When her phone buzzed again, she said, "My mom's outside. I have to go."

"But you have to believe me."

"No, I have to *go*."

"Becca, I think my mom was in contact with her before she—*before*. They were friends. I think Miss Winters went after her all those years ago, and now she might have done something to my stepmother, too."

Becca glanced at the portrait again, then pressed the whole stack of papers into Robby's hands. "I believe *you* believe, Robby. I'll be home on Sunday. We'll talk more then." She glanced at Zeus and Robby again, her expression softening. "Neither of you do anything stupid while I'm gone, okay?"

19

The Duel in the Dark

Abby paced around her darkened bedroom, glanced at her clock, and started pacing again. Across the hall, her mother's furious typing slowed to an occasional *tap-tap-tap*. It wouldn't be long before she flicked off her office light and trudged downstairs for bed, which meant it wouldn't be long before Abby would be out of excuses.

Nearly midnight, she thought. *Nearly time to meet Olivia at the lighthouse.*

When the typing finally stopped, Abby padded back to her bed and slipped under the covers. Her door creaked open, flooding the room with light from the hallway. Abby closed her eyes tighter when she felt her mother's gaze on her, suddenly worried she might have left her jacket or snow boots out. She held her breath and waited.

"I know you're awake," her mother whispered from the doorway. "I could hear you moving around."

Just go to bed, Abby thought to herself. *Please, Mom.*

"I'm not going to lecture you, honey. Well, not much." Mrs. Shepherd chuckled quietly. "I just want you to make sure you're taking care of yourself. You've been so busy lately with your new friends and all that extra credit work, and you… weren't yourself at dinner tonight. You barely touched the pecan pie." She waited for Abby to reply. Finally, she said, "If you need to talk about whatever's going on, I'm here."

When Abby still didn't reply, her mother sighed. "Well, good night, sweet girl."

Abby lowered the covers to her chest. "Mom?"

Mrs. Shepherd stopped, half in, half out of the room. "Yes?"

"Good night."

Abby waited a few minutes after the door clicked shut and her mother's footsteps faded to silence before throwing off the covers and retrieving her wand. The wand felt good in her hand, like a mug of hot cider thawing her fingers after a chilly day outside. She'd adapted to using it more quickly than she'd expected, and now it felt odd to think of casting a spell without it. A familiar warm sensation spread through her whole body until a dim blue light glowed from the wand's tip, just bright enough to reveal her snow boots hidden under her desk.

It was only after she'd put on her jacket and knelt to lace her boots that she felt like she was being watched. She glanced at her bedroom door certain she'd find her mother there—but it remained closed. Slipping on her other boot, she scanned the room, then spotted a streak of purple outside her window and breathed a sigh of relief.

"Amethyst." She unlatched the window with a flick of her wand. "What are you doing here?"

Amethyst slipped inside, eying Abby's boots. "The better question is what are *you* doing? You moped around all day. Not even the snowman cheered you up for long."

"That's the last time I invite you to Thanksgiving dinner."

"Tell me what's going on."

"Nothing."

"It sure doesn't look like nothing."

"And that gives you permission to spy on me?"

"I'm checking on you, Abby. It's different. This is what friends do."

"Stalker friends."

"*Best* friends. There, I said it." Amethyst brushed a thin coating of snow onto Abby's rug and shook out her hair, sending wet droplets everywhere. "You're my best friend. Which means I'm practically obligated to stalk you when you're acting all strange."

"That's not how it works."

"Well, I'm still new to this whole friendship thing." Amethyst sank her hands into her pockets. "I'm pretty sure keeping secrets from each other isn't how it's supposed to work, either."

Abby glanced at her clock and then sighed. "Fine. Come with me. I'll explain on the way."

It would feel better having someone on her side tonight, anyway.

The cold air stung and tiny flecks of ice peppered their cheeks as Abby and Amethyst neared the rocky headland. Abby checked the time on her phone.

"Are you sure… she'll even… show up?" Amethyst shouted over the wind.

That had occurred to Abby too. Olivia didn't seem like the type to suffer in this kind of weather just to make a point. *She's probably laughing at me from her toasty warm bed.* Still, she wasn't going to risk it. "Olivia will break her neck if I'm not there to stop her."

"How is that not a good thing?"

"I can't let her do something dangerous just to prove she's better than me."

Amethyst snorted. "I think a broken neck might do her a world of good."

"That's because you have no moral compass."

The first-floor windows of the lighthouse glowed dimly as they approached. Abby touched the tip of her wand to the hexagram, and the door slid open with a faint creak. A seagull rocketed within an inch of Abby's head, and then another fluttered unsteadily past—Flapper, looking plumper than ever. Abby waited another second to make sure there weren't any more surprises before slipping inside.

The warm smell of chocolate filled the room as Piper flailed wildly at five floating mugs while a steaming pitcher charged after her. "Oh good, you're here!" she said, dodging the pitcher. "I made some hot—*ouch*—hot cocoa!" A mug dive-bombed her head, grazing her left ear. "Bit of a problem with the—*oomph*—the animation spells on these mugs, but I'll have it under control in a second." She darted to her left, feinted right, and spoke the proper incantation. The mugs wobbled before floating resentfully toward their intended recipients. Abby trapped hers between her hands, holding it firmly until it stopped struggling, and then noticed Daisy and Delphi sitting off to one side.

"'Unquiet meals make ill digestions,'" said Daisy, holding her still-struggling mug at arm's length. "*Comedy of Errors.*"

"What are you guys doing here?" Abby asked. She glanced at Amethyst, who looked just as surprised.

"Jupiter's rising," said Delphi as if that explained everything.

Piper's hands rested on her knees, but she took occasional drags from her inhaler. "We're here… to… support you," she huffed. "Try the hot chocolate."

Abby sipped her cocoa but barely tasted it. She sent the mug floating to a small table next to the cauldron, then hung her jacket on the wall near the other coats still speckled with ice.

"Who told you I needed support?"

"Flapper," said Piper. "He followed Olivia the other night—he *can* fly, you know—and overheard you two talking in the woods. He finally thought to tell me about it today, and then I texted them. I would have texted you, too," she added, in Amethyst's direction, "but you refuse to get a phone."

"I told you to come alone." Olivia slid through the door and flung it shut behind her. She held a wet broom in her right hand and her wand in the left. "Where's your broom?"

Abby stepped into the center of the hexagram. "I'm not here to fly."

"Because you can't."

"She can," said Amethyst. "I saw her."

Olivia laughed. "Well, if *Amethyst* says it's true."

"I'm only here to make sure you don't get yourself killed," Abby interrupted. "That's it."

Olivia studied Abby through narrowed eyes. "You're just looking out for me?"

"That's right."

She shoved past Abby and marched toward the stairs. "I can look after myself."

Abby pointed her wand at the stairway door and slammed it shut. Olivia spun around, her face twisted in irritation, and leveled her wand at Abby. They glared at each other, and then Olivia spun back and shot a blast at the door that splintered the wood. She stomped up the stairs.

"*Now* do you hope she breaks her neck?" asked Amethyst.

"Little bit."

Abby rushed after Olivia, taking a second to seal the smoldering remains of the door behind her in case one of her friends tried to follow. It wouldn't hold any of them for long, but it might give her a minute or two.

Olivia was waiting around the first bend. She slanted her wand at Abby. "Just admit I'm the alpha here."

Abby glared at her. "Do you actually like being hated by so

many people?"

"I don't care if you freaks hate me as long as you respect me." She thrust her wand at Abby, lightning fast. A thousand invisible threads crackled in the air between them, hanging like a spider's web waiting to be woven.

Abby hooked the strands to her wand first.

"You want respect? *Earn it.*"

Olivia's wand and broom clattered to the steps. She stumbled back, glassy-eyed, then lurched forward as she steadied herself.

"Satisfied?" Abby shouted.

"We're just getting started."

Olivia snatched her wand from the steps and stabbed it into the space between them. Abby hooked another thread and sent Olivia tumbling to her hands and knees. "That was for your stupid Romeo and Juliet comment in front of Robby last week," she said, her cheeks burning with a wave of fresh anger. She raised her wand like a club. "It's not enough for you that my best friend replaced me with someone else?"

She sent a fresh blast at Olivia as she climbed the winding steps toward her. Olivia abandoned her wand, scrambling backward on all fours. Abby fired another shot, angrier now.

The door at the top of the lighthouse hung open, and sleet pounded the boards of the catwalk. Olivia crawled outside, her hair blowing in the wind.

Abby's wand quivered between clenched fingers as she followed Olivia outside. "It's not enough to mock and ridicule me and my friends?" Her wand flared blue-white, channeling her rage. "You just can't help yourself, can you?"

"Abby, please…"

Blood streaked the ancient glass casing of the beacon light. Olivia's hair and face were awash in it, too, and her lips were swollen. She held up a shaky hand. "Please… stop…"

Abby gasped. She dropped her wand and rushed to Olivia's

side. "Oh God, Olivia, I didn't mean to—"

Concerned voices floated up the stairs. Amethyst reached them first, shining her wand quickly from Abby to Olivia with an unusually serious expression on her face. "You okay?" she asked Abby.

"I didn't mean to do it." Abby repeated it, louder this time, loud enough that everyone would hear her. "I just got so angry at—"

Everything, she thought. *Everything in my life.*

"It's okay," Amethyst said gently. She touched Abby's shoulder. "It's all right."

Olivia tried to sit up. She coughed, then winced as she allowed Amethyst to ease her back down. Abby put one hand under Olivia's left shoulder, Amethyst took the other, and together they propped her against the wall. A glob of bloody phlegm trickled down her chin, glowing blue in the wandlight.

"I hate you so much," Olivia croaked weakly at Abby.

Delphi leaned over the railing. "Guys? Big problem."

"No more predictions," said Amethyst, not looking up.

"I'm pretty solid on this one, actually."

Miss Winters floated out of the darkness. Her cloak whipped wildly above her broom. Her eyes were stone. She leapt onto the catwalk and waved her wand at Abby and Olivia. Translucent threads of purple and red that Abby had never seen before spun shapes in the air. All at once, the threads surrounded Abby, squeezing her, flowing through her. She suddenly felt hollowed out, as if she'd been cut off from her own life force.

"What happened here?" Miss Winters demanded.

"She challenged me," Abby said numbly. She glanced down at Olivia and then away. "I didn't mean to hurt her."

"Then you failed spectacularly."

Abby stared at her left hand. Her wand hand. It looked the same, but now it felt like a blunt object.

"To keep you from doing any more harm," Miss Winters explained. "It will wear off." She touched Olivia's forehead and whispered something Abby couldn't hear. Olivia's head lolled to one side and her breathing eased—the sound of sleep. Miss Winters surveyed the remaining girls. "Five against one, was it?"

"No, just… one against one," said Abby.

Miss Winters eyed her coldly. "The rest of you may go. *Now*," she added sharply when no one moved. "Abigail, a word."

Amethyst squeezed Abby's hand, and then she and the others headed down the stairs. Once they were alone, Miss Winters invited Abby to stand with her at the railing. They watched the girls file out of the lighthouse.

"What was your biggest mistake tonight?" Miss Winters said at last.

"I let my anger get the best of me."

"It certainly seems so. But that wasn't your mistake. This was." She handed Abby her wand. "Never discard your wand, Abby. *Never.* Someday, you may pay a terrible price for it. You went too far, but probably not as far as Olivia would have if she'd had the upper hand. This may be the best outcome for you both. Perhaps you'll arrive at a truce now."

"I don't think she's going to forgive me."

"You don't need her forgiveness. You need her fear. I think you earned that tonight." Miss Winters placed a hand on Abby's shoulder. "Not many girls could have done what you did here. You are the strongest in your coven, but that also means you have a responsibility to them—even to Olivia. You represent the best of what she could be. Don't take that lightly."

"I'm not the best. I haven't been able to fly since that first night when you—"

"I remember what happened that night," Miss Winters said, her voice surprisingly gentle.

Abby slumped against the rail. "Olivia wanted me to prove that I can fly so she could race me. She said *she* could fly. I hate her, but I didn't want her to hurt herself. *Ironically*," Abby added, shaking her head.

"She came to me a week ago for private lessons. I see now what motivated her." Miss Winters eyed her broom as it bobbed against the bloodied beacon light, then seemed to come to a decision. "Next week, I will teach you all to fly."

Abby smiled uneasily, ducking against the wind. Miss Winters probably meant for it to sound reassuring, that she thought they were all ready to take the next step in their learning. But as Abby risked another glance in her teacher's direction, then again at her own fingers, still powerless and empty, it was more evident than ever that she still had only scratched the surface of what it meant to be a witch.

If Miss Winters could strip away Abby's powers with a flick of her wand, what chance did she have—what chance did any of them have—of stopping her from doing even worse things if they discovered that she actually was responsible for the disappearances of Tina and Mrs. Vickory?

20

All for One

The trail to Becca's house zigzagged up the steepest part of the Heights, ending at the foot of a two-story colonial not far from her street. At the top, Robby stopped to catch his breath while Zeus lumbered slowly around the final switchback, huffing in the cold. Though it was only late afternoon, the moon glowed pale and low in the sky.

Victorian-style lampposts lined both sides of the street, while wreaths dotted with red bows and dusted with fresh snow hung from most of the doors. Becca's was not one of them. A menorah flickered in the living room window instead.

Robby knocked on Becca's front door, shifting nervously while he waited for someone to answer. Zeus flashed Robby a reassuring smile as he huddled beside him, his hands shoved into his pockets. They were both puzzled that Becca had asked them to come over as soon as she'd returned from visiting her father.

As Becca opened the door, a gust of warm air swept over Robby—or maybe it was just the blood rushing to his cheeks.

"Zeus, you can leave your jacket and shoes over there," she said, pointing to a coat rack by the door. "I need a second alone with Robby."

Zeus caught Robby's eye. "Good luck," he mouthed.

Robby followed Becca around a corner to the foot of the stairs, catching a glimpse of her mother poking at a fire in the living room. Spotting them, she waved and then turned back to the fireplace.

"Becca—" he began.

"Shush."

"I'm sorry I—"

She shushed him again, then stood on her tiptoes and gave him a peck on the forehead. "Happy Hanukkah."

"Is this some kind of Jewish tradition I don't know about?" Robby asked, feeling more confused than ever.

Becca's mother laughed. "I think she just missed you. Becca, leave your door open if you go upstairs."

Robby shook his head. "Then... you're not breaking up with me?"

Becca poked him hard in the shoulder. "It would serve you right if I did, all that sneaking around. But no." She studied him thoughtfully. "We need to talk about Miss Winters."

They returned to the hallway to find Zeus examining the floor. Robby gave him a thumbs-up, ditching his own jacket and sneakers by the coatrack before they followed Becca upstairs. She led them down a hall, flicking on a light in a room that looked like an office—probably her mom's.

"We're not supposed to be in here," Becca whispered. "We're right above the living room, so try to walk quietly." She tiptoed to the desk and fiddled with something under the keyboard tray, pulling out a small metal key, which she fitted into the lock on one of the drawers. It slid open with a click, and she riffled through a series of files before removing a thick manila folder.

"At first I thought you were out of your mind," she explained. "But then you mentioned Whispering Hill, and I got... curious. My mom is the one who handled the sale of that place."

Robby eyed the thick folder. He remembered Becca telling him that her mother was a realtor, but he was sure he would have made the connection if he'd seen her mother's name on the SOLD sign.

"Mom uses her maiden name professionally. Elena Rosenberg. She changed it back after the divorce." Becca opened the folder and legal documents, photos, and surveyor's drawings spilled across the desk. "Paperwork from the sale. My mom keeps copies of everything in her office, so I decided to take a look." She pointed to one of the pages with a half dozen signatures at the bottom. "Look who actually bought the property at Whispering Hill. It's not Miss Winters. It's a company—*the Greylocke Corporation.*"

Robby's breath caught in his throat. Zeus picked up a few pages and began shuffling through them.

"It gets even more interesting. I looked for a connection between the Greylocke Corporation and other places in town via the town auditor's website just before you got here—it's all online if you know how to look," she explained when Robby raised an eyebrow. "Greylocke owns the old lighthouse, Willow Hill, half the buildings in the Hex... even the right-of-way on the trail between the Heights and the Hollows. There's something in here about cave access, too."

The hexagram, Robby thought.

"Did you know that trail used to be the main carriage road between Boston and Salem in the seventeenth century?" Becca continued. She didn't wait for him to answer. She flipped through the folder, then pulled out another document. "There's almost nothing about the Greylocke Corporation online beyond a shell website, but look at this letterhead." She placed the sheet on the desk and tapped a spot near the top of the page with her finger. "The CEO is a woman named Joanna Winters."

"Winters and Greylocke," Zeus whispered.

Robby stared at the name on the page. "We were right, then. Miss Winters is Joanna Greylocke. The names can't be a coincidence."

"I don't believe in coincidences, anyway," Becca said, placing her hand on the small of his back. "And here's what I really don't understand. Why would the CEO of a company that's bought up all this property around town decide to become a substitute history teacher at the middle school?"

Robby raised his head. "Abby."

Becca's face tensed. "What about her?"

"Not Abby," Zeus cut in, locking eyes with Robby and shaking his head a fraction. "You mean the diary, right?"

"What? Oh, right. The diary."

Becca rubbed her chin. "The diary mentioned in the *Secret History* book?"

"Yeah," said Zeus. "Maybe she knows Mrs. Vickory found out about it and she wants to figure out how."

Robby knew Zeus had just been trying to protect Abby's secret, but the mention of the diary actually gave him an idea. He pulled out his phone and tapped the screen. "I took pictures of all the pages from *The Secret History*. The diary where Mrs. Vickory found the portrait of Joanna Greylocke is mentioned in one of the footnotes. Here we go: 'Bound journal with cherrywood cover. Carved with her initials. From the author's personal collection,'" he read.

Zeus rubbed his temples. "Read it again."

"'Bound journal with cherrywood cover. Carved with her initials. From the author's personal—'"

"Her initials," Zeus said. "Joanna Greylocke's initials? J.G."

"Probably."

"I think I've seen that diary before."

"What? Where?" said Robby and Becca together.

"That day at Mrs. Vickory's house." Zeus shook his head. "I was holding it when we heard the noise upstairs."

"'From the author's personal collection,'" Robby whispered. "Of course! Mrs. Vickory wrote *The Secret History*, so the diary would be from *her* personal collection. Guys, if there's even a chance that book can give us a clue about what Miss Winters has planned, or what happened to Tina or my mom—"

"We need to get the diary," Becca said.

"Are you sure you want to get involved?" Zeus asked. "It could be dangerous."

"My mom sold her that house. Robby's stepmom is missing because of her. And *your* dad," she pointed at Zeus, "is investigating what happened to Mrs. Vickory. I already told you guys that I don't believe in coincidences. I think we're supposed to be in this together, all three of us."

"She's right." Robby wrapped his fingers around Becca's hand and squeezed. "All for one and one for all."

21

Return to Whispering Hill

Abby found the note in her locker just before school on the first day back after Thanksgiving. She read it three times before tucking it into her gym bag and heading to meet the others. They crowded around her in the girls' locker room. "My house at sundown," they read in a hushed whisper. "Bring the others. Tonight, you fly!"

Amethyst looked up, wide-eyed. "For real?"

Delphi and Piper both grinned. Daisy borrowed Piper's inhaler and tried to look excited between gasps, but she ended up looking more seasick than anything. Abby felt a surge of anticipation at the idea of flying, then pursed her lips, remembering how Miss Winters had cut her off from her powers that night at the lighthouse. It had only lasted an hour, but the memory of it still lingered.

"All of us, you think?" said Amethyst. Her eyes flicked toward Olivia, who was changing at the other end of the locker room. The purplish bruises on her face matched Amethyst's hair. Even Sarika had steered clear of her that morning.

"Pretty sure," Abby said. She crossed the locker room before she had a chance to think about it. Her stomach knotted and somersaulted as she risked a glance at Olivia's bruises. Over the past few weeks, Miss Winters had taught them some rudimentary healing spells to treat cuts and bruises along with their other lessons. But whether out of pride or some other form of grudge-holding, Olivia had refused to let Abby or any of the others perform them on her. Now any lingering anger Abby felt toward her disappeared as she studied those bruises, replaced by a more familiar feeling—guilt. She cleared her throat.

Olivia tied and retied the laces of her gym shoes without looking up.

I deserve this, Abby reminded herself.

She placed Miss Winters's note on the bench and waited.

"If this is some kind of apology—"

"It's from Miss Winters."

Olivia unfolded the note, glanced at it, and then squeezed her eyes shut. "I'm assuming you know where she lives."

"Whispering Hill." Abby motioned over her shoulder toward the other girls. "We're going to head over there together this afternoon."

Olivia crushed the note and shoved it back at Abby. "I would rather die than be seen in public with you."

"That can be arranged," muttered Amethyst when Abby returned to the group and repeated Olivia's response. Amethyst studied the bruises on Olivia's face from across the room. "Remind me to never make you angry."

"You make me angry every day," Abby said, giving Amethyst a frustrated look.

"Not that angry."

"I've never been *that* angry before."

Amethyst made a show of chewing her gum and then blew a huge bubble. She patted the spot in her gym bag where she'd stashed her wand. "I bet there's a spell to make her like you."

Abby shook her head. She didn't want Olivia to like her. She just wanted Olivia to forgive her. And there probably wasn't a spell powerful enough to ever make that happen.

As the sun dipped below the horizon, the limousine driver Abby and Robby had seen on Halloween met the girls at the foot of Whispering Hill. Olivia was already waiting by the gate, blowing into her hands and tugging down her hat to keep warm.

The driver, a long-limbed man with graying hair and a gaunt, bloodless face, creaked open the iron gate and stepped aside to allow the girls to pass. An unlit brass lantern dangled from his hand, jangling in the breeze as he closed the gate behind them and introduced himself as Bishop. There was a storm in the air, and the icy wind cutting through Abby's jacket made her shiver. It was the bitterest day she could ever remember for so early in December.

When they neared the top of the hill, Abby noticed a stone fountain near the front entrance, which she swore hadn't been there on Halloween. The boarded-up and broken windows had been replaced, and the vines that once threatened to engulf the entire structure were now trimmed back to reveal square, gray bricks. In the fading daylight, the house no longer looked haunted, but it still gave the inescapable impression of an old mental hospital.

Abby had expected to find Miss Winters waiting on the front steps, but the double doors remained shut.

When the others hesitated at the bottom of the steps, Olivia rolled her eyes and marched up them. She made it to the fourth step before the smell of sulfur choked the air. The nearest chimera turned its head and opened its eyes to peer at her. The bloody glow looked no less terrifying in dusk's dim light. Olivia gasped and lost her footing.

Abby yanked her back to the safety of the group. *She must be in shock. She didn't even bother to insult me.*

"Miss Winters invites you *to* her house, not inside it," Bishop explained. "Now, I suggest we hurry. She does not like to be kept waiting." He led them down a cobblestone trail to the right of the main house. His lantern now blazed with dizzying wisps of red and green and yellow.

Miss Winters stood at the cliff's edge facing the sea, not turning until the girls formed a silent semicircle around her. Bishop retreated to the woods, leaving them to their lesson. A sliver of pale yellow peeked out from the clouds, reminding Abby of when she'd last stood at the edge of this very cliff. She wrapped her arms around herself, breathing in air so cold it hurt.

If Miss Winters were keeping any secrets from them—if she had anything to do with Tina's disappearance—then the answers were likely to be hidden somewhere at Whispering Hill. It was just a matter of finding the right opportunity to poke around.

Six brooms bobbed in the air, bundled tightly by gauzy threads that trailed back to Miss Winters's wand. She cast off with a flick of her wrist and the brooms sprang apart and toward the girls. Abby had to fight the instinct to dodge hers, while the other brooms darted and lunged as if daring the girls to catch them.

The broom rumbled like a jet engine beneath Abby's fingers, pulsing with a familiar warmth. She grinned despite her other concerns. Whatever magic she'd harnessed the first time she'd flown, wherever it had been all this time… she felt it again tonight.

"Abby, please assist me with a demonstration." Miss Winters surveyed the other girls before adding, "Olivia, join Abby by the ledge. You'll ride with her."

Abby's mouth fell open, but no words came out.

"I don't want to go shotgun on her broom," said Olivia.

"Noted. Now off you go." She prodded Olivia until they

stood side by side. Even at high tide, a tangle of sharp rocks gaped up at them from below like jagged teeth. Olivia looked like she wanted to assume her usual sneer but couldn't quite bring herself to do it. Her face had gone white.

"How should we…?" Abby began.

"Simply mount the broom," Miss Winters instructed. "You'll remember the rest."

Abby took Olivia's hand in hers. "Trust me?"

Olivia closed her eyes. For an eternity she stood motionless. At last, her chin made the barest of nods. With the broom between their legs, Abby closed her eyes and stepped off the ledge, pulling Olivia behind her. The wind rushed through her hair, drowning out every other noise. They fell faster. Abby gripped the broom tighter as she struggled to force the handle upward. There was a sound like a *whoosh* and then, just as she opened her eyes, they rocketed skyward. Olivia squeezed Abby's ribs tight enough to leave a bruise.

Miss Winters had already begun to line up the other girls for liftoff by the time Abby steered them back to the ledge. Amethyst raised her broom excitedly in Abby's direction. Behind her, Daisy choked hers with both hands and shoved a booted foot hard onto the bristles, triumphantly driving the straw into the frozen ground. The shaft shuddered and relaxed, finally hers to command. Daisy exhaled and looked up, only then realizing everyone was staring at her.

"What?" she said.

Abby and Olivia bobbed on an air current while Miss Winters demonstrated the proper way to grip the broom handle, where to position one's feet when braking, and how to accelerate for maximum control or velocity. She didn't appear to be forcing any of the others to ride tandem. Judging by the tense breathing over her shoulder, Abby guessed Olivia had reached the same conclusion.

"It seems kind of complicated," Piper said.

"I managed when I didn't even know I was a witch," Abby reminded her. "You can do it."

"I'll go next," said Amethyst. She peered over the edge with her broom between her knees, and then dropped out of sight before quickly shooting back into the sky like she'd been fired from a cannon. She circled a few times and then descended, settling a few feet away from Abby and Olivia. "Epic," she whispered breathlessly.

It went just as well for Daisy and Delphi, and by the time it was Piper's turn, even she managed to launch without any difficulty. Miss Winters mounted her broom and joined the group. Her hair whipped in the wind and her face looked somehow different—rosier, friendlier.

"Broom magic," she intoned over the wind and the waves, "is not like the other spells you've learned. It requires more than simply knitting together the disparate threads of the unseen world. It requires you to ride them. Your broom is not a tool like your wand. It is a vehicle. And your first flight, so fraught with nerves, forges a sort of bond with that vehicle."

Abby understood then what she'd sensed earlier. This wasn't just any broom—it was the same broom she'd flown on Halloween.

Miss Winters caught Abby's look and smiled. "You left it right out in the open, dear. I thought you might want it back someday."

"I couldn't fly without *this* broom," Abby realized.

"It's a kind of symbiosis. Your first flight left a unique imprint on your vessel. You put yourself into it, and that means only you can fly it. It also means that you can only fly on your own broom, at least until you've learned a bit more. Now, shall we go for a little trip?"

Olivia's grip tightened around Abby's waist.

"No one will spot you as long as you stay near the hill, but take care to keep close," Miss Winters shouted over her shoulder as she lifted into the darkening sky.

Abby hung back until it was just her and Olivia hovering alone. "Why isn't there a broom for you?" she asked.

Olivia's fingers dug deeper into the skin around Abby's ribs. "I left mine at the lighthouse."

"Oh," said Abby. "The night we...?"

"Let's just go."

"You're sure?"

"Just. Go."

Abby leaned into the wind and willed the broom up into the night air. The rest of the girls had fallen into a V formation behind Miss Winters, already shrinking into the distance.

I might never get a better chance, Abby realized, her stomach churning with sudden nerves. She eyed Miss Winters again, now a dot on the horizon, and then circled above the tree line until the whole Whispering Hill complex was the size of a postage stamp below.

Olivia pulled in so close that her hair tickled Abby's neck and ears. "Miss Winters said to keep close to her."

Abby looked over her shoulder. "I'm sure she didn't mean me. I've done this before."

From the air, the main building looked like a castle on a hill, with two staggering stone towers and a sweeping hexagonal courtyard spread between them. The wind screamed louder the nearer she flew toward the north tower, so she doubled back and swooped toward it again.

Could it be an *actual* scream?

She kicked the broom into a slow glide and floated toward the noise.

"Do you hear that?" she shouted over her shoulder.

Olivia shook her head. "What?"

Abby still heard it, though, and it definitely *wasn't* the wind. She drifted alongside the tower. Ice caked the windows and spilled from the mouths of a half dozen gargoyles. Thick snowdrifts hung along the ledge between the windows, making any sort of dismount all but impossible.

The screaming grew more insistent. It almost sounded like someone calling her name.

"I think someone's in that tower," Abby shouted. "Hold on."

She glanced over her shoulder again, catching Olivia shaking her head, before attempting to guide the broom closer. They lurched as another gust hurtled them back.

A warding spell?

She saw it now: a tangle of gossamer threads clinging around the top of the north tower like barbed wire, crackling with power, making turbulent ripples on the wind. Abby leaned forward to examine the spell, unbalancing the broom.

"Abby, I'm slipping…" screamed Olivia.

"Just hold on a sec." Abby traced the design of the warding spell in her mind. Not impossible to unravel, she decided, but it would take time. If she could just—

"No, Abby, I—I can't!"

The broom shook as Olivia's weight shifted and then vanished. The warding spell knocked Abby back again and she held on with her lead hand, clutching behind her to secure Olivia. But Olivia was already gone.

Abby dove toward her, all thoughts of the warding spell gone as she pushed the broom to go faster, faster…

"Abbbbby!"

"Got you!" Abby yelled, wrapping her free hand around Olivia's jacket.

But it was too much weight. The broom spiraled out of her control again as they plummeted toward the ground, and then suddenly Olivia's coat slipped from Abby's grasp. Abby snatched her wand from her back pocket and screamed Olivia's name, but the spell fizzled against the trunk of an ancient elm. She raised her wand again, one last chance, but she knew it would be too late.

There was a scream as Abby's spell misfired again. Then a flash of scarlet as Miss Winters snatched Olivia from her fall just as she grazed the ground.

The other girls zoomed into view, and within seconds they were all back on the ground near the main house's front steps. Olivia dropped to her hands and knees, gasping.

Abby ran to her side.

"I think that will be all for today," Miss Winters said coolly.

You're hiding something in that tower, Abby thought, looking up from Olivia long enough to lock eyes with Miss Winters. *Someone.* But Miss Winters's face remained unreadable as she turned her attention to the other girls.

"What happened?" Amethyst asked as she and Abby drifted down the driveway behind the rest of the girls. "Did Olivia—"

"She didn't do anything," Abby said. "Just slipped."

Amethyst slowed to a stop near the gate. "You are a terrible liar."

"I—" Abby plunged her hands into her pockets. "Maybe it was nothing, but I swear I heard someone in the north tower shouting my name." The more she replayed the moment in her mind, the more the voice echoed like a hazy memory.

She thought it belonged to Robby's mother.

22

House of Secrets

Robby squeezed through the narrow gap in the side of the hill. Inside the cave, the air reeked of mildew and brackish water, but at least it wasn't as windy.

"You're sure you want to do this?" he asked Becca again, shining his phone's light to cut through the darkness.

"It's not every day I get to play Dora the Explorer before homeroom."

"I think you're more the Lara Croft type," he said.

She snorted. *"¡Vamanos, Robby!"*

Water dribbled from the low ceiling as they inched together into the darkness, bumping heads and shins and elbows. Becca sniffled in rhythm with the drips. "Sorry," she said after blowing her nose loudly into a tissue. "I think I got a cold when I was at my dad's. How far are we from this secret passage?"

"It's just around the bend."

A nagging voice inside Robby's head said they shouldn't have come to the Hollows at all. They should have gone straight to Mrs. Vickory's house for the diary—every minute they wasted felt like it gave Miss Winters an advantage. But Becca had asked to see the hidden cave, and he couldn't think of a logical reason to tell her no. What difference would it make if they waited until after school to get the diary?

He felt along the uneven surface of the east wall, which was beaded with ice, until he found the secret opening and passed through it. He'd grown used to it by now, but Becca looked less certain when he poked his head back out of the wall.

"It's *magic*," she whispered, sinking her fingers into the rock and staring wide-eyed when they plunged through to the other side.

"I told you I wasn't making it up."

"Trust but verify." She kissed him on the cheek and followed him through to the other side.

Robby shined his light around the tunnel to let Becca get a sense of where they were, pausing to look at her when the light illuminated her face.

She reached for another tissue. "Sorry, I know I'm gross right now."

"It's not that."

"Then what?" she asked, stuffing the tissue back into her pocket.

"You seem… different since you got back."

"I have a cold."

"No, I mean—"

"And I guess I like having a puzzle to solve. Together, I mean. One that doesn't involve me trying to figure out why my boyfriend is always sneaking around behind my back."

"I wasn't *always* sneaking." He tilted his head hopefully. "Did you say boyfriend?"

She sniffled again, and then smiled. "Assuming you want to be official?"

"If you need proof…"

She averted her head when he leaned in to kiss her. "I wouldn't do that just now. Snotty nose, remember? But I'll definitely take a rain check."

Robby hunched into his phone to adjust the brightness on the flashlight app, hoping Becca wouldn't notice his disappointment. She squeezed his hand encouragingly and eyed the tunnel ahead.

"This place is so creepy, Robby."

"Wait till you see the hexagram. *That's* the creepy part."

They crawled on all fours before emerging into the narrow chamber that ended with the six-pointed star. He ducked a few protruding stones and pushed ahead until the light from his phone revealed the hexagram on the back wall.

"Fluffy bunny feet," Becca whispered under her breath.

Robby stared at her. "What?"

"Hmm? Oh, sorry. It's what I think about when I get nervous—fluffy bunny feet. It calms me." She smiled weakly. "You can't be scared when you're thinking about fluffy bunny feet."

Robby held up the light as she traced the hexagram with the tips of her fingers, then pushed—hard, like she expected it to budge with a good shove. She gave it a swift kick for good measure and then danced back, shaking her foot. "Definitely solid."

"Zeus and I can't figure out what it's for," Robby said as Becca poked around the edges. "It must have *some* purpose. Zeus saw Miss Winters come this way. Do you think it looks like an altar?"

Becca nodded noncommittally and continued to inspect the wall. After a minute, she stepped back and retrieved her phone from her pocket. She tapped away at the screen, repositioned herself a few times around the chamber, and then nodded as if a puzzle suddenly made sense.

"What are you doing?"

"Getting the GPS coordinates."

"You get reception in here?"

"Mom got us on a really good plan because of her job." She returned to the hexagram and craned her neck to one side and then the other before pocketing her phone again. "Can you shine yours over my shoulder?" she said between sniffles. "No, not there." She pointed about a foot to the left of the hexagram. "There. Better. Hold it steady." She ran her fingers along the wall, paused to inspect a chipped nail, and then turned back to him. "It's not an altar."

"Then what is it?"

"Your problem," she replied cheerfully, "is that you don't have long fingernails." She trailed her fingers down the wall while blowing hard in the same direction. Dust billowed out of a narrow crevice along the length of the wall. She repeated it three more times until all four corners were revealed.

"A door," she said proudly. "And I bet I know where it goes."

"Aren't you going to tell me?" Robby asked as they sprinted into school just ahead of the morning bell. Knowing that the altar was actually a door hadn't gotten them any closer to unlocking it.

"Not yet," said Becca, barely out of breath. "Soon, though." She flashed Robby a smile before disappearing into the crowd crisscrossing the hallway. Robby didn't see her again until study hall in the library, where she spent most of the hour on her laptop, occasionally swatting him away when he tried to distract her.

"I could help you," Robby insisted. "I'm a good helper."

"Awesome." She clicked the print icon on her screen. "You can help by grabbing those pages for me."

Robby shuffled over to the printer, then rejoined Becca by the window. She spread the documents across the table, opened an envelope containing photocopies from her mother's file on Whispering Hill, and spread those out, too. On top of everything, she laid a topographical map of Willow Cove, smoothing it flat.

"Right here," she said, pulling a fine-tip black sharpie from her back pocket and drawing a small dot, "is the entrance to the cave." She scribbled the GPS coordinates next to it in short efficient strokes. Then she shifted the marker and drew a hexagram about a finger's width away, eyeballing the measurement. "Right here is the point where the cave dead ends." She drew a line connecting them. "That door is about three hundred feet directly below Whispering Hill."

"Wow," said Robby.

"Don't be too impressed. We still don't know *why* it's there. But these old records might be able to help." She pushed the map aside and pocketed the sharpie. "These are property records from the town auditor. It's so easy now that they've digitized all this old stuff."

She rearranged the pile until she found a page that interested her. The writing at the top indicated the years 1600 to 1699. "If we can figure out what the cave was used for and who owned it, maybe we'll understand what Miss Winters was doing there when Zeus—"

"What do we have here?" said T-Rex, peering at the scattered mess on the table as he and Joey emerged from the stacks. Sarika and Olivia flanked the boys. T-Rex flicked a metal lighter absently between thumb and forefinger, barely registering its flame. Robby had a vision of T-Rex burning the library to the ground just for something to do.

Olivia elbowed her way past T-Rex and stuck her finger onto the spot where Becca had drawn the hexagram. "What is *that*?" she demanded.

Robby rose from his seat and slipped between Olivia and the map. She only came up to his eyes, but he had to fight the urge to shrink from her glare. "None of your business," he replied coolly.

The bell rang before Olivia could demand anything else. She was still eyeing the map when T-Rex grabbed her by the elbow and pulled her away, but she glanced back over her shoulder, her expression unreadable, just before passing through the door.

Becca thumbed through the papers again as the library emptied. "Remember how I said the Greylocke Corporation owns the right-of-way and some of the caves around the carriage road? Guess who sold it to them."

Robby leaned in for a better look. "William Winslow," he read, "in 1695."

Becca looked up at the clock. "We'll have to dig deeper some other time. None of this is going to help us get *through* that door. But it has to mean something."

"Maybe the diary will give us another clue," Robby said. "See you right after school?"

"Wouldn't miss it."

Zeus joined them on the carriage road after school. "Ten bucks says that door leads to a vampire's tomb," he said once Robby and Becca brought him up to speed.

"There aren't any vampires in Willow Cove," Robby told him.

"You don't know that." Zeus turned his collar to the wind as they approached Mrs. Vickory's house. "It could be werewolves, though. Maybe zombies."

"Speaking of the dead..." said Becca.

Yellow police tape sagged between snow drifts, forgotten and faded by the elements. The police had boarded up the windows and hammered a sheet of plywood across the door frame. Robby pried one side loose until he and Becca could squeeze into the house.

"What am I supposed to tell my dad if we're caught?" Zeus

said from the other side. "It's still a crime scene."

"Tell him your prefrontal cortex isn't fully developed," Robby suggested.

Zeus peered at him through the gap in the plywood. "What?"

"It's not your fault if you make bad decisions. It's just biology."

"I don't think he'd buy that." Zeus just managed to squeeze through the gap. He let the plywood settle back into place, then added, "My dad still keeps an eye on this house. Can we just get the book and get out fast?"

There was an empty space on the countertop where the toaster had been, and a clear patch in the dust next to the overturned couch. A chalk outline filled the space where they'd found Mrs. Vickory's remains. "The diary should be somewhere around here," Zeus said, pointing to the chalk lines.

Only it wasn't.

Zeus dropped to his knees, prepared to sift through the ashes if he had to. But there weren't any ashes, either. "It's not here," he said, mostly to fill the silence.

"Do you think Miss Winters came back?" Robby asked.

Becca didn't reply, but as she looked around the rest of the room, her gaze settled on the stairwell that led to the second floor. She wandered over, peering into the darkness. "What did you find up there?"

Robby thought of the faded photos tucked inside his wallet—one of Abby, the other of Mrs. Vickory and his mother. He hadn't thought much about Mrs. Vickory lately. She'd obviously known Abby and the other girls were different, but how? And why? He thought of his mom's letter again. *Do not involve your new mentor or the Council.* What Council?

Zeus crossed the room to join Becca by the staircase. "That's where we found Attila," he said.

"Achilles," Robby corrected. He pulled back the shutters to let in a thin column of light, then shifted aside as Becca and Zeus came to join him.

His eyes fell on the sagging police tape across the front yard. "We've been so stupid."

"What do you mean?"

"Miss Winters didn't take the diary—the *police* did."

Zeus tapped his forehead against the window, hard. "I can't believe I didn't think of that." He rubbed his temples thoughtfully. "I can find out where dad's keeping the evidence."

"You think he'd let us have a look?"

"Not exactly. But we don't have to let that stop us."

23

Footsteps in the Dark

"This is the worst," Olivia complained, absently kicking at a jagged wet rock and then hopping back an instant before a frothy wave swept over it. She shook ocean water from the hem of her jeans and glared at Abby. "*You're* the worst."

Under the circumstances, Abby found it hard to disagree.

"Ready?" yelled a voice from above. It sounded like Piper, but the wind tended to distort sounds at the base of the sea cliff. Miss Winters stood with the other girls about a hundred feet above them, supervising their broom launches. A steady drizzle only made their situation more miserable.

Abby sent up a green flare from the tip of her wand, signaling she was ready to catch Piper if she fell. Seconds later, Piper leapt into the air and swept gracefully upward, hands free, hair whipping in the wind behind her, just as she'd done at least a dozen times already tonight. Just as they'd *all* done at least a dozen times—all except Abby and Olivia. Miss Winters hadn't allowed them anywhere near a broomstick in the weeks since the incident at the north tower.

"Pointless," muttered Olivia.

Abby had to agree. Miss Winters was obviously punishing them. She'd remained unmoved by Olivia's protests, and Abby was too wrapped up in her own thoughts to mount much of an argument. She'd heard *someone* in that tower, and all of her mental energy since that day had gone to figuring out how to get back up there to confirm her suspicions. *All I want for Christmas is to know what Miss Winters is up to,* she thought.

She had to be sure before she could tell anyone else.

Especially Robby.

She pocketed her wand and stepped carefully back to the shoreline, where Olivia sat puffing into her hands for warmth.

"Ready?" yelled another voice from high above. Abby thought it might be Daisy.

"Your turn," said Abby. Olivia shrugged but didn't move. If Miss Winters thought that forcing the two of them to spend more time together would lead to them bonding, she'd underestimated Olivia's ability to hold a grudge.

Abby crawled back toward the rocks and fired another green flare. She watched without much enthusiasm as Daisy managed a successful liftoff and landing. "How many times do you want me to say I'm sorry?"

Olivia twisted just enough to give Abby a dirty look. She lifted her phone to her ear, covering the other with her free hand.

"Who was that?" Abby asked when Olivia finally turned back around.

Olivia rolled her eyes as she stood and brushed sand and salt from her jeans, then shoved her phone into her back pocket. "Who do you think?"

T-Rex and Joey. And probably Sarika, too.

"Your friends can't come here."

"Says who?"

Abby had her wand out before Olivia could finish her sentence. "Says me."

Olivia's jaw clenched. Abby could tell Olivia was thinking

of the last time they'd squared off. "Fine. I'll call off mine if you call off yours."

"What are you talking about?"

"Your little friends are getting nosy."

Abby's confusion must have shown in her eyes.

Olivia gave a dismissive snort. "Do you pay attention to *anything* going on around you? A few weeks ago, I caught Robby and Becca in the library with a map of Willow Cove—"

"So what?"

"So, they'd drawn a *hexagram* on the map, that's what. Where do you suppose they saw one of those?"

"I don't know." Abby let out a deep breath. *A hexagram?*

"And to think you made a big deal about *my* friends hanging around near the lighthouse. Robby and Becca are up to something."

"Ready?" one of the girls called down.

Olivia made no move to follow as Abby stepped back into view of the cliff. When the launch and landing were complete— Amethyst this time—Abby wandered back to the small beach where Olivia was gathering her things.

"And where do you think you're going?"

"Deal's a deal. I'll handle my friends. You handle yours."

"You can't just leave. We still have another hour."

"Because this is such a productive use of our time."

Abby watched Olivia's back as she made her way down the beach. She hated to admit it, but Olivia was right. Spotting the others was pointless—unless Miss Winters intended to keep her as far from the north tower as possible.

"Ready?"

Abby fired another flare and then cast a voice-activated charm to send a signal flare whenever someone yelled that they were preparing to launch. They'd be fine without her. And if she wanted to get a look inside the north tower, Olivia had just given her the opening she needed. The sooner she discovered what

Miss Winters was hiding, the sooner she'd know just how much danger they were all in.

The drizzle had turned to steady rain by the time Abby reached the top of the hill. Her friends' voices drifted through the trees. She crouched behind a rotting elm, but all she could see of the group was a gash of scarlet against the darkening sky—Miss Winters.

Abby scurried ahead until she emerged from the woods. Chimeras guarded the perimeter of the main building, staring ahead with stony eyes. Abby reached for her wand and then changed her mind. She stuck to the tree cover until she spotted a bare maple that brushed against a second-floor window. Pulling herself level with the lowest branch, it was an easy climb after that.

Below her, the nearest chimera remained motionless. There were more spaced along the upper floors, but she couldn't see any from her position. Hopefully they couldn't see her, either.

She stretched until her fingers brushed the window, and then found a groove below it. She pushed up and the frame trembled. She pushed harder, straining every muscle in her body, and this time it moved an inch, creaked, moved another inch, then finally shifted wide enough for her to climb through.

She scrambled off the branch and fell to a floor awash in darkness. Her shoulder throbbed. The rain had soaked through her clothes to the skin, but at least she was inside. She shivered and let out a deep breath. There wouldn't be much time to look around, especially if the weather drove Miss Winters inside early.

Lightning flared as she closed the window, revealing an unmade bed with jumbled sheets and loose blankets. As Abby's eyes adjusted to the darkness, she made out a wardrobe and a reading chair with a blanket thrown across one arm. A steady drip echoed inside a cold fireplace.

Abby tilted the light from her phone around the room. Her heart raced when she saw her own reflection staring back from a mirror near the door. A lacy bra and a pale satin nighty dangled from one of the mirror's arms, sending alarm bells howling in her head. *Of all the rooms to stumble into!*

She crept toward the door, wincing with every creak of the floorboards. She turned the handle—and froze at the sound of footsteps on the other side. Voices drifted toward her, louder with each heartbeat. She slid under the bed just as the door opened and Miss Winters stepped inside. Abby watched the hem of her cloak cross the room.

"Soaked to the bone," Miss Winters said with a weary sigh. She crouched near the fireplace and touched her wand to the damp logs. Flames leapt to life, filling the room with a warm glow.

"Something's troubling you," said a voice from the hallway. Bishop.

"Nothing is troubling me." Then Miss Winters laughed—a wet, choking noise. "Nothing more than usual."

Abby shifted and risked another look. She couldn't see Bishop, but now she could make out the fireplace clearly enough. Miss Winters had spread her cloak over a drying rack nearby.

"Weather like this reminds me of the first time I came here. Do you remember? I often wonder how things might have been different if I hadn't come."

"That was a very long time ago, Joanna."

"Time does seem to have its own rhythms, though, don't you think? Nights like this, I feel I might reach back and touch them. But they're never…" Her voice trailed into silence. "They're just memories now. Echoes."

"Perhaps I should fix your tea," said Bishop.

"Not tonight."

A pause, and then: "You're going to them, again?"

Miss Winters's eyes remained fixed on the fireplace. "That will be all."

"Joanna."

"That will be *all*."

The door creaked. "It will not bring you the comfort you seek."

"It brings me no comfort at all. But it reminds me why I must not fail with these six."

Bishop said something else, a low whisper Abby couldn't make out, and then the door creaked closed behind him. Miss Winters crossed the room again. The wardrobe door scraped open, and she reappeared a moment later. She lifted her cloak from the drying rack and pulled it again around her shoulders. "My life for theirs," she murmured.

The flames sputtered when she left the room, as if she'd taken all of the oxygen with her. Abby huddled in the sudden darkness and waited—*one-one thousand, two-one thousand*—before scurrying out from under the bed. She inched the door open and peered down the hallway. Miss Winters disappeared around the corner, her shadow momentarily stretching along the opposite wall before blending again into nothingness.

Abby hesitated. If she left the same way she'd come, she might still escape undetected. But she didn't *want* to leave—not with so many new questions piled on top of the old ones. She thought she could still make it to the tower, but the cry for help seemed like a distant memory after what she'd just overheard. She took a step toward the hall Miss Winters had just passed through, then another and another until she reached a narrow back stairwell, where she watched Miss Winters's back disappear again into the shadows.

One-one thousand, two one-thousand.

Abby followed her.

Miss Winters's footsteps echoed like a distant drumbeat. Though even the largest shapes were difficult to make out in the dark, Abby guessed by the feel of the floorboards and the angle of the steps that the staircase corkscrewed sharply downward. She stuck to the far edges where the steps were widest.

At the base of the staircase, a hallway extended in both directions. She followed the dim creaking of floorboards, catching a glimpse of red wandlight before it disappeared around another bend.

That brief glow revealed a low cobwebby ceiling and narrow walls stained with mold. A lone light fixture dangled inches from Abby's head, and as she crouched to avoid it, she tried to make sense of what she'd seen: a large picture frame hanging empty on one wall; something long and couch-shaped shoved against the other draped in pale sheets; doors spaced evenly every ten feet.

The air grew musty as Abby trailed Miss Winters down another flight of stairs. Wooden steps gave way to an uneven floor—the basement. Abby hung close to the wall and followed until Miss Winters turned another corner and the wandlight again vanished. Abby clutched her own wand, worried she'd been discovered. But a moment passed, and then another.

Abby counted to a hundred. Still no sign of Miss Winters. She illuminated the darkness with her wand, revealing unusual silhouettes draped in foul sheets. She tugged on one, leveling her wand to see better. It looked like an ordinary chair until she noticed the leather straps set six inches apart, one level with the waist, the other with the chest. Two smaller straps on the arms would have been used to restrain someone's wrists.

Abby stumbled back, bumping hard into something metal—a cage. She swung her wand around and peered inside. It was empty. She threw another sheet to the ground, revealing a long porcelain tub filled with rusty tools: a jagged-toothed hacksaw, a hand-crank drill. She surveyed the room again. More cages, more chairs. Another tub. A tangled pile of manacles.

This was how they treated the mentally ill?

She bent over, fighting the urge to vomit. That was when she noticed the faintest hint of red light coming from a seam in the floor.

A trap door.

She waited for the red light to disappear before dropping to all fours and tracing her fingers along the seam. The small door lifted easily when she grabbed at a leather loop near the front edge, opening to reveal a narrow ladder into the depths. Abby couldn't see the bottom or any sign of the wandlight that had drawn her to the door.

She extinguished her own wand, clenching it between her teeth as she climbed down. The rungs were slippery. She tested each step before lowering her full weight onto it.

Plunk-plunk-plunk. She held out a hand to catch a drop of water. It smelled like the ocean.

She relit her wand, but beyond the small glow, the darkness seemed to stretch on forever. A rough passage narrowed and widened at random intervals. What she'd thought was a puddle turned out to be a black pool that rippled in a half dozen places where water dripped from the ceiling. She poked at the surface with the toe of her sneaker and watched the pool shudder.

Her eyes fixed on a small section of the tunnel wall, five or six paces from the foot of the ladder, and as she approached, the darkness resolved into the shape of a hexagram etched into the coarse granite. She traced it with the tips of her fingers, and it pulsed with an electrical charge—a warning.

No turning back, she thought. *Open sesame.*

The six-pointed star flared to life, briefly illuminating the chamber in a fiery burst before dissolving again to blackness. A hidden door ground open, revealing more darkness.

Abby heard a sound behind her.

Breathing.

"That's far enough," said Miss Winters coldly.

A searing pain separated Abby from her wand. The next blow sent her reeling into the icy pool. She clawed frantically for something she could use as a weapon—her wand, a rock, anything—until her fingers closed around a softball-sized chunk of granite.

The red glow of Miss Winters's wand filled the cavern. Abby squinted, still unsteady on her feet, but the hardness in Miss Winters's eyes dissolved into recognition. She lowered her wand and took a step forward.

"Abby, what are you doing here?"

"You knew I was following you. Don't pretend you didn't."

"I knew *someone* was following me. I never dreamed it was you."

"Then who?" Abby squeezed the rock again.

"I will ask the questions. What are you doing here?"

Excuses rattled around Abby's head, none of them believable. Finally, she settled on the truth. "I heard someone in the tower the night you taught us to fly. Someone I think I used to know."

"I very much doubt that." Miss Winters raised her wand again, but this time she used it to retrieve Abby's wand from the pool. Abby accepted it hesitantly, half expecting a trap, and only let the rock fall to the ground when the wand's familiar pulse coursed between her fingers.

"You are a long way from the towers now," Miss Winters observed. "I admire your bravery, but you've been very foolish. I might have hurt you."

"Why didn't you?"

Miss Winters looked Abby up and down and frowned. "You're shivering."

Abby's teeth chattered. She *was* shivering—and soaked. Her shirt and jeans clung to her skin. She hadn't realized Miss Winters had unfastened her cloak until it was already wrapped around her shoulders.

Miss Winters was wearing jeans and a T-shirt with the words The Clash emblazoned across the chest. She caught Abby's eye and nodded.

"My dark secret: I like punk music. You must never tell." She touched her shirt self-consciously just below the neck. The scarlet glow of her wand gave her face unexpected warmth. "I suppose that's hard for you to imagine."

"I'm not used to thinking of you as anything other than a witch," Abby told her.

"Is that all *you* are, Abby? A witch? Nobody is just one thing. Not even me."

"I know that," Abby murmured. "I mean, I *should* know that. I just never really thought of it that way."

Miss Winters's eyes narrowed. "You heard something from the tower that upset you—scared you, even. But you snuck around instead of coming to me. You don't trust me?"

Abby's cheeks burned. She opened her mouth to protest but choked back the words. They'd both know she was lying. "I overheard you tonight," she said, surprised at her own honesty. "I didn't mean to, but—"

"They used to lock up women like us in this place. Maybe you didn't know that. They called it a mental hospital, but prison is a far better word. They caged people here, mostly women. Beat them, lobotomized them. They did it in the rooms and the corridors and the basement—and then they did it everywhere else when the overcrowding began. They strapped girls down and tortured them to see what they could learn. It's what this town has *always* done with unusual women, no different than hanging them from trees, strapping them to posts, crushing them, stoning them, burning them—always trying to put an end to their unusualness. Or worse, to cure them of it."

Her features had taken on a new intensity, the soft curves sharpening. She looked like the familiar Miss Winters again. "The cry you heard from the tower—I can only assume it was an echo from a time long past."

"That's an awfully long echo," Abby said.

"'There are more things in heaven and earth than are dreamt of in your philosophy.'"

"What does that mean?"

"It's Shakespeare. Perhaps Daisy would recognize it. It means a thing can be true, even if you don't understand why it's true. Time doesn't forget. *Places* don't forget. You'll see. But first—" The hexagram flared a fiery orange before fading again. The heavy stone door slid closed.

"Where does that lead?" Abby asked.

Miss Winters stared into the darkness for so long that Abby thought she might not have heard. "Nowhere pleasant," she said at last.

She led Abby past the ladder and deeper into the cavern. Abby walked faster to keep up, dragging the heavy hem of Miss Winters's cloak over the uneven ground. She could hear a faint dribble of water in the distance that grew into a steady downpour—the rain from outside.

They emerged into the large courtyard between the two towers of the main building. Ancient trees ringed the space, their branches so thickly entwined that Abby could easily imagine what it had been like as a natural grove long before the buildings were erected around it.

"We're in the very heart of the place now," Miss Winters said, pointing her wand at a solitary oak tree near the center of the grove. Abby hugged the cloak closer as Miss Winters raised her arms to the sky as if to summon the elements. "They built the entire complex around this one tree." Her flimsy T-shirt clung to her frame, soaked through in the downpour, but she didn't appear to notice. "An oak can live for six hundred years. Can you imagine what that must be like? Rooted in place and doomed to watch as everything it's ever known withers and dies around it. You see, Abby, this hill, this tree, even the walls—they all retain memories. Imprints of the past."

Miss Winters exhaled and lifted her face to the highest branches. Abby shielded her eyes with her free hand and followed her gaze. "This is where they killed the Winslow sisters. You can still hear them sobbing if you listen closely. Close your eyes and try it."

Abby did as she was instructed. The cold wind continued to swirl through the grove, pelting rain in a steady sideways drumbeat against her skin. But there were still no other sounds. After a long moment, she opened her eyes again to find Miss Winters watching her closely.

"I don't hear them," Abby told her.

"Listen for the sounds between sounds, Abby. When you hear the whisper of the wind, ask yourself, 'What is it saying?'"

Abby slowed her breathing, still not entirely sure she should trust Miss Winters.

"Listen." Miss Winters squeezed Abby's hand. Heat rippled where their fingers touched, spreading first through Abby's hand and then her arm and then to her whole being, driving the downpour from her mind. "Now close your eyes again."

A faint sob arrived on the wind, choked and muted, followed by a whispered cry for help.

"Feel the past come alive," Miss Winters said.

Something, maybe a fly, buzzed near Abby's face. Still, she kept her eyes shut. The smell of unwashed bodies stung her nostrils, and then hooves were thundering all around her. Heavy wagon wheels of timber and metal creaked over hard-trod earth. Ropes tensed against branches, swaying in a new breeze, hot, dry, and thick with the smoke of a hundred lit torches.

Abby's eyes shot open.

Men and women in peculiar clothes were shouting at her, rushing her—rushing *through* her as if she weren't there at all. The oak tree stretched above her, six girls swaying from its branches, each of them bound and gagged, struggling for breath. Their faces tugged at Abby's memory like a hazy vision from another time, another place.

She darted toward them, but the world flickered with each step. She gasped and fell to her knees as the vision washed away with the return of the cold December rain.

"Living history," Miss Winters said, helping Abby to her feet. "It's all around us. Whispering to us. Haunting us like ghosts, if we let it."

"It seemed so real."

"It is real."

Abby wrapped her arms around Miss Winters, needing to be anchored again in the present. She never wanted to feel anything like that again.

"Albert Einstein theorized that the distinction between the past and the present is only an illusion."

"Are you saying that's what I heard from the north tower— the past?"

Miss Winters nodded. "I'm afraid it has a way of clawing its way into the present."

"That's horrible." She shivered and wrapped Miss Winters's cloak tighter. "That night, I heard—I mean, I *thought* I heard someone who went missing a long time ago."

"It's a hard thing to accept, Abby, but those of us with gifts have always been burdened with special insights as well. What- ever you heard in the north tower, whatever tragedy from a time long past, don't fear it. The past can't hurt you, and the present... I won't let any harm come to you, either."

"'My life for theirs'—I overheard you. What does it mean?

Are we in danger?"

"We are witches. We are always in danger. What you witnessed just now is a reminder of what happens to girls like us in this town. If I must give my life to protect you girls, I will."

"To protect us from what, though?" Abby asked. "From who?"

Miss Winters stared at Abby, her eyes dark. Raindrops lit scarlet by the dim light of her wand glistened like tiny stars in her hair. She looked fierce and powerful.

"Perhaps it's time you heard the truth about Mrs. Vickory."

24

Underground

The day before Christmas, Becca inspected herself in Robby's bedroom mirror, her lips pursed in a frown. She wore a black turtleneck, black leggings, black gloves, black ankle socks, and a black ski mask pulled halfway down her face. Only her cheeks were pink.

"I look like a dork," she complained.

"You look like a ninja," Robby assured her.

She tugged the mask all the way off, grinning as her hair spilled down around her shoulders. "I was going for cat burglar, but I'll settle for ninja. Think it'll work?"

"Put the mask on again," said Robby. Becca pulled it back over her head until only her eyes showed. "You could be anyone under there. No identifying features at all."

She mumbled something unintelligible.

"What?"

She lifted the mask. "I said, it's hard to talk under this mask."

"If you find yourself having to talk to anyone," said Zeus, "we have bigger problems. The goal is to not be seen or heard."

"Silent as a ninja," Robby added.

Becca shook her head but smiled as she pulled on her winter jacket. She bounced up and down until her feet fit snugly inside her snow boots. "And now I look sweet and innocent," she announced. She checked the time on her phone—her flight to her father's house for Christmas vacation left in five hours. "Not at all like someone planning to break into the police station and then skip town."

Zeus looked around as if expecting his father to jump out from under Robby's bed. "Not so loud."

Robby peered out his window, in part to hide his impatience. His dad was standing in the driveway with a snow shovel in one hand and a steaming mug in the other. Abby's mother huddled beside him. Thick gobs of snow fluttered around them from a slate gray sky.

"I think we're going to have to risk being seen," he said, turning his back to the window. It was all he could do not to pace. "There are a couple of inflatable tubes and a Flexible Flyer in my garage. We can pretend we're going sledding."

Becca shook her head. "That won't work if my mom comes to pick me up before we get back."

"Why not?"

"I broke my arm the one time I tried sledding. Almost broke my neck, too. Mom knows I'd never agree to do it again."

"We'll just say we're going to Hex-Mex for hot cocoa, then," suggested Zeus.

Becca pulled a fluffy pink hat over her head. "*That* she'll believe."

The trees in Robby's backyard drooped under the weight of heavy snow as the trio exited the house, leaving behind a trail of deep footprints. Christmas lights sparkled through the woods like red-and-green beacons, the only sign of human life in the wintery scene. Even the old skating pond was just an empty white sheet in the middle of the woods.

In the tunnels, Zeus shook snow from his head and shoulders, then unpacked three flashlights he'd hidden inside his jacket. He handed one each to Robby and Becca. As they moved through the tunnels, Zeus pointed out where each passage led. Robby was only half listening—he'd heard it all before.

"—all the way back to the Hex," Zeus said. "But we're going this way." He aimed his flashlight straight ahead where the floor angled sharply toward a steep jumble of rocks. The light ended in a pinpoint about fifty feet overhead; it was like staring straight up from the bottom of a well. "And here we are."

"You're sure you're okay with breaking and entering?" Robby asked for the thousandth time.

"It's not breaking, just entering." Zeus kicked at a loose rock. "But don't get caught," he added hastily. "My dad would probably throw us in jail just to make a point."

"How about you?" Robby asked, turning to Becca.

She bobbed her head as she tugged off her snow boots. "Cold!" she shrieked when her feet touched the ground. "*Cold-cold-cold.*"

"Sorry," said Zeus. "Ninjas don't wear boots. Too loud."

"Stupid ninjas," Becca muttered, hopping up and down. She unzipped her jacket. "Tell me again what to do if I get caught?"

"Don't," said Robby and Zeus together.

"You guys are so helpful."

"Are you positive the diary will be here?" Robby asked.

Zeus shrugged. "Process of elimination—that's why it took so long for me to be sure. Evidence is usually transferred to the state police barracks or the district attorney's office, but that doesn't always happen until a trial is underway. Right now, the police don't even have a suspect." Zeus raised his flashlight again. "There's a very small hole up there that you should be able to squeeze through. I snuck in a few years ago to see where it goes."

"Am I the only one who's concerned that there's a secret entrance into the police station?" Becca asked.

"It's not technically the police station," Zeus explained. "It's an annex. The building next to the police station is one of the oldest in Willow Cove, and the town deeded it to the police a few years back. Dad says they used to hide munitions from the British down here during the Revolutionary War, and then later to hide slaves escaping into Canada as a stop on the Underground Railroad. The police converted the first floor into the new evidence room last year."

"And you've been inside?" Robby asked.

"Before they converted it," Zeus admitted. He handed Becca a claw hammer. "You might need to pry some boards loose."

Robby directed his flashlight to the spot above, squinting at where the passage narrowed. It looked like a dangerous climb, even in full light. "How small is the hole?" he asked.

"Becca should fit."

"*Should?*" asked Becca.

"Almost definitely. When you get inside, you'll be in the basement. Stick to the perimeter until you reach the stairs. The lights will be off, so wait until your eyes adjust. When you get to the top, turn right and stay low. You'll already be in the secure area."

Becca tugged on one of her gloves. "What about security cameras?"

"They're not actively monitored. By the time anyone sees you on the tapes, we'll be long gone."

"Anything else?" asked Becca as she pulled on the other glove.

"Just… good luck," said Zeus.

"Be careful," said Robby. His heart thumped as he watched her scamper up the rocks and disappear into the dark. He and Zeus stood in silence as the seconds stretched into minutes, jumping at every dull echo coming from above. Robby checked his phone; time seemed to be moving at a glacial pace. Eventually, he scooped up Becca's jacket and boots and tucked them into his backpack in case they needed to make a quick exit.

"I'm worried," Zeus said into the silence. He talked softly, almost a whisper, but his voice echoed off the uneven walls.

"She'll be back any minute," Robby said hopefully.

"I don't mean about Becca. She really is like a ninja."

Robby smiled. "What do you mean, then?"

"Abby." He leaned against the granite wall, tapping his flashlight like a drumstick. "The more time she spends with Miss Winters, the more concerned I get."

"Abby can take care of herself."

"I know that. But are we sure *we're* on the right track? The portrait of Joanna Greylocke, the hexagram in the cave, this diary we're looking for—we still haven't actually learned anything helpful yet. All we're doing is collecting puzzle pieces."

"That's how you start to solve a puzzle."

Zeus clicked his flashlight on and off. "I just wish I could talk to Abby alone, you know? To warn her about Miss Winters. But she's always with Amethyst and the other girls. If I could tell her what we've learned, though, maybe she'd—"

The sound of Becca scrambling through the shadows prevented him from saying more. He angled his flashlight toward the break in the cave wall until a small, lithe figure dropped into the tunnel.

"Go!" Becca whisper-yelled. *"Go-go-go!"*

They raced through the tunnel's twists and turns until it was clear that no one had followed her. Becca hunched over, breathing hard, before reaching under her shirt and pulling out a large plastic baggie. "I triggered some sort of alarm and I panicked. I'm sure I contaminated the evidence from, like, a hundred other cases." A wide grin split her face. "Mission accomplished, though."

She unzipped the bag and pulled out the remains of the diary. Robby shined his flashlight onto the blackened pages, grinning when he saw the J.G. etched into the cover. "You found it," he said.

Becca returned his grin. "I found it. We all did."

Zeus shined his flashlight back the way they'd come, shaking his head. "I can't believe you pulled it off."

"Didn't you say it would be easy?"

"Yeah, but I never actually believed it."

Becca shook her head, still amused. "I will literally never trust you again."

Robby stuffed the diary back in the bag. "Let's go straight to Hex-Mex and read it. I brought money for the hot cocoas."

"I really should go home now," Becca said, glancing at her phone. "Mom likes to get to the airport early. But you guys need to call me the second I land and tell me what's in there."

25

The Order

A bby dropped onto her bed and turned up the music playing on her phone while Amethyst riffled through her overnight bag for something to wear. She pulled on a pajama top and then stuffed her day clothes into the backpack, before shoving it inside Abby's closet a bit more forcefully than seemed necessary.

"What's the deal?" Amethyst asked.

Abby muted the music. "With what?"

"With you." Amethyst scowled. "You've been acting weird since the other night."

"Have not."

"Have too. Or have you always liked punk music?"

Abby took off her glasses, rubbed her eyes, and put them back on. "Maybe you should spend Christmas Eve at your own house if you don't like my taste in music. Mom is already asking why you're not spending it with your grandfather."

Amethyst sighed and then collapsed onto the bed next to Abby. "Your music is fine. I like The Clash as much as anyone. It's *you* who's not okay. What's going on?"

Abby lay back until her head hit the pillow next to Amethyst's. She felt a migraine coming on, and she wished she'd taken something for it. She wished she could just go to sleep, too. More than anything, she wished she knew whether Miss Winters had told her the truth the other night.

Finally, she said, "Something happened."

Amethyst propped herself up on one elbow. "What is it?"

"While you were practicing flying last weekend, I snuck into Miss Winters's house."

"Wait, why am I just hearing about this now? You know you can tell me anything."

"I know, I should have. But listen—Miss Winters caught me. And I thought it was going to go bad, but instead she just… showed me something. The past. I don't know exactly how to explain it, but it was like I was right there in 1691. I could see the Winslow sisters hanging there, dangling—dying. I could *feel* it. And it made me think of something else, but I couldn't quite… I couldn't completely remember it at the time. I think I've seen those girls before."

She closed her eyes and her wand shot into her hand from across the room, settling between her fingers with a familiar thrum. "The night we got our wands," she said, staring up at her ceiling, "when I tried to see what Miss Winters was doing in the lighthouse—I'm almost certain I saw those same faces then."

"Did you ask Miss Winters about it?"

Abby shook her head. "I'm only just remembering it. Bits and pieces, anyway." She shifted until she was face to face with Amethyst. "Miss Winters told me something else. Something about Mrs. Vickory."

Amethyst rubbed her temples. "Go on."

Abby closed her eyes and saw Miss Winters standing in the grove, her face slick with rain, her eyes gleaming with intensity. "She told me that Mrs. Vickory was part of a group called the Order. They're like knights or something. Warrior witches."

Amethyst snorted. "Old Mrs. Vickory?"

"She can't always have been old." Abby sat up and tucked a wisp of hair behind her ear. "Miss Winters says the Order serves a group called the Council. Those are the elder witches—the most powerful in the world, one from each continent."

"Powerful like Miss Winters?"

Abby nodded. "Except Miss Winters isn't *on* the Council. She says they're bad news."

"What kind of bad news?"

"Manipulative. Controlling." Abby swallowed. "Wicked."

"Real-life wicked witches? I don't like the sound of that at all. And Mrs. Vickory was one of them?"

"She *worked* for them. But everyone does. That's basically the choice you get when you become a witch. Join the Order and do what they say, or…"

"Or what?"

"They cut you off. Take away your powers."

"They wouldn't. They *couldn't*." Amethyst sat up to look Abby in the eye. "How would they even do that?"

"Miss Winters did it to me the night I hurt Olivia in the lighthouse. Just long enough to make sure I wouldn't hurt her any more, but it can be done." Abby shook her head. "It felt like I was being hollowed out. And that was only for an hour. I can't imagine it being permanent."

Amethyst stared straight ahead for a long moment, then hopped off the bed and began pacing. When the bedroom door creaked opened, Abby and Amethyst both jumped, but it was only Abby's mother holding a plate of cookies.

The smell of gingerbread wafted into the room. "There's eggnog, too, but I couldn't carry it," she said. "You can come down for it if you want. Amethyst, you're sure your grandfather doesn't mind you spending Christmas here?"

"He won't even notice," Amethyst said mechanically.

Abby's mother eyed her doubtfully. "Eggnog's in the fridge," she said as she closed the door. "Don't stay up too late."

After her footsteps faded, Amethyst plopped back down onto the bed. "Do you believe Miss Winters?"

"I don't know. I thought I did when she told me. She says she's teaching us to be independent of the Council. To be our own witches, free from their control, able to defend ourselves against them—just like her." The clock in the hallway ticked loudly, filling the silence. "But there's a small part of me that wonders if she only told me all about the Council to distract me from what I heard in the tower."

"You think she actually has someone chained up inside there?"

"You already know Robby thinks Miss Winters did something to his mom. I swear it *sounded* like… I don't know. It could have just been my imagination. I mean, it probably was. But what if it wasn't?"

"Suppose she does have some kind of ulterior motive." Amethyst hopped off the bed again. She paced between Abby's desk and window. "What would it be?"

"I've been asking myself the same question." Abby took a deep breath. "It's not like she hasn't had a million chances to hurt us if she wanted to. Why *teach* us?"

Amethyst frowned. "Maybe she likes to toy with her prey."

"I've got to get inside that tower. That's the only way we'll know. Next chance I get, I'm going to have to—"

"Abby, if you get caught again…"

"I know."

Amethyst craned her neck. "Hold that thought. You hear that?"

Abby did hear it: a clanking, clunking sound, like someone tripping over a tin can. Amethyst lifted the window shade and peered outside.

"Anything else you've forgotten to tell me?" she asked.

"Sometimes you snore. Who is it?"

"The Incredible Hulk."

"The what?"

"It's Zeus—Robby's friend. The football player."

"What's he doing here?"

Abby opened the window to reveal Zeus staring up at her with his hands stuffed into his jacket pockets. He called her name and freed one hand long enough to wave. "I was hoping to talk to you about—"

"Rapunzel, Rapunzel, let down your very red hair," Amethyst said, squeezing into the window beside her.

Abby swatted at her. "What's up, Zeus?"

"Oh, I thought—I mean, I was hoping… maybe you'd be alone tonight." He backed up a step. "I guess I should have known."

"What did you want to talk to me about?"

His breath misted in the air. He rubbed his hands together, then tucked them under his arms. "It's nothing."

"You came to my house on Christmas Eve for nothing?" she asked, raising a skeptical eyebrow. "It's freezing outside. I'll come downstairs and let you in. Hold on."

"No, it's okay, I'll just go."

"Stay there," she told him. "I'm coming down."

"Abby," Amethyst whispered, "we still have important things we need to finish talking about *up here*." She poked her head back into the window and raised her voice. "Five seconds."

"What?" asked Zeus.

"You have five seconds to say what you came to say," Amethyst told him, "then I'm closing this window." She waited a beat. "Four."

Zeus took a deep breath and brushed his hands through his hair.

"Three. Two."

"Amethyst," Abby said, shaking her head.

"One second. Nothing? Okay, we're done."

"Wait!" Zeus frowned at Amethyst. "There is something."

"What is it?" Abby asked.

"I had this idea that maybe we could… I mean, if you wanted to…"

Abby strained to hear him, missing a word or two. He looked as if he hoped she might know how to fill in the blanks for him. But she had no idea what he wanted to say. "That we could do what, Zeus?"

"There's a dance coming up." His voice came out uncharacteristically high. He cleared his throat. "The winter social?"

Abby stared at him.

"I know it's a few weeks off, but I was just wondering if you"—he met her gaze, obviously screwing up his courage—"you'd want to go?"

"With you?"

"Just hanging out," he said hastily. "But, you know… together."

Abby answered without thinking. "I don't know, Zeus. I'm so busy with…"

He dropped his gaze to the ground, looking anywhere but at Abby. Amethyst fell back into the bedroom, trying not to laugh. Abby was frozen in the window, still staring at Zeus, her mouth open. Butterflies fluttered in her stomach.

Where did those come from?

"Sorry I bothered you." Zeus backed up another step, his head bowed low. "I'm sure I'll see you at school. Merry Christmas, Abby."

Before she could stop herself, Abby yelled, "Zeuuus!"

He looked back up at the window.

"I think—I mean, maybe…" The hopefulness in his eyes sealed it. "Maybe we *could* go together."

"We could?"

"Yes," she said, surprised to discover she meant it. "It's been way too long since we've hung out."

26

The Diary of Joanna Greylocke

Robby awoke on Christmas morning to the sound of Becca laughing in his ear. Something that felt like a Brillo Pad nuzzled his chin and then disappeared before he could swat at it. He squinted at his clock—five in the morning, too early for presents—and attempted to sit up. A pile of books and papers scattered to the floor as Einstein leapt into his lap.

Becca laughed again. She sounded close enough to be in the same room, but Robby was awake enough now to remember that she was at her dad's house across the country. He fumbled for the glowing tablet next to his pillow and saw her grinning back at him on the screen.

"Merry Christmas, sleepy head."

He rubbed his eyes until her face came into focus. "You too." He swiped an unruly swath of curls from his eyes. "Did we fall asleep chatting?"

"Must have. Einstein was licking your cheek when I woke up."

Robby followed her eyes to the iguana, shaking his head. "How's your dad?"

"It's like the North Pole here." She yawned. "Dad goes all

out at Christmas trying to buy my affection since it's the one holiday where Mom can't even pretend to compete. I can already hear him moving around downstairs preparing to shower me with gifts."

Robby hoisted Einstein onto a pile of blankets at the foot of the bed and climbed to his feet. He carried his tablet with him as he lifted the window shade and peered outside. The world had gone gray with predawn fog. He dropped the shade and propped the tablet on top of his dresser. "Hold on," he said, dipping out of sight to change. He reappeared a moment later in a rumpled sweatshirt and a fresh pair of jeans. "Want to finish going over the diary before everyone wakes up?"

Becca pulled her hair into a ponytail. "Sure."

After walking back to the bed, Robby rearranged the tablet so he could still see Becca as he flipped through the diary. He and Zeus had read the entire thing through from cover to cover already, but he'd been bringing Becca up to speed the night before. Opening to the first page, he read, "'My name is Joanna Greylocke. It is not my real name. I do not have a real name anymore. Today, I set sail across the Atlantic in search of a new beginning—'"

"Don't start at the beginning again," Becca complained. She scrunched her nose. "Joanna was already on the ship before I fell asleep."

"She was an orphan," he reminded her. "She came here when she was thirteen to live with her only remaining family. That was in 1680, so she would have been in her mid-twenties in 1691." He flipped through the pages to the last passage he remembered reading to Becca. "'I have spent the morning retching in the hold of this miserable ship, though whether from the churning sea or the stench of these sailors or the memory of my own horrible deeds, I cannot say. The captain was ill-inclined to take a girl of my years, yet he was less inclined to refuse the last of my family's coin with which I secured this voyage.'"

"'The memory of my own horrible deeds,'" Becca repeated.

Robby flipped to the next page. "Here we go. 'The only hope remaining for me now is the grace of a distant uncle whom I have never met.' That would be William Winslow. 'Would that I had never been born—that my mother, at least, still lived and breathed instead of me. But though I have seen greater wonders than I ever dared imagine, I do not know how to bring her back to me.'"

Einstein nudged Robby's knee. Robby shooed the iguana away and turned back to the tablet. "There's a long gap after that. Some of the pages are too burned or smudged or just… gone. It seems like she was happy here. Her uncle accepted her into his home. And her cousins— When she started writing in the diary again a few years later, she says, 'We are like sisters. The seventh sister, they call me. It is as if I have always been one of them. I never dared to dream of having a family once more.'"

"So, what happened?" Becca asked. "Where did it go wrong?"

"January 1691." He flipped ahead until he reached a passage near the end of the diary. "'The young men whisper about me behind my back while the elders leer when they think I am not looking. Some of them do not even hide it. I only hope Jeremiah does not see, for I fear what he would do to them. Or that he would blame me for their weakness.'"

"Jeremiah?"

"Winters. The son of a judge, apparently. She was in love with him."

"Winters," Becca repeated under her breath. "She took his name."

Robby nodded. Then he sighed, frustrated as he neared the final few pages. "That's one of the last entries. No mention of where she went or what happened to Jeremiah. No clues about the tunnel or the door in the Hollows. Nothing I can see that gets us any closer to figuring out what happened to Tina or my mom—or what Miss Winters wants. Maybe Zeus is right, and this is just another dead end."

"I bet we're just missing something."

Robby sighed. "The last entry is the longest one. Want me to keep reading?"

Becca twirled her silver pendant between her fingers, then stopped suddenly, pursing her lips. "Actually… Can you send me the sketch of Joanna Greylocke from the *Secret History* book? The one from 1691."

Robby opened the photos tab on his phone and scrolled through the images until he found it. "What are you thinking?" he asked as he hit SEND.

"It's probably nothing." She crinkled her nose again. "Read me the last entry while I check something." She peered intently at the screen and began typing.

The final diary entry was written in the same crisp cursive handwriting as the letters to his mother. It was dated in early January 1691, more than three hundred years earlier.

"'A thick gray fog had already settled over the village by the time I left my uncle's house. I wrapped myself in Catherine's scarlet cloak, nervous, excited, and acutely alert despite the midnight hour. My heart beat with anticipation for a life full of new promise. For the unborn life growing within me.'"

"She was pregnant?" said Becca, looking up.

Robby nodded. "'I made certain that no one could hear my boots crunching against the packed dirt of the village road nor see me wade through the yellow-brown heather at the edge of the village. No one watched me climb to the top of the orchard hill, and no one witnessed Jeremiah rush to me, silent as a shadow, just as I knew he would.'"

Becca stopped typing. She looked up at the screen again. "So, he loved her, too."

"I think we're getting to the part Miss Winters alluded to when she brought us all to Willow Hill that first day in school.

Remember when she said the Winslow sisters' fate was sealed on
Willow Hill, even though none of them could have known it at
the time? Listen to this." He shifted the diary into the light:

> "My love," he called me, though he
> had already planted the seeds of his be-
> trayal. "We cannot continue to meet like
> this. There are too many whispers. Bishop
> suspects us already, and if we should be
> discovered—"
>
> "It means nothing," I told him.
> "Whatever they say about me. They can-
> not harm me with words."
>
> "They say you bewitch men."
>
> "Is it true?" I asked him, twirling the
> single gray lock of my dark hair between
> my fingers, my lips curving into the secret
> smile I saved only for him. "Have I be-
> witched you?"
>
> "You must be serious, Joanna."
>
> "Jeremiah Winters, I am always seri-
> ous about our love."
>
> "But we cannot be together. Not any
> longer. For *your* safety."
>
> Even then I did not understand. I was
> still a fool.
>
> "I won't listen to this," I told him.
> "Next time, please do not—"
>
> "There will be no next time," he said.
> "There cannot be. If only you heard what
> they say about you. They speak of witch-
> craft. The devil's lure."
>
> "Then they speak of things they do
> not understand." Barren branches shud-

dered in the wind as I spun in the moonlit mist, my hair trailing like a silky web behind me. Surely, I could make him see. "These people don't fear some Christian devil. They fear *women*: our casual power over witless men. They call us the weaker sex, but it is they who cannot resist us. And in their shame, they seek to discredit those who hold sway over them."

He backed away, horrified at my words. I pressed on. I had no choice but to make him see. "I tell you, it is not witchcraft—not as they know it. It is good. It is natural. *Pure*." My skin burned hot in the night, my spirit blazing with conviction. I had grown so weary of hiding that which I had become. It was time to show him, finally, the woman he loved—the whole of me. I raised my arms above my head and probed for the silky strands of the secret world around us. At last, I revealed my power to him. "What their superstitions call witchcraft, Jeremiah, I call a miracle."

"God help me," he cried. "You *are* a witch."

"It is not evil as they say. I am learning to control it now. I *am*." Even as I stepped toward him, he backed away. "This power is a wonder, my love. Just as our child will be a wonder."

"We cannot," he protested.

"We already have. I feel her growing inside me now."

I reached out my hand to him, and I

swear, in that instant he nearly took it. If
only he had.

I fear now as I write this that he plans
to turn the village against me, once and for
all. That he will name me as a witch.

But I vow on my own life's blood, if
he tries, then I shall show him fury such as
this village has never seen.

"That's the last of it." Robby swallowed. His throat had
gone dry from reading. "Except, we know from *The Secret History* that Joanna Greylocke never did stand trial. Jeremiah turning
on her has to be the treachery she meant, only it was the Winslow
sisters who were hanged. And then she just disappeared from history for three hundred years."

Becca gasped, then looked up suddenly. "Robby," she said.
Her eyes narrowed. "She *didn't* entirely disappear."

"What do you mean?"

Becca dropped out of view, reappearing a moment later
holding a newly printed sheet of paper. "We thought the internet
was a dead end, but we were just looking at it the wrong way."
She held the printout in front of her camera. "While you were
reading, I ran a reverse image search on the portrait."

Robby squinted at a sepia-toned photo of someone who
looked just like Miss Winters in Victorian-era garb. Einstein
crawled over to see.

"This is from a newspaper article in 1889," Becca said. "She
was going by the name Joanna Grey at the time. She was a
schoolteacher in Willow Cove."

Robby traced the now-familiar face. The woman's uncertain
smile reminded him of the girl in the diary entry—the Joanna
Greylocke who seemed so frightened and alone.

"Why was her picture in the newspaper?"

"The article isn't about her, actually. It's about six girls in her class."

"What about them?"

"They vanished, Robby. They all vanished."

Part Three

27

Promises to the Dead

Abby hopped from foot to foot on the slushy path to school. Amethyst lumbered along beside her, rubbing her mittens together for warmth. The new year had swept into town in a wet gray blur, leaving everything feeling dim and dull. So far, the first three weeks of January had been nothing but cold rain and icy sidewalks.

"I never thought I'd miss the snow," Abby said, wiggling her toes inside her boots to keep them from freezing. She nearly stepped in a puddle and had to grab hold of Amethyst's arm for balance. "Sorry, I was just trying to avoid the slush."

"That's not all you've been trying to avoid."

Following Amethyst's gaze, Abby's chest tightened as she caught sight of Zeus and Robby climbing the school's front steps. She ducked into the shadows and tugged her winter hat tight over her head. When she peeked out from beneath it, they'd both disappeared inside.

"You know you can't keep avoiding Zeus, right?"

Abby sighed. "I know. I'm the worst."

"Eventually, you have to actually go to the dance with him."

"I *know*."

"Then why are you avoiding him?"

Abby removed her glasses and began to polish them with the hem of her shirt. "Because I think I made a mistake. It was selfish of me to say yes. I can't risk bringing him into this."

"It's not like you're inviting him into the coven, Abby."

"Obviously. But it still feels... *dangerous* right now. Don't you think?" She scrubbed at a speck of ice on her lens that turned out to be a scratch. "Between Miss Winters and the Council and the voice in the tower—it wouldn't be fair to involve Zeus in any of it. Even if he does just want to hang out."

Amethyst glanced at her sharply. "Oh, he definitely wants to do more than that."

"And that's just the thing. Maybe I do, too. I don't know! I can't even think about it until I know what we're dealing with, though. And speaking of avoiding people..." Amethyst ducked into the shadows beside her, narrowly dodging Daisy and Delphi as they stepped onto the school steps.

"They have bad poker faces," Amethyst said. "You know we can't trust them not to accidentally blab our suspicions to Miss Winters."

"It would be easier if we told everyone, though. They could help create a distraction so we could sneak into the tower and see what's going on in there. At this rate, we'll be seniors by the time Miss Winters gives us another opening."

"Daze and Delphi have many wonderful qualities, but subtlety isn't one of them. Same goes for Piper. There's no way they'd be able to act normal around Miss Winters if they knew." Amethyst frowned. "Or around Olivia."

Abby and Amethyst slipped through the school doors after the first bell, only to find Zeus waiting by Abby's locker.

"We'll never make it to gym if he doesn't move," Abby whispered.

"I'll distract him. You go the long way."

Abby whispered a thanks and then slipped away.

"It's just a temporary fix," Amethyst reminded her. "You still have to go to the dance with him!"

A few girls were still changing when Abby slipped into the locker room just ahead of the second bell. Olivia paused in the middle of a heated discussion with Sarika to shoot Abby a withering glare before resuming their argument.

"They've been going at it since homeroom," explained Becca, nodding in Olivia's direction.

Abby tossed her school bag onto the bench in front of her locker, then unclasped her lucky pendant and placed it carefully inside the front pocket. She didn't normally talk to Becca, but today her curiosity won out. "What are they fighting about?"

"Sarika thinks Olivia's been messing with her."

"Messing how?"

"Hypnosis." Becca rolled her eyes. "Apparently, she has all kinds of weird memory gaps and Olivia's always there when she comes to."

She's not wrong, Abby thought as Sarika thrust her phone in Olivia's face, acting like it proved something. Abby tossed her shirt and jacket onto the bench in front of her locker and opened her bag to pull out her gym clothes. They weren't there. She'd brought them home on Friday to wash and must have forgotten to grab them from the dryer.

"I forgot mine last week," said Becca, glancing at Abby's bag. "Mondays are the worst. I keep spare clothes in my bag if you want to borrow?"

"No, it's okay."

Becca stood on her tiptoes to unlatch her locker. "I don't think Mr. Rexman will agree with that." Her eyes flicked toward

Olivia and Sarika, who looked ready to come to blows. "Look, most of the girls in this school are awful. The rest of us should have each other's back." She opened the locker and pulled out her gym bag. "I promise they're clean."

Abby's gaze drifted in Olivia's direction again. "All right," she said after a moment's hesitation. "Thank you."

Becca placed her gym bag on the bench next to Abby's and began to rummage through it. An artist's sketchpad fell open onto the floor between them as she produced a spare shirt and gym pants. Abby crouched to help retrieve it, and then froze.

"I'm such a slob," said Becca, snatching the sketchpad away from her.

Abby had only glimpsed it for a second, but she'd recognize a hexagram anywhere. What she didn't recognize was everything around it—a cavern or tunnel. It looked similar to the door that Miss Winters had stopped her from entering in the passage under Whispering Hill. "What is that?" she asked.

"Nothing." Becca's cheeks flushed. "Just something I drew."

"Have you seen something like that around here?"

"No," said Becca, too fast. "Sometimes I just draw things."

Becca handed Abby the spare clothes and then scooped everything else back into her locker. Abby eyed Becca's back. Drawing might be another of Becca's talents, but she still didn't give off a spark, which meant whatever she was up to, it wasn't because she was secretly a witch, too.

"Thanks, again," Abby said, poking her head through the borrowed shirt.

Becca smiled. "Don't worry about it."

All I do is worry, Abby thought. *And now I'm worried about you, too.*

"You should ask Zeus about it," said Amethyst after school as she and Abby slogged behind Miss Winters in the general direction of the seashore. "He's always with Becca and Robby lately." Tiny flecks of frozen rain pelted their faces through the coastal fog. Piper, Daisy, and Delphi were right behind Miss Winters. Olivia moodily trailed at the back of the line.

"You know I don't want to get Zeus involved in this."

"It seems like maybe he already is."

Abby sighed. "What do you think they're up to?"

"I don't know, but they'd better hope Miss Winters doesn't find out about it."

Miss Winters stopped at the edge of the salt marsh on the outskirts of town. They gathered in the icy cordgrass near a rounded haystack as the sky dimmed. The mud flats in the distance reeked with the rotten-egg smell of low tide.

Olivia wrinkled her nose at the air. "Why are we even here?"

"We are hunting," said Miss Winters, barely concealing her excitement.

"For what?" Piper asked. Flapper peeked out from a side pocket of her jacket, peering at the horizon.

Miss Winters held up a hand to quiet them. The sky had grown darker, though a small sliver of light still hung low on the horizon, pale as snow.

"I see something," Piper whispered in awe, and then Daisy and Delphi echoed her. Abby followed their gaze. Hundreds of tiny lights sparkled red and green and blue in the distance, zipping about like fluorescent fireflies.

"They're so pretty," said Daisy.

"They are will-o'-the-wisps," said Miss Winters. "*Tenuis Borealis*, to be precise, the common North American wisp, more abundant than mosquitoes in the salt marshes of New England." She placed a hand on Piper's shoulder as the young witch began to drift forward, as if in a trance. "Observe them, but do not follow yet."

Piper stiffened and then looked around in surprise. "I didn't mean to. It just happened."

"Are they dangerous?" asked Daisy.

"They are the spirits of the dead," said Miss Winters. "And not the happy kind."

"Ghosts?"

"In a manner of speaking."

The lights drew closer. They weren't each a single color as Abby initially thought. They blinked from hue to hue like a traffic signal gone haywire.

Olivia stared at them, transfixed. "What are we supposed to do with them?"

"Catch them," said Miss Winters, "like this." She raised her wand and stepped toward the swirling lights. They scattered like ripples in a pond before regrouping a few steps ahead. Miss Winters followed them confidently. "As you can see, they are trying to lure me deeper into the marsh." Her wand zipped through the air in a flurry of movement, and this time when the lights dispersed, one wisp remained behind at the tip of her wand. Miss Winters repeated the motion twice more, each time capturing another wisp before returning to the girls with a quivering ball of light clinging to her wand.

"As a witch, you will encounter many creatures that you may have considered little more than myth and legend. Griffins and goblins, giants and jabberwockies, unicorns and vampires—"

"Unicorns?" said Daisy.

"Vampires!?" said Delphi.

"And worse still. Basilisks and brownies, dryads and naiads, gargoyles and chimeras, and many things even more frightening. But wisps," Miss Winters said, holding out the tip of her wand for the girls to study, "are a good place for us to begin our observation of magical creatures. A wisp cannot hurt you—it cannot even properly touch you—unless you allow it to. Follow them recklessly, however, and you will find yourself in a very unpleasant situation, where you are likely to remain until you eventually become one of them."

Piper blinked nervously. "A lost soul?"

"Indeed. Now, let us begin. Your assignment is to each catch and release a wisp. You will pair off and take turns preventing your partner from wandering." She surveyed the girls for a moment. "Daisy and Delphi, you two together. Piper and Amethyst." Miss Winters tilted her chin toward Abby. "You and Olivia."

Amethyst squeezed Abby's hand and then drifted toward Piper, who steered Amethyst into the thickening darkness with a *sorry-not-sorry* look on her face.

"You again," Olivia complained as Abby joined her.

"This doesn't exactly make my day, either."

"Let's just get it over with."

They wandered through crunchy knee-high grass guided only by the dim glow of their wands. Ahead, Miss Winters stood to one side, her hands on her hips, watching as Daisy waded into a swirling cloud of wisps. Delphi hung back a few paces, her wand at the ready.

"Nothing to fear now," Miss Winters called out. "Raise your wand—like that, very good—and keep it high. Excellent form. Now, let them come to you, and… Well done, dear. Very well done."

Daisy lurched backward, holding her wand away from her body like a burning match. Her sister caught her as she stumbled. A wisp twinkled at the tip of Daisy's wand, flickering through the colors of the rainbow before settling into a pale blue glow. "'Blue circles stream'd like rainbows in the sky,'" Daisy whispered reverently.

"And to release it from its earthly bond," Miss Winters said, "simply reverse the pattern."

Daisy flicked her wrist. She gasped as the wisp faded to dark, like a matchstick flame suddenly extinguished.

"Don't be sad for it," Miss Winters said gently. "It has been waiting for someone like you to come along and set it free. The eternal void is better than its aimless wanderings." She surveyed the darkened marsh for a moment. "Look in the distance now, and you will likely see—yes, there they are—several other swarms just like this one. Pick one and then return to me with a wisp before releasing it. Partners, stay close. Good luck!"

"Do you want to go first?" Abby asked.

Olivia stared straight ahead. Abby followed her gaze to one of the new swarms. Three shadowy figures blinked in and out of view.

"Does that look like…?"

"T-Rex," Abby finished for her. She squinted and made out the other two shapes. Joey and Sarika. "I thought you said—"

"I know what I said," Olivia snapped. "It's not as easy as I thought. They won't stop following me."

"Is that why you were arguing with Sarika this morning?"

Olivia nodded stiffly. "I can't make them forget it all anymore, and they keep—"

"I could help you," Abby suggested.

"Excuse me while I vomit. You'd only make it worse."

But it quickly became obvious that things had already gotten worse. The wisps were just pinpricks of light in the distance now. Only an occasional lurch from Joey or T-Rex gave any indication that they hadn't been swallowed whole.

"Everything all right here?" asked Miss Winters, appearing suddenly behind them. Abby jumped.

"Fabulous," said Olivia. Her eyes narrowed, daring Abby to contradict her. Abby held her tongue until Miss Winters drifted away to observe Piper and Amethyst.

"Why would you even want to help me?" Olivia whispered.

"We'll all pay for it if Miss Winters finds out what you've been doing."

"Come on, then."

"They can't hurt us if we stay together." Abby and Olivia broke into a run. When they reached the swarm, the wisps scattered before regrouping thicker and brighter than before.

Abby shielded her eyes against the dazzling lights. "We need to get your friends out of there!" she shouted. Joey was closest to her, so she pushed him as hard as she could. He just stared back at her, slack-jawed, even when she called his name.

"I can't move T-Rex," shouted Olivia, her voice panicked.

"Maybe like this?" Abby grunted as she bull-rushed Joey out of the swarm. They stumbled a few steps together before Joey landed on his back in the cold muck and Abby toppled down on top of him, closer to him than she'd ever want to be. Several wisps broke free, regrouping around them.

Abby scrambled to her feet. Olivia had given up on T-Rex and was tugging Sarika by the arm. They'd escaped the swarm only to have another form around them. Now, instead of one swarm, there were three.

"This situation is not improving!" Olivia yelled.

Joey tottered after the lights again. Abby grabbed him by his shirt but had to let go before he dragged her away.

A few wisps fluttered toward her, flickering between colors with dizzying frequency. *Let them come to me*, she thought, repeating Miss Winters's instructions. *And then...* She swiped her wand through the air like a rapier. A tremor stretched from her fingers to her elbow as she captured her first wisp, which glimmered a hundred different colors at the tip of her wand as it struggled to break free.

One down. Thousands to go.

Olivia seemed to have the same idea.

Abby watched T-Rex out of the corner of one eye. Every time she glanced at him, he'd drifted a little farther away. She couldn't see any of her friends now—the wisps were leading them away from safety just as Miss Winters said they would.

"Got you," Abby crowed as she captured a second wisp at

the tip of her wand, where it struggled and pulsed on top of the first one. She went after the others with more confidence, capturing them in twos and threes until her arm felt sluggish with the unfamiliar weight and her wand pulsed with variegated lights.

"Abby!" shouted Olivia. "A little help?"

Abby turned in time to see Olivia stumble to one knee. Her wand glowed red and green while wisps swirled around her in quick circles. She looked like she was wrestling a Christmas tree.

"Coming!" Abby yelled. She spared one final look at Joey lying face up in the muck—groaning, but unharmed—before sprinting after Olivia and wrangling the last of the wisps onto her wand. Sarika sat up in dazed silence, rubbing her brow with unsteady hands. Joey stumbled over and sank to the ground next to her. Other than the wisps at the end of Abby's and Olivia's wands, the sky was once again dark.

"We did it," Olivia said, breathing in wheezy puffs.

"What… about… T-Rex?" Abby asked between her own labored breaths. She scanned the horizon. A tiny bead of light flickered in the distance, fleeting as a firefly. "That way. Come on!"

Olivia turned to Joey and Sarika. "You two stay here," she told them as they blinked at her, bewildered. "If you see any more lights, try not following them this time!"

Abby and Olivia broke into a run, wands at the ready. The glow made it easier to find a path through the marsh grass. It also made it easier to see that Amethyst, Piper, Daisy, and Delphi were already there, blocking T-Rex from drifting any deeper into the endless night—and that Miss Winters was methodically dispatching the wisps.

"What is the meaning of this intrusion?" Miss Winters growled at T-Rex through gritted teeth as Abby and Olivia came to a stop a few paces away. She pressed her free hand into his chest like a spear. "This is not some school field trip. You are not welcome here."

T-Rex lumbered to his feet. Blood trickled like spittle from his puffy lower lip, mingling with the mud and muck smeared across his chin. He leveled a shaky finger at Olivia. "She… She's been… *doing* something to us," he rasped. "Erasing… erasing our…" He stopped and rubbed his eyes. "Where am I?"

Miss Winters spun toward Olivia. "Is this true?"

Olivia's eyes briefly met Abby's, the defiance gone. She lowered her head.

"Who else?" Miss Winters demanded.

"Joey and Sarika."

"No," said Miss Winters sharply. "Who else in this coven *knew* you were doing this?"

Joey and Sarika tottered toward them, blinking like raccoons in the wandlight.

"I told you to stay put," Olivia grumbled under her breath.

"I want answers," T-Rex snarled. "We *all* want answers."

Miss Winters's free hand moved so quickly that Abby almost missed it. With the slightest flick of her wrist, T-Rex's expression changed from pit bull to puppy, all soft lines and rounded corners. "You are not entitled to them," Miss Winters said. "Who. Else. Knew?"

Olivia met Abby's gaze, and for the briefest of moments, Abby thought she might actually keep it to herself. But Olivia had never been the type to go down alone. "Abby knew. I'm sure they all knew. That's how they work, five against one."

"Oh, like you'd even *want* to be one of us," said Delphi.

Olivia thrust an angry finger in Abby's direction. "Her friends are snooping around, too. I've seen them."

"Shut up, Olivia," Abby warned.

"Enough." Miss Winters glared at all of them. "The five of you, release the wisps you've caught. Olivia and I will clean up her mess."

"They don't remember most of it," Olivia said. "They barely know what's going on when they're completely lucid."

"And yet they keep finding you. Memory charms are, by their nature, imprecise. Something of what they have seen remains, rattling around in those empty heads of theirs, ready to rise to the surface at unpredictable times."

"It's just T-Rex," grumbled Olivia. "He's too dense to cause us any trouble."

"And you are just a foolish child," Miss Winters snapped. "Never set something in motion unless you're certain you can control the outcome. These three friends of yours are now a problem. Anyone who learns too much about what we do is a problem."

Abby risked a glance at Amethyst, who caught her eye warily. *Robby, Becca, and Zeus. They're a problem too.*

"I am *so* not going to the dance with you this weekend," Olivia snapped at T-Rex.

"That's the first wise decision you've made all night," Miss Winters said, giving her a sharp look. "One fewer of you for me to keep an eye on there. The rest of you, I said to release your wisps and go home. Olivia, you will come with me—*now*." She yanked Olivia by the hand and led her away, T-Rex and the two others following like wayward pets.

Piper stared regretfully at the tip of her wand. "I want to keep one."

"You'd better not," said Delphi.

"Why not?"

"They're the spirits of the dead. We promised to set them free. You can't break a promise to a dead person, or they'll come back and haunt you." Delphi shook her head. "I thought everyone knew that."

Abby watched Miss Winters disappear into the darkness, her long cloak flapping behind her. She looked like someone straight out of a gothic romance, striding across the misty moors, haunted by a long-lost love. But who, Abby wondered, was haunting her?

Amethyst followed Abby's gaze. "You don't think Miss

Winters would really hurt Robby or his friends?" she said, low enough for only Abby to hear.

"I hope not." Abby tucked her hands under her arms and eyed the others as they released their wisps. "I'm not sure we should leave it to chance, though. Did you hear what she said to Olivia about the dance?"

"Miss Winters must be a chaperone."

"Not even she can be in two places at once," Abby pointed out.

Amethyst's eyes widened. "If she *is* hiding something from us—"

"Then this is the opening we've been waiting for."

28

The Bloodline

On the night of the dance, something scraped loudly outside Robby's window, a persistent *scratch, scratch,* pause, *scratch, scratch,* like fingernails on a chalkboard. He closed the Greylocke diary and placed it on his desk next to the newspaper clippings and real estate documents he'd been studying all afternoon, then lifted the shade to peer outside. The weather had finally turned back to snow. Peering down at the driveway, he saw his father clearing ice from the car's windshield.

Was it already time to leave?

He frowned at his reflection in the window. His reflection frowned back, red-faced and scowling in a stiff button-down shirt. He stuck a finger under his collar and tried to loosen it, but that only made him choke. Right now, Becca was probably putting on makeup or painting her nails or doing whatever else it was girls did to get ready, and he couldn't even find a shirt that looked good. Sometimes, he wondered why she liked him at all.

He dropped the shade and returned to his desk, where he glanced at the old letter addressed to his mother and the crumpled photo of Abby he'd found at Mrs. Vickory's house. He knew he should finish getting ready, at least comb his hair, but he also felt like he was close to a breakthrough. He kept coming back to the fact that Joanna Greylocke was pregnant in 1691. It seemed too important. But despite searching, he couldn't find any mention of the child anywhere. What happened to her baby?

Then a thought occurred to him. He kicked it around inside his head, poking and prodding for holes, but he couldn't find any. What if Joanna Greylocke's child had been hiding in plain sight all along?

He tapped his fingers impatiently against the keyboard while he waited for his computer to whir to life. The truth about Joanna Greylocke's bloodline might be right there in the family history project they'd done for Mrs. Vickory earlier in the year.

He pulled up the genealogical diagram of everyone in class who could track their family history back to the seventeenth century in Willow Cove. Trailing a finger down the screen, he found the name he was looking for.

Victoria Snow.

An orphan born to unknown parents in the year 1691. It couldn't be a coincidence. She'd had four children and eleven grandchildren before she died in 1755. Robby scanned names, generation after generation, until he found another that sounded familiar: Mary Courage, born in 1876, believed to have died in 1889 at the age of thirteen. He riffled through the newspaper clippings on his desk, and there it was: Mary Courage, one of the six girls who'd vanished the last time Joanna Greylocke returned to Willow Cove.

He checked the diagram again, and then skimmed the article Becca had found about the disappearances. The five other girls who vanished were also descendants of Victoria Snow. If his theory were right, they were all originally descended from Joanna Greylocke herself. But why would she be going after her own bloodline?

A knock at the door pulled him from his thoughts. The door

cracked open. His father poked his head inside and then edged the rest of the way into the room, dripping wet snow onto the floor with every step. He jangled his keys. "Car's running."

Robby checked the time. "Still a little early, Dad."

"Teachers have to help set up. Better to get there early in this weather, anyway."

He peered over Robby's shoulder at the computer screen. Robby inched to one side to block his view. "I'm not quite ready yet. I'll walk over in a bit."

"What have you been doing up here all this time?"

"Just thinking."

His father smiled, but then his expression creased into something more complicated as his gaze settled on the stack of papers next to the keyboard. "Thinking about what?" he asked with concern.

Robby followed his father's eyes to the crumpled photo of Abby. "It's not like that, Dad."

"It would be natural if it were, you know. Even if everything is great with you and Becca. You've known Abby for a long time."

"We're just friends." Robby shook his head. "And lately it doesn't even feel like we're that."

"There's no such thing as *just* friends, Robby."

"What do you mean?"

His father leaned against the desk. "I suppose I mean that real friendship isn't always easy. Sometimes you want different things from each other. Sometimes you want the same things at different times. But being there for each other, being part of each other's lives through all the ups and downs—there's no *just* about that. It's everything." He patted Robby on the shoulder. "Have you tried talking to her? I bet she feels the same way."

Robby's phone buzzed with a call from Becca. He stared at the screen and let it go to voicemail. His father joined him in staring at the missed call. "Sometimes we want two incompatible things, Robby. But sometimes we only think they're incompatible. I hope Becca isn't the reason you and Abby have drifted apart."

"I told you, it's not like that."

His father removed his glasses and rubbed his eyes. "Good. Becca is a nice girl. If you really like her, don't give her any reason to doubt how you feel." He glanced at the clock on Robby's bed stand. "You're sure I can't give you a ride?"

"You go. I just need to finish up here."

"Don't stay too long." He patted Robby on the shoulder one more time and then left the room. "Never keep a pretty girl waiting," he added as he drifted down the stairs. "More free advice!"

Robby watched by the window until the car pulled out of the driveway. His gaze wandered to Abby's bedroom across the way, but the shades were down and the room dark. Everything about it seemed so familiar and yet so alien. Everything about *her* seemed that way lately, too.

He returned to his computer and studied the names and dates on the screen again, drawing invisible lines between all the connections to Joanna Greylocke. The six girls in 1889 were all descended from Victoria Snow. Abby and the other girls she'd started hanging out with all came from the same bloodline, too—Joanna Greylocke's bloodline.

It had to mean something.

But what?

Abby paced back and forth across Amethyst's bedroom, pausing every few minutes to peer out the window as the sky slowly darkened. Amethyst's house shuddered each time the wind whipped up the snow on the bare fields beyond.

Laying on the bed, Amethyst surveyed Abby with narrowed eyes until finally it seemed she couldn't take it any longer. "Stop pacing," she said. "You're making me nervous."

"You *should* be nervous." Abby took one final look outside before shuttering the window and turning her back to it. It didn't help. It still felt like Miss Winters could see her all the way from Whispering Hill. "We should both be nervous."

"Fine, you're making me more nervous." Amethyst blew a giant bubble of purple chewing gum and then floated the wad to the trash can with her wand. "Even though chances are we won't find anything in that tower."

"I hope you're right." Abby caught herself pacing again. She stopped, then began twirling her lucky pendant between her fingers. "It's just—Don't you wonder what Miss Winters did to T-Rex and the others? They've been acting like robots since the salt marsh." She adopted a mechanical voice. "'Yes, Miss Winters, whatever you wish, Miss Winters.' It's creepy."

"Personally, I think it's an improvement." Amethyst pulled out a new stick of gum and popped it into her mouth. "I'm more worried about what she'll do to *us* if we're caught."

"We'll only be at Whispering Hill for a few minutes. Then we'll arrive fashionably late to the dance and no one will ever suspect a thing."

"Now I hope *you're* right," Amethyst said.

"Aren't I always?" Abby glanced at her phone again. "It's time, by the way."

Amethyst hopped off the bed, grabbed her broomstick, and unhooked the latch to the widow's walk on the other side of the room. Spooks, who'd been watching them from a pile of laundry at the foot of the stepladder, gave her a dirty look before resettling a few feet over.

Abby zipped her jacket and followed Amethyst up the ladder to the roof of the house. Outside, the wind howled even louder. Abby tied her hair into a ponytail and pulled her winter hat down over her head.

"Ready?" Amethyst asked.

"What could possibly go wrong?"

"Never say things like that!" Amethyst swatted at Abby with her broom. "Now hop on and let's get this over with."

Abby mounted the broom and then wrapped her arms around Amethyst for support. As they lifted off into the icy breeze, she huddled closer, ducking from the wind while they buzzed barren treetops at the edge of the farm. Amethyst brought them swiftly upward until suddenly Whispering Hill came into view ahead. The north tower stood stark black against the sky, spiraling up and ending in a sharp point that split the night in two. The moon lit the clouds from the inside like a giant paper lantern.

Amethyst coasted to a ledge near the top of the tower that looked like it could support their weight. She hovered close while Abby tried to peer inside, but the glass was too caked with snow and ice to make out anything clearly. Abby leaned forward until her hat brushed the back of Amethyst's head. "Can you get any closer?"

"I'll try, but it's—Oof!" They lurched away from the tower as if shoved by an invisible hand. "It's no good, Abby. You were right about the warding spell."

"That only makes me want to get in there more."

Amethyst steered them outside the spell's orbit. "It could take hours to unravel that spell, though, and even if we do—"

"There's always the old-fashioned way."

Amethyst peered over her shoulder, hesitation written across her face. "What's that?"

"I jump."

"What? You can't jump, you'll never—"

"Look at the spell, Amethyst. The threads go *around* the tower, not above it. Just get us higher, okay?"

"You'll fall!"

"Then catch me before I hit the ground!"

Amethyst groaned but pointed the broom toward the roof's slate-black pinnacle. Foot-long icicles draped the edges like jagged teeth.

"A little closer, I think—There!" Abby leapt before she could change her mind. She hit the roof with a thump and flailed as she slid down. Finally, she slowed, and then dropped to the ledge.

She gave Amethyst an unsteady thumbs-up before groping around the window for some kind of crack or crevice in the glass. It was as thick and unbreakable as pond ice.

Thunk!

She felt her feet slipping and steadied herself before prying at the window. *Thunk!* There it was again.

It was coming from inside the tower.

The glass creaked. The frame trembled. A latch clicked and then the window opened inward, revealing more darkness. An invitation… or a trap?

This is why I came.

She waved to Amethyst and then climbed inside.

The sun had slipped beneath the treetops by the time Robby left for the dance. The woods shielded him from the worst of the wind, but something about the way the snow-laden branches loomed over the path behind his house had him on edge even before he heard a twig snap behind him.

He stopped short, then turned, listening. Only the howling wind answered, carrying with it the smell of the ocean at low tide. Maybe it was just the emptiness of the woods that spooked him, like even the birds were hiding.

His phone buzzed from somewhere deep in his jacket. After

fumbling around for it, he saw Becca's name on the screen, and tapped a quick reply to let her know he'd be there soon.

Snap.

A twig, a branch. Something in the woods, just to his left. And suddenly the woods didn't feel empty anymore.

He took a step back toward his house, searching for the source of the sound.

T-Rex emerged from the bushes, Joey and Sarika just behind him. Robby took another step back. Something about them was different. The set of T-Rex's jaw. The quiet certainty with which all three of them moved toward him, like wolves surrounding their prey. Robby turned to run, but Joey grabbed his arms and pinned him in the middle of the trail before he'd made it more than a few steps.

"Come on, guys," Robby said, struggling to break free of Joey's grip. "Stop it!"

It was their silence that most concerned him. Joey and Sarika said nothing. T-Rex, standing a few feet from Robby and facing him head on, silently tilted his chin from side to side, studying him.

"T-Rex," Robby began, aware of the pleading note in his voice. "Whatever this is about—"

T-Rex launched at him like a battering ram. Robby hit the snow, facedown, gasping for breath. Someone kicked him in the face and his head exploded with bright white waves of pain. He thought it might have been Sarika, but everything had gone blurry and all he had to go on was the sound of cackling from somewhere above him. He tried to call for help, but his words came out as a gurgling whimper.

"No girlfriends to protect you this time," T-Rex said.

Robby groped around for his phone. He managed to click something before Joey smooshed his face into the snow and he couldn't focus on anything other than the pain. Someone yanked him to his knees and propped him in the middle of the trail. Sarika had one hand on Robby's shoulder. Joey jerked him up by the hair, holding him while T-Rex spit in his face and then punched him. Robby fell to the ground again.

"Where does she want him?" asked Sarika.

"Somewhere they'll never look," said Joey.

"Why?" Robby rasped. His voice sounded wrong somehow. Distant, not his own.

T-Rex loomed so close that all Robby could make out were the bloody red lumps of his knuckles. The world swam around him, hazy and unbalanced. "We have a message for you," T-Rex said in an eerily robotic voice as he reared back to punch him again. "Joanna Greylocke sends her regards."

29

The Prisoner

A lantern flickered to life in the tower, bathing the room in pale blue light. Chains and manacles were bolted to one wall, rusted but unbroken. A painted hexagram filled the floor. Abby squeezed her wand between her fingers and scanned the room.

"Hello, Abigail," said an old tired voice.

Abby spun toward the sound. "Bishop?"

The old man latched the window without taking his eyes from her. Abby's heart thumped as she risked a glance at the lantern in his hand. Inside, a small, iridescent wisp flittered like a frantic firefly.

"I thought you might come," Bishop told her. "When Miss Winters discovers your presence here tonight—she *will* discover it—you will deny you ever saw me. I was not here. I certainly did nothing to help you. But until then, you may come with me. Quickly now, before I change my mind."

"Amethyst is out there. She's waiting for me."

"Fool of a girl," Bishop snapped. Then he sighed and shook his head. "All right, I'll return for her momentarily."

"To do what?"

"To tell her where you've gone."

"Which is where?"

He shook his head impatiently. "You came here for answers. Follow me if you want them."

He lifted a wooden panel in the floor and led her down a narrow stairwell. Abby risked a final glance at the window and imagined Amethyst hovering just outside. She wished she could tell her to go.

"How long have you worked for Miss Winters?" Abby asked. Bishop turned, bringing a finger to his lips. Abby pressed her lips together and followed him.

They reached the bottom of the stairs and entered a long corridor similar to the hallway outside Miss Winters's bedroom. But every angle was just slightly off, and strange shapes flitted across the walls before revealing themselves as shadows cast by Bishop's lantern. The air grew colder as they descended another stairwell and followed a new hallway, which ended at yet another set of stairs, these spiraling downward through the darkness like a corkscrew into what Abby felt certain was part of the basement. *Or a dungeon*. At the bottom, a tall wooden door curled into an arch. A red hexagram had been burned into it beneath a barred window.

"This is as far as I can take you," Bishop said. "If you wish to pass this door, you'll need your wand. But your magic will leave a signature. She will find out you've been here, but at least you will know."

"Know what?"

"Some things are better seen for yourself."

"Why can't you just tell me?"

Bishop frowned, and Abby got the distinct impression she'd failed some crucial test. As he turned to leave, she reached out her hand to touch his shoulder. "Why are you here with her? Why are you helping me now?"

"Often, there are no good choices. Only good intentions."

He hesitated. "I will fetch Amethyst now. Once you have seen what you came for, follow the corridor until you reach the main foyer. Do not stray from this route. Your friend will be waiting for you outside. And Abigail?"

"Yeah?"

"Don't judge her too harshly."

When he was gone, Abby turned back to the door. It looked like it belonged in a medieval castle—thick broad planks, black metal hinges, an iron ring. Something metallic rattled on the other side. "Is someone there?" she called.

When no answer came, she took a deep breath and released the seal. The door creaked open. Dust glittered like tiny stars in her wandlight, and then the smell hit her: blood and sweat and urine. But when she peered inside, she saw only darkness.

"Hello?" she said.

Her eyes narrowed as they adjusted to the room. A woman was slumped against the far wall, little more than skin and bones, all but unrecognizable except for the torn blue scrubs.

"Tina?" Abby gasped.

Robby's stepmother struggled to rise. Invisible shackles crackled around her wrists like electric vines, snapping her back to the floor. She screamed and then slumped again, knocking aside a tray of half-eaten food. Abby scrambled to her.

"Abby." Tina's voice was raspy from disuse. She coughed and blood gurgled onto her chin as Abby eased a steadying hand under her back. Tina lifted a bony hand to Abby's face. Her eyes were cloudy and unfocused, but her lips cracked into a weak smile. "You found me."

"I thought I heard someone calling my name."

"I hoped you would. I sensed you near me. She moved me soon after that." Her gaze darted around the room. "Where are the others? Piper, Amethyst, Olivia—"

"You know about them?"

"I was sent to teach the six of you."

Abby's throat tightened. "Sent by whom?"

"For millennia…" Tina's voice cracked. A cough racked her body. She grimaced before continuing. "The Council of Witches has sent the Order to train and protect each new generation. You were supposed to be… my students. I came to Willow Cove to teach you. I'm sorry… I failed."

You're a witch? But part of her knew it had to be true. *The costume on Halloween. The broomstick. Inviting Piper to work at the clinic.* Tina must have been preparing to tell them what they were. "You haven't failed us. I'm still alive. We all are, and I'm going to get you out of here."

Tina clutched Abby's wrist. "It's too dangerous now."

"But you need a doctor! Or maybe…" Abby twisted her wand to cast a healing spell, but Tina shook her head.

"I'm… too far gone… for simple healing arts," she said.

"Then we need to tell the police. Mr. O'Reilly—"

"No! No, Abby, especially not James." She coughed again. "I won't lose him to Joanna."

"Joanna." Abby suddenly hated the sound of that name. "Who is she, Tina? Why did she do this to you? What does she want with us?"

"Only Agnes knew everything. I just have pieces. She comes to me sometimes now. Keeps me alive and then takes my power… to sustain… herself."

"Agnes," Abby repeated. "You mean Mrs. Vickory. She was a witch, too?"

Another cough shook Tina's body. Finally, with great effort, she nodded. "She was my teacher. She knew about the bloodline… Joanna always follows the bloodline." Tina's eyes clouded. She looked as if she might pass out.

Abby needed to keep her talking. Distract her until she could find a way to free her. "Miss Winters—Joanna, I mean—she told me the Council wants to control us."

"No, Abby, the Council protects us." Tina clutched at Abby's face and then let her hand fall weakly to the floor. "Agnes had another apprentice... before me."

"An apprentice. Good. Who?" *Keep talking.*

"Emily... O'Reilly."

Abby froze. "Robby's mom?"

"She would have joined the Order... herself one day. I was sent to replace her... Until then, I thought Greylocke... just a ghost story..."

"Greylocke?"

"Her real name. Joanna Greylocke."

"Robby needs to hear this. I'm getting you out of here right now." She glanced at Tina's wrists, the skin red and raw. The shackles that had jolted her back to the wall were obviously a restraining spell, but what was the counter pattern?

"Someone's... coming," Tina croaked. "Listen."

Footsteps in the distance. Doors opening and closing. Voices.

I shouldn't have trusted Bishop.

"Go, Abby. She can't know... you've found me." Tina guided Abby's wand hand toward the door. "I can hide your presence for a while. You must contact the Council... They can help."

"Contact them how?"

Tina whispered something Abby couldn't make out. She reached for Abby's wand hand. "May I borrow... your power... for just a moment?"

In answer, Abby clutched Tina's hand. It was like thrusting her fingers into a bucket of ice—her arm went numb, and then her chest, and then all of her strength dissolved, and she collapsed to the floor, a wasted husk, trembling and weak.

"Tina..." Abby groaned, suddenly terrified she'd trusted the wrong person after all.

"I think"—Tina's voice sounded stronger—"yes, that should be enough." She wrapped her fingers between Abby's until they held the wand together, two hands as one, and then she tilted Abby's wand toward the hexagram. It flared to life, a circle of green flame. When she released the wand, warmth returned to Abby's fingertips. Her arms tingled as if they'd fallen asleep.

"When this is all over, I will teach you properly about your abilities," Tina whispered. "Until that day... I know you'll find your own way. You always have. Now, go! Go, and don't look back."

Abby stumbled toward the door. It closed behind her, and she flared her wand to life as she slipped into the darkened corridor. Part of her wanted to turn back and save Tina, despite her protests.

Find your own way. You always have.

She hesitated.

Go, and don't look back.

She exhaled and then followed the route Bishop had described. Near the end of the corridor, she stopped mid-stride, because there it was again: the unmistakable *click-clack* of hurried footsteps in the darkness. Getting closer.

Lights out, she thought, and blackness swallowed her again as her wand went dark. Still, the footsteps grew louder. She leaned into the wall and stopped. The footsteps stopped, too, replaced with voices. Was it Bishop and Miss Winters? But that didn't fit. She recognized Bishop's voice, but the other was younger. Angrier.

"Amethyst!" Abby shouted. Her wand blazed to life again as she raced the rest of the way to the main foyer. Bishop was wielding his lantern between them like a shield. When Amethyst spotted her, she gave Bishop a quick kick to the shin and then darted in her direction.

"Are you hurt?" Amethyst asked.

"I'm fine. What are you doing here?"

"Creepy Mr. Filch over there wouldn't tell me where he'd taken you."

"It's Mr. Bishop," he corrected her.

Amethyst rolled her eyes. "You're okay?"

"We need to get out of here—now."

They ran the rest of the way, and when Amethyst slammed the heavy double doors behind them, Abby still wouldn't slow down. "We have to get to the dance," she huffed.

"You're that desperate to see Zeus?"

"Not Zeus, Amethyst. Robby. I have to see Robby."

30

Reunion

Robby lurched awake with a gasp. His jaw hurt. His neck and stomach and shoulder hurt, too. An orange glow lit the room and foggy voices whispered in hushed tones just out of sight. He tried to sit up, but a flurry of stars washed over him in a wave of nausea.

He blinked and tried to prop himself up again, then immediately wished he hadn't moved at all. Now he could see the vague shapes of two big, white orbs at the end of a long snout. The snout drew nearer, snuffling hungrily, and Robby was suddenly aware of the creature's yellowed canines, which looked as if they could cut wire.

"Spooks, leave him alone!" said a girl's voice, and then she appeared in his line of vision just long enough to swat the creature aside. Robby blinked again and the girl reappeared in front of him. She had purple hair and eyes the size of golf balls. *Amethyst Jones?*

"Give it a few more minutes before sitting up," she told him. "This isn't an exact science."

"What isn't?"

"Magic." Amethyst looked over her shoulder. "Guys, I think

he's okay."

Abby leapt into sight, pushing Amethyst out of the way. He mumbled her name. Abby wiped her eyes and then touched his forehead hesitantly, as if afraid she might hurt him.

"The dance!" Robby suddenly remembered. He tried to sit up again but felt another wave of nausea. He winced and covered his mouth until it passed. "Becca—"

"I'm here." Becca crowded into the space between Abby and Amethyst. Her eyes were wet-rimmed as she leaned in close, her fingers brushing his jaw, her minty breath mingling with his. She was wearing the same pink cashmere turtleneck as the day they'd met. "Zeus came, too."

Behind her, Zeus's dark face towered over the three girls, his lips pressed tight with concern. "I texted your dad on the way here and told him we all left together. I didn't want him to worry."

The metal coils of a tattered old couch pressed into Robby's back as the room took shape around him. "Where are we?" he asked, managing to sit up without the room spinning. The creature with the wet snout—apparently a raccoon—leapt into his lap and settled there without further consideration for the couch's current occupant.

"That's his spot," said Amethyst, apologetically.

"We're at Amethyst's house," Abby said. She'd pulled away from Robby long enough to wipe the tears from her cheeks, but she and Becca continued to hover, sniffling indiscreetly.

Robby's breath misted in the air as he glanced around the room at the cracked walls and cobwebs, and then back to Amethyst. "You live here?"

"Happily."

"We found you in the woods near Mrs. Vickory's house. We dragged you here," Abby explained. "Luckily, you were giving off a pretty strong signal."

"Magic?"

"GPS." Becca waved her phone. "Abby found me at the dance, and I pinged you before your battery died."

"*You* could have died," Abby said. "Who did this?"

"T-Rex." Robby rubbed his chin. It still hurt, but not nearly as much as it should have. "He came after me out of the blue, like that time in the library. But this was… different. I think he might have actually been trying to kill me."

"Good thing we have magical healing powers," Amethyst said, twirling a knobby willow switch in her left hand. "It took both of us to fix you up. You're welcome, by the way."

Robby glanced from her to Abby, only now noticing the way they were slumped together. Their faces were drawn and colorless, and sweat beaded Abby's forehead.

"We're still new to healing magic," Abby explained. "It takes a toll."

Becca lifted a thick blanket off the back of the couch and wrapped it around his shoulders. She trailed her fingers over what felt like a giant angry lump until Robby winced and pulled away. "Sorry," she said, wincing herself. "Just so you know, there are easier ways to impress a girl than getting beaten up."

"So, you *are* impressed?" Robby replied, trying to smile but mostly grimacing.

Becca rolled her eyes. She tilted her chin in Abby and Amethyst's direction. "With them, definitely."

A willow switch materialized in Abby's left hand. She pressed it to the bump on Robby's forehead and furrowed her brow, concentrating. His forehead itched as the wound stitched itself back together. "Better?"

"A little."

"It's not purple anymore, so that's progress. Assuming green counts as progress."

Robby's eyes drifted to Becca again. She smiled at him between sniffles. "Abby explained everything. Halloween, the flying…"

"I'm on record as strongly advising against telling them," Amethyst pointed out.

"We didn't have a choice," Abby countered. Turning back to Robby, she added, "And I had no idea you'd already told Zeus everything, anyway."

"He knew I could keep your secret," Zeus said.

Abby grinned at him. "Well, now I know it, too."

"You should have told *me*," said Becca, raising a finger to silence Robby's protests, "but I understand why you didn't." She turned to Abby. "How do you do it, though?"

Abby scrunched her nose, considering the question. "Imagine everything you see has its own unique thread wrapped around it." She moved her wand in a slow arc until a second blanket lifted off the back of an old armchair and came to rest on top of Robby's shoulders. "Magic is just a matter of knitting those threads into new possibilities."

"Miss Winters taught you to do that?" Robby asked.

Abby's features hardened and she lowered her eyes. "You were right about her. I was trying to protect you, but instead I just made a mess of everything."

"I think we both did. Friends again?"

Abby squeezed his hand. "Friends forever."

"Took you guys long enough," Becca said. "What we really need to do is put all our heads together and compare notes."

"I don't think it was really T-Rex who came after you," Abby told Robby. "Not entirely, I mean. Miss Winters did something to him this week—brainwashed him or mind-control or something. I don't know. But I'm sure she would only have sent him to attack you if she thought you were getting too close to the truth."

"What truth?"

"Her name's not really Miss Winters. It's—"

"Joanna Greylocke."

Abby's eyes widened. "You know?"

"Some of it. You?"

"Some of it."

Robby adjusted Spooks in his lap. His head throbbed, and even the dim glow of the firelight hurt his eyes. "I need to talk to all of your new friends as soon as possible. Mrs. Vickory knew all about you and the other girls. I think she'd been tracking your bloodline for years. She wasn't just a history teacher."

"I know." Abby smiled at him as if she'd never been happier to see anyone in her life. "And Tina isn't just a veterinarian. I found her. She's alive." Robby gasped, but Abby plunged ahead before he could say anything. "And there's something I need to tell you about your mom, too."

31

A Council of Witches

Abby awoke to the smell of bacon and the sound of voices drifting upstairs from the kitchen. She pushed aside her covers and sat up, blinking back the sunlight streaming in through her bedroom window. Amethyst had spent the night in her room after helping her bring Robby home, but she wasn't there now. Abby's stomach rumbled and she glanced at the clock above her bed—nearly eleven. Amethyst was probably downstairs looking for breakfast.

The voices were louder in the hallway, and so was the sizzle of bacon. Abby followed them both downstairs to the kitchen but stopped short of the doorway when she realized one of the voices belonged to Chief Madison, not Amethyst. Mrs. Shepherd lingered over the stove in her silk pajamas, waving away smoke from a frying pan while the police chief asked questions. Abby's stomach twisted.

"I'd just like to talk to her myself, Carolyn."

Abby's mother frowned, but she hid it quickly, checking the coffeemaker, fetching a mug, pouring. She handed the coffee to the chief. "I've already told you what time she came home from the dance."

"There were some fires last night," Chief Madison said as Abby inched closer. "Intentional, by the look of things. The Vickory house burned to the ground. The old lighthouse. A few more places on the other side of town. It seems like kids from what we've turned up."

"What kids? Not Abby."

"We found this not far from the Vickory house." Chief Madison extended his hand, palm open. "Are those Abby's initials on the back?"

Abby reached instinctively for her lucky pendant, but it was gone. As she leaned back, her mother locked eyes with her for a moment, but instead of saying anything, she snatched the pendant from the chief's hand, setting it down on the counter next to her coffee mug.

"I'm going to need that back," the chief began.

"Oh, Abby lost this ages ago—"

No, I didn't, Abby thought. *She knows I didn't.*

"—and while I'm sure she'll be grateful to have it back, I'm equally sure that my daughter was not setting fires last night. Really, how could you accuse her of something like that?"

"I'm not accusing her of anything," the chief said, accidentally sloshing coffee onto the floor. He swore under his breath as he bent to mop it up, but Mrs. Shepherd waved him away. "I'd just like to know if Abby saw anything that could help. I'm concerned, that's all. People disappearing, fires, evidence going missing—"

"Evidence?"

"Something's not right in this town, Carolyn. I don't want our kids mixed up in it."

Mrs. Shepherd lifted the frying pan from the burner, setting it aside, and the sizzle faded. "I'll talk to Abby when she wakes up. If she says anything helpful, I'll let you know."

Chief Madison nodded, looking resigned. He returned the still-steaming coffee mug to Abby's mother and grabbed his jacket from the hook by the door, then stopped short as he was about to step outside. "Zeus says they were together at the dance all night, and that Abby left with a few friends. Who drove her home?"

Abby's mother blinked, but otherwise her expression remained unchanged. "She came home with Amethyst Jones, and I've already explained to you that they arrived before their curfew."

The door rattled in its frame as the chief shut it against the cold.

Abby waited outside the kitchen in case he came back, certain her mother wouldn't let her go back upstairs without an explanation. Her stomach rumbled again, and she eyed the bacon. After a moment, she shuffled into the kitchen, shoulders slumped, waiting to be yelled at.

"Sit," Mrs. Shepherd said. Abby settled at the table while her mother added bacon to a plate of eggs and toast, then set it down in front of her. "You eat. I'll talk."

Abby chewed her bacon without looking up. She didn't want to catch her mother's eyes in case she found genuine anger there. Or worse, disappointment.

"I always thought I'd be a cool mom, you know." Mrs. Shepherd scraped a chair away from the table and slouched down into it until she sat across from Abby. "But the truth is I'm just muddling through it like I do everything else. Trying to figure it out as I go."

"Are you mad?" Abby asked.

"Furious," her mother said calmly. "But I don't think you burned down a house, even if I'm not quite sure how this"—she held up the pendant—"ended up near a crime scene."

"It's not—"

"I know, sweetie. This is me trusting you." She brushed the top of Abby's head. "I think you and Robby just had a lot of catching up to do last night."

Abby looked up from her plate. "You know about that?"

"I caught Amethyst sneaking out this morning. She wilted under questioning and told me you all went back to her house together. Honestly, I'm more impressed that Zeus didn't confess it all to his father."

"But you're not yelling at me or… grounding me?"

"That didn't seem to be particularly effective last time," her mother replied, chuckling. "I thought maybe we'd try a different approach. Talking to each other."

Abby took another bite of eggs and then studied her mother's face. "I like this approach."

"Good. Now, just so that we're clear, I'm *not* okay with you sneaking around or leaving the dance without permission. I know I can be a little overprotective sometimes, though, and… I suppose I've been having a hard time accepting that you're growing up." She sighed. "Lately, you've seemed like you're a million miles away. I miss you. But I don't want to keep pushing you away."

Abby forced a smile. She thought, for just a moment, of telling her mother everything. That Tina was locked in a dungeon on the other side of town, maybe dead by now; that Miss Winters had been lying and manipulating her from the very start; that her entire world seemed to have changed in a single night.

"See, a million miles."

Abby blinked. "Sorry. Not a million miles, Mom. Just a few."

Abby finished her eggs and brought her plate to the sink. She felt a sense of purpose crystalizing. Her mother wanted to protect her, but she couldn't—not from Miss Winters. And while Chief Madison was right that something was definitely wrong in Willow Cove, he was wrong about the solution. It wasn't up to the adults to stop Miss Winters. They couldn't.

It was going to have to be Abby and her friends.

Moonlight streamed in through the windows of Amethyst's living room, painting the faces of Abby's friends in a ghostly hue as they huddled by the fireplace. Daisy and Delphi watched while Flapper crawled out of Piper's jacket and hopped to the floor, shaking out his feathers with as much dignity as he could muster. Amethyst was sitting in the corner armchair, stroking Mrs. Vickory's cat, having rescued him from Robby's attic. Only Olivia stood apart near the door, rosy-cheeked and visibly annoyed.

Abby poked at the logs in the fireplace and rubbed her hands together as orange flames danced in the reflection of an old fire extinguisher near the hearth.

From the couch, Daisy and Delphi's conversation rose above the others. "I'm just saying, the Pleiades aren't *that* bright tonight," Daisy told her twin. Delphi had produced a pocket-sized crystal ball to illustrate an astrological point.

"And I'm telling you, the seventh Pleiad is far brighter tonight than—"

"What's a Pleiad?" asked Piper. Spooks hopped into her lap, making sad raccoon eyes at Amethyst and Achilles.

"The Pleiades are a potent astrological constellation known to influence the fortunes of all mankind," said Delphi airily. She glanced about, surprised but pleased to have an interested audience. "According to legend, the stars represent seven heavenly sisters—"

"I thought there were only six stars in the constellation," said Amethyst.

"You can only *see* six stars, but there's a seventh that goes through various permutations. It's almost impossible to see the seventh sister with the naked eye, but tonight it's expected to be at its brightest in more than a hundred years."

"Is that a good thing?" Abby asked.

Delphi shook her head. "The barrier between the living and the dead is at its thinnest when the Pleiades reaches its highest point in the sky. That's actually where Halloween comes from.

It's derived from an ancient druid rite that coincides with the culmination of the Pleiades at the end of October. I've been tracking it since fall, and the cluster is burning brighter and longer than anyone's ever seen it."

"Tell them what that means in English," Daisy said, annoyed.

Delphi lowered her voice to a whisper. "The veil between life and death that should have closed on Halloween is still open, but only until tonight."

Abby's skin prickled with goosebumps. "What exactly *is* your prediction, Delphi?"

"The Aztecs used the Pleiades to figure out when to hold ritual sacrifices, so I'm just a tiny bit concerned about their position in the sky right now given that you told us you needed to discuss a matter of life and death."

The front door flew open. Everyone turned as Robby stumbled inside, a gust of snow barreling in behind him. Zeus and Becca followed, slamming the door shut.

Daisy eyed them with surprise. "'Hoyday, a riddle!' What are you guys doing here?"

"I invited them," Abby said.

"Why am I not surprised?" said Olivia. "You get away with everything, while I—"

"Just hear me out," Abby told her. "They're part of this, too."

"Part of what?" asked Piper, even as she spotted Achilles padding away from the armchair toward Robby. She scooped him up and retreated a safe distance away, her voice a soothing whisper that sounded almost like a purr itself.

"Yeah, why *are* we here?" grumbled Olivia.

"Because Miss Winters isn't who she says she is," Abby explained. "Her real name is Joanna Greylocke. She was born in the seventeenth century, and she's trained girls like us before." The others stared in silence as Abby explained everything. Robby unzipped his backpack and distributed the documents they'd decided would be most convincing—the diary, the photographs, the newspaper clippings.

"What exactly is this supposed to prove?" said Olivia, only half glancing at the newspaper clip showing Miss Winters's nineteenth-century students.

"That Miss Winters killed Mrs. Vickory, and she's coming for us next," Abby said. "She's keeping Robby's stepmother prisoner—Tina's a witch, too. I saw her locked up in Miss Winters's basement with my own eyes. She told me about a witch's council meant to protect us, but I don't know how to…" Abby's voice trailed off. Piper's eyes bulged out, her mouth gaped in a circle. "Piper?"

Achilles nudged her chin, and then Piper worked her hand free of the cat and pulled out her inhaler. "I used to wonder why Tina invited me to help out at the clinic all the time," she said, breathing deeply between gulps from her inhaler. "I should have figured it out once I turned thirteen. I've always liked animals, but I never realized I could *talk* to them. Not all of them, obviously, just the ones that could become familiars."

"Familiars?" repeated Zeus.

"A witch's animal companion," Piper explained. "A magical assistant. Like Amethyst's raccoon. And Flapper, obviously—and Achilles."

"You and your animals again," said Olivia dismissively.

"It's a legitimate form of magic," Piper shot back. "You're just mad they don't like to talk to you."

Achilles yowled, rising onto his hind legs to paw at Piper's shoulder.

"What's he saying?" Abby asked.

Piper looked as if she wanted to reach for her inhaler again. "Mrs. Vickory wanted to protect us from…" Piper looked up, whispered something to the cat, and then listened to his mewed reply. "From Miss Winters."

"You can't be sure that's what he said," Daisy suggested. "Maybe you're misunderstanding."

"I'm not," Piper snapped. "I know what I'm doing."

"Hold on." Olivia's hand fell to her wand. She twirled it like a pistol between her fingers as she paced the room, finally stopping by the fireplace. Even in the dim light, her face had gone pale. "Miss Winters taught us everything we know! She came to us when we needed someone to show us what we were becoming. I don't believe she wants to hurt us. She cares about us. About *me*."

"I thought she cared about us too," Abby said. "I wanted to believe her. I admired her, Olivia. But it was all an act. She's not looking out for us. She doesn't care about us. She's been manipulating us from the start."

Olivia shook her head. "How can you be so sure?"

"We could at least tell the police," suggested Daisy. "Let them sort it all out."

"No one's calling the police," Zeus interrupted. "I don't want my dad going anywhere near Miss Winters."

"Even if the police could help, which I don't think they could," Abby added quickly when Zeus shot her a look, "there's no way they'd believe us."

"She's right," said Becca. "No one's going to believe any of this."

"Only magic can defeat her," Abby insisted.

"What about that council you mentioned?" asked Delphi. "Maybe they could—"

"There's no time. Remember what you said earlier? The veil between life and death closing tonight? I don't think it's a coincidence. Last night Miss Winters sent T-Rex and his friends after Robby to—to—" She shivered at the memory of finding him lying in the snow. "To silence him," she finished. "And she had someone, probably T-Rex again, set fire to all the evidence of what she's been up to. Mrs. Vickory's house. The lighthouse.

She's tying up all her loose ends. Whatever Miss Winters is planning, it *must* be happening soon. Maybe even tonight. Besides," Abby added, after a deep breath, "we have our own council of witches: *us*. We can confront Miss Winters together, all six of us."

"Nine," corrected Robby. "There are nine of us."

"I have to be home by ten," Piper said nervously.

"We can stop her if we all work together." Abby glanced at Olivia, who'd sunk farther into the shadows. Their eyes met. "Didn't you ever wonder why she always played you and me against each other? I bet it's because she didn't *want* us to get along. We're weaker when we're divided." She took a step toward Olivia, holding out her hand.

Olivia pursed her lips. "You really think…?"

"It's the only explanation that makes sense," Abby said, nodding. "But it doesn't have to be that way anymore."

For a moment, Abby thought Olivia might take her hand and join them. Then Olivia raised her wand. The tip exploded with a wild green light and Abby's wand flew from her back pocket. Four other wands joined it midflight before Olivia snatched them all with her free hand.

"She warned me you might do this," Olivia yelled. "Try to turn everyone against her." Streaks of purple and red forked into the space between them like lightning. Abby gasped as if someone had punched her in the throat. Her insides felt hollow, and by the time she recovered her breath, she knew what Olivia had done to her—to all of them. Miss Winters had done the same thing to her that night at the lighthouse when she'd fought with Olivia.

"It'll wear off," Olivia told them. "Eventually."

She waved her wand again and the windows flew open. A dark shape crossed in front of one before disappearing into the night. "I'm going to Miss Winters now, and you can just wait here for her to come and deal with you."

"We won't stay here like sitting ducks," said Robby.

"Oh, I think you will."

Olivia crossed the room and kicked the front door twice. It opened from the outside to reveal T-Rex and Joey in the doorway, each gripping a canister of gasoline. Sarika peeked out between them. "My friends will keep an eye on you until Miss Winters and I get back."

32

Toil and Trouble

Robby dashed upstairs with Abby on his heels. He cracked open the first window he came to and stuck his head out for a better look. The smell of gasoline drifted inside as T-Rex and Joey circled the house, spraying it as if they planned to burn the whole place down. T-Rex glowered at him, while Sarika recorded the entire scene. Robby reached into his back pocket for his phone, but Abby put a hand on his shoulder.

"The way T-Rex is right now…" she said, shaking her head. "They'll torch the house as soon as they hear someone coming. We can't risk it."

Robby slammed the window in frustration. He leaned against the wall and slid to the floor as everyone else flooded into the room.

"We're surrounded," said Daisy.

Zeus stood up straighter. "I'm not afraid of T-Rex or Joey. Robby and I can hold them off while one of you—"

"They'll burn my house down if you try anything like that," Amethyst pleaded.

"But if we ran—if one of us snuck out, I mean—we could get one of our parents…" said Becca.

Abby shook her head again, and Amethyst shrugged help-lessly. "What could a parent do?"

Piper looked like she wanted to cry. "I don't want Miss Winters to hurt my parents."

"I knew T-Rex would be a problem someday." Abby frowned. "He followed Olivia around like a lost puppy for months, but I never thought Miss Winters would use that."

Robby sat up. "T-Rex knows you can do magic?"

"I'm sure Olivia told him what she did to us." Abby stared at her hands, as if willing them to respond to her magical commands. "I can *see* the threads, but I can't touch them."

"What if he thought you still could…?" Robby stood and began to pace as the idea took shape. It was a long shot, but it could work. It would work. Only if they were really lucky, though—and only if they had everything he needed to pull it off. "I'll need my gloves," he said, rubbing his chin. "And a pillow-case."

Amethyst disappeared from the room, returning a heartbeat later with a threadbare cotton pillowcase under one arm.

Robby nodded. "Duct tape?"

Amethyst shook her head.

"All right, I can improvise."

"What are you thinking?" Abby asked.

"We need to put on a show for them. Make them believe you all still have your powers." Robby raced down the stairs two at a time. The fire still blazed in the hearth, and there beside it, exactly where he remembered seeing it, was the most important piece of the puzzle. His stomach clenched as he turned the metal canister over. If he was wrong, if it was just a normal fire extinguisher, the whole idea would fall apart.

"CO_2," he said triumphantly. Amethyst's grandfather must have kept the carbon dioxide fire extinguisher for electrical fires or for the tractors and other heavy farm equipment. Robby scooped it up under one arm and ran toward the basement.

"We need hot water, three or four bowls of it. Boiling if you can."

"On it," Amethyst called. "But why?"

"No time to explain." He paused by the basement door. "And I need a drama queen. Someone who can pull off the part of a vengeful witch."

"Daisy," called out four voices in unison.

She bowed. "I'm Shakespearean-trained."

"Open the window and stand where T-Rex and Joey can see you," Robby instructed. "Act like you're going to cast a spell. Amethyst, put the bowls around her. When I give the sign, Daisy, I want you to give the performance of your life. I'll be in the basement where none of them can see me."

"What's in the basement?" asked Amethyst.

Robby grinned. "That's where the magic happens."

Robby pulled out his phone to light the way. Abby and Becca followed close behind, ducking to avoid a cluster of pipes before stopping beside him.

"They're ready for you upstairs," Zeus called.

Robby pulled his gloves tight, then wrapped the opening of the pillowcase around the nozzle of the CO_2 canister. "Open the valve."

Abby did, and the pillowcase began to inflate. Robby's fingers burned icy cold even through his gloves. Some of the vapor escaped from the pillowcase, but there was still a reassuring rattle inside when he shook the fabric.

"Dry ice," Abby said. "It actually worked." She killed the valve on the fire extinguisher and then kicked the furnace pipe that ran from the basement up to the rest of the house. "Daze, you're on!"

Robby grabbed the pillowcase and sprinted upstairs as Daisy stuck her head out the window, then raised her arms above her head, fingers spread wide. "'Double, double, toil and trouble,'" she intoned. "'Fire *burn* and cauldron *bubble*!'"

Robby shook loose a few chunks of dry ice into the bowls at her feet. A wispy gray mist burst instantly into the space around her, hissing and spewing like a geyser.

"'Eye of newt and toe of frog, wool of bat and tongue of dog!'"

Robby eyed T-Rex and Joey over Daisy's shoulder. It wasn't working. They looked confused, but not particularly scared. Then Piper shouted something behind him, and a mass of teeth and claws and beaks streamed through the roiling mist and out the window.

"'For a charm of powerful trouble, like a hell-broth... *BOIL AND BUBBLE!*'"

The animals overwhelmed T-Rex and Joey just as Daisy reached a crescendo. Joey scrambled back to his feet and shrieked, sending Sarika and her phone tumbling to the ground. They both ran as T-Rex climbed to his knees and raced after them.

"And... scene," said Amethyst.

Daisy beamed. "How was I?"

"Perfect," said Robby and Abby together.

Robby dashed outside to make sure T-Rex and the others were really gone. He found Sarika's phone still recording in the snow and picked it up, pocketing it for later. Back inside, he found Piper kneeling in front of Spooks, Achilles, and Flapper.

"That was amazing!" he told her.

"I can't take all the credit." She scooped up a small green iguana and held him up for Robby to see. "It was actually his idea."

"Einstein?" Robby blurted. His eyes flicked to where he'd

left his backpack. "You stowed away?"

"He says his name is Perseus," Piper told him.

"No, it's Einstein. Tina had a dog named…"

Perseus. Could it be…?

"Transmogrification," Piper explained. "Tina turned him into something that wouldn't bother your allergies."

"You're Tina's familiar?" Robby said. Perseus wagged his tail like a hyperactive metronome. Robby scratched him tentatively on the head, and then the iguana rolled onto his back and let his tongue loll out in satisfaction.

Just then, T-Rex appeared at the window, staring at them mutely while some silent battle played out across his face. The others went quiet. Becca hovered close to Robby, one hand on his shoulder, as she craned her neck to see out the window. "What's that in his hand?"

Robby shoveled Perseus into his backpack and slung it over his shoulder. "We have to go! Now!"

The lighter tore through the air in a perfect arc before skittering to a stop near the front door. Robby reached for it and then dived back when the first blue spark struck gasoline.

It made a sound like *whoomph*, and the porch burst into flames.

33

Into the Depths

"**M**y house," Amethyst whispered, shaking her head. "All my things…"

"We have to go!" Abby shouted, yanking her friend's arm while Daisy pulled from the other side. A beam cracked and then split in half as they dragged Amethyst out into the night.

"My house," Amethyst repeated.

"I got Spooks," Piper yelled over the wind, lifting the wriggling raccoon by the scruff of his neck. Becca grabbed Achilles and followed her outside. Flapper rocketed through one of the open windows and landed near the barn.

"Good idea," Abby yelled, sprinting toward the barn, the others staggering after her. Piper and Becca released the raccoon and cat into the haystacks while the remainder of the group cowered by the double doors, watching Amethyst's house burn.

"We can't stay here for long," Robby said.

Piper stroked Achilles, plucking at a few singed tufts of fur. "I vote we run away."

"If we run now, we'll never be able to stop," said Amethyst.

Piper blinked twice. "I can live with that."

"I can't," said Daisy.

"Me either," said Delphi.

"No wands, no magic, no way into Miss Winters's house even if we *wanted* to take the fight to her," Piper began.

"Do you want to end up like her other students?" Abby yelled over the wailing of the wind and the crackling flames. "Maybe she got away with it back then, but this is our time, and we have to be the ones to stop her. Not the police, not our parents, not some council we've never even talked to—*us*." Abby took a deep breath, looking at the faces of her friends. "We're the only ones who can."

Daisy nodded. "I'm in."

"Me too," said Delphi.

"And me," Amethyst said.

"Piper?" asked Abby.

Piper sighed. "I guess, but we can't just march in through Miss Winters's front door."

Becca was digging through Robby's backpack. She rose up, clutching her sketchpad triumphantly, then thrust her drawing of the hexagram toward the girls. The thick strokes of the drawing glistened orange-black in the firelight, almost as if they'd already unlocked the seal.

"What's that?" asked Piper.

Abby beamed at Becca. "We may not be able to march in through the front door, but who says we can't use the back one?"

The wind faded to a breeze when Abby pushed inside the dark cave. She reached for her wand before remembering it wasn't there. Zeus's phone flickered to life, illuminating a long wide tunnel with no end in sight. "It's this way," he said, ducking as he led the group down a low, narrow path off the main cavern. When they reached a rough granite embankment beaded with ice, Zeus took a deep breath and plunged *through* it.

Abby gaped, but then Robby took her hand and said, "Come on."

Minutes later, the tunnel opened into the wide antechamber where Robby and Zeus had discovered the hexagram. It looked exactly as Becca had sketched it. Abby traced the symbol with the tip of her index finger; it tingled. It was sturdier than any seal she'd encountered before. Every fiber of her body thrummed as the hexagram radiated its warning—no trespassing, keep out.

Moment of truth, she thought as she touched the center of the symbol.

The six-pointed star flared to life, briefly illuminating the entire chamber in a harsh red glow before dissolving back into darkness, leaving only their cell phones to light the way. The door slid open.

"It's like entering the Mines of Moria," Robby whispered under his breath. "'Speak, friend, and enter.'"

"What?" said Abby.

"Tolkien. Never mind. Ready?"

"*I'm* ready," Abby told him. "But you're not." She turned to Zeus and Becca. "You three need to stay."

"You can't just leave us here," Robby protested.

"You've seen what Miss Winters can do. That first night with the chimeras—that was nothing for her. She's more powerful than you can imagine. You guys would get hurt... or worse."

Robby shook his head. "You know what she's taken from me."

"And I don't want her to take you from *me*." Abby motioned Amethyst to lead the other girls through the opening, then backpedaled until she stood within reach of the seal. "If I don't come back—"

"Don't talk like that," Robby said. "You'll come back. We

all will. Because we're going with you."

She squeezed his hand. "Robby, you've done your part. It's my fight now."

Turning to Zeus, Abby rose to her tip toes and kissed him on the forehead. When she pulled back, he stared at her wide-eyed. "Thank you, for everything. You too, Becca." She touched the seal and smiled bravely as she slipped through the door.

"You'll come back," Robby said again. But the door was already scraping closed.

Robby heaved himself against the door. When it didn't budge, he pried at the grooves in the wall, pushing and pulling until his fingers bled. Nothing happened. When he touched the seal, it stayed closed—even if he thought for a second it sparked like a flicker of static electricity. "We have to find a way to follow them."

Becca shined her phone's flashlight onto the door, nearly blinding him as she leaned in to inspect the seal. "Robby, maybe she's right."

"We can't just let her fight Miss Winters alone," Zeus said.

"She's not alone. There are five of them, and only one Miss Winters."

"How'd that work out for the girls who vanished the last time she came to Willow Cove?" said Zeus, kicking at the loose rubble on the cave floor.

Becca took a step back from the hexagram, shaking her head, then scanned the rest of the cavern. "Well, I don't see how we can go after her unless we actually *do* march in through the front door, and from what you told me about the chimeras... What is it?"

Robby closed his eyes. "The front door."

"What about it?" said Zeus.

The corners of Becca's mouth curled into a smile. "I know that look. You have an idea."

"I have an idea," Robby agreed. "Only…"

"What?"

"You're going to hate it."

34

Whispers

"Flashlight?" said Piper. "Anyone?"

Abby reached out to reassure her but found only empty air. She knew Piper couldn't be far, though. She could hear her teeth chattering.

"I think I dropped my phone," Daisy said from a few paces back. There was a touch of panic in her voice.

"My phone's dead," muttered Delphi.

"I miss my wand," said Amethyst.

Abby thought of the strange tingling in her fingers and the way the witch's seal had responded to her. "*Lumos*," she whispered experimentally. The tips of her fingers flared like tiny Christmas lights, illuminating the nervous faces of her friends. Amethyst shivered. Piper pushed the buttons of her phone uselessly. Daisy and Delphi were holding hands.

"Olivia's spell must have worn off," said Abby. "It can't have been easy to cast it on all five of us."

"Or maybe she just expected Miss Winters to have come for us by now," Amethyst muttered.

The others cast their own spells, and soon a vaulted ceiling, like the inside of a church, came into focus. Underfoot, the stone floor looked like the work of a skilled craftsman.

The glow revealed a vast hexagon cut into the bedrock. A half dozen rectangular shapes, carved stone blocks six feet long and about half as tall, were arranged near each of the six points. A raised dais, like an altar, rose in the middle.

"I know where we are," Abby whispered.

"It's a tomb," said Piper. She didn't try to conceal the horror in her voice.

"It's *their* tomb," Abby said. "The Winslow sisters. It has to be." The others all started to speak at once. Abby shushed them. "Listen—What's that?"

It sounded like the wind whistling through a leafy grove: indistinguishable murmurs, whispers on top of whispers. But the air in the chamber was still. Abby squeezed her eyes shut and let go of her thoughts the way Miss Winters had shown her by the oak tree weeks before. There were sounds between the sounds now. Individual voices.

Sister…

Please…

Do not…

Mustn't…

Not for us…

Rest now…

Abby's eyes shot open. She took a step forward, and then another, crossing to the center of the chamber. As she listened again, the world around her shifted. The voices grew louder, more insistent, each individual thread part of a larger tapestry. The chamber flickered.

Miss Winters knelt just a pace or two away, her cloak shimmering in the green glow of Abby's illumination spell. Pulling back the hood of her cloak to let her dark hair fall to her shoulders, she looked up at Abby—*through* Abby. Because she wasn't really there. This was another memory.

An echo from another time, Abby thought. Miss Winters had

come to this tomb to be among her dead sisters before. To speak to them. To make a promise to them. "My life for theirs," Abby murmured.

Miss Winters rippled. Faded. And then the chamber went quiet again.

"Guys, Miss Winters comes here to visit her sisters." Abby waved her illumination spell around the chamber in search of another seal. "I think this is where she was going the night she caught me sneaking around her house—which means there should be another way out."

"*There*," said Delphi, pointing.

As the light of Abby's spell passed over them, a few murky lines in the granite wall resolved into a six-pointed star.

"Let's go find her," Abby said, raising her hand to the hexagram and hustling the group through to the other side before the stark red glare of the witch's seal began to fade.

"You were right," said Becca. They'd stopped at Robby's house after leaving the Hollows, and now she held a flimsy red saucer sled in front of her as she looked up at Whispering Hill. "I hate this plan."

Zeus rattled the rusty chain that held the iron gate closed. "I don't like it, either." He let the metal clatter back into place. "It should be all three of us going in. All for one and one for all."

"We've gone over this." Robby peered through the gate into the shadowy trees beyond. "There's no way all three of us can get past the chimeras."

"But Abby—"

"I'll find her, Zeus, and I won't let anything happen to her."

"I don't see why it can't be me who goes inside," Zeus countered.

"Because my stepmother is in there somewhere. It has to be me. This is only going to work if we each do our part. All for one, like you said."

Rather than answer, Zeus brushed snow from one of the pillars. Loose mortar crumbled to the ground along with it. He put his weight against the bricks and the whole thing wobbled. "Are you sure you'll be all right?" He glanced back at Becca. "Both of you?"

"The chimeras seem to respond to movement. They'll chase her, but they can't leave the estate. At least, I'm pretty sure they can't. Becca will get their attention and then sled down the driveway and through the open gate to safety. *If* you can bring the pillar down."

"I'll bring it down."

"She won't have time to climb the fence," Robby warned. "They're fast. They'll be right on her heels."

"I said I'll bring it down."

"All right. Then *I'll* slip right in through the front door." Robby turned to Becca, who was hiding behind the saucer. He gently pushed it down until they were eye-to-eye. "You can still change your mind."

Becca shrugged, trying to look brave. "How hard can it be?"

She tossed the sled over the fence and watched it slide to a standstill on the other side. Robby helped her climb over and then landed in a heap next to her. Zeus was already hard at work pushing and pulling on the gate.

"Be careful, both of you," Zeus warned. "I got this."

Robby scooped up the sled and scrambled up the rocky slope, huddling with Becca against the driving snow. He reached for her hand, partly to steady their footing, but mostly to reassure himself she was still there. She squeezed back.

The main building appeared through the snow. The windows on the upper floors glimmered yellow in the night, and a strange red glow mingled in the moonlit space between the two towers.

Robby and Becca crouched low under the cover of the trees, eyeing the winged chimeras, which slumbered along the sides of the staircase leading to the entryway.

"Which ones are the chimeras?" Becca asked.

"All of them."

Robby's phone buzzed with a picture from Zeus—the iron gate lay flat across the driveway. He held it up for Becca. She nodded, then took the sled from him, all the while eying the house doubtfully. She tugged her hat tight against her ears and took a tentative step into the driveway where the chimeras could see her. A dozen stone eyes flared red. Becca raced back into the bushes. The eyes faded to gray again.

Her breath came in quick, short bursts as she gripped the sled like a shield. "Wish me luck."

Robby touched her shoulder. "Becca?"

"Yeah?"

"Fluffy bunny feet."

She smiled, then stepped out into the open. The chimeras turned their gazes toward her. A dozen eyes flashed red. And then the chimeras took flight.

Robby thought Becca had gone rigid with fear, but no—she was waiting for them to get closer. All of them. More eyes flared to life, more chimeras broke free of their stone restraints, crawling and flapping toward her until Robby couldn't keep track of how many there were. When Becca was sure she'd gotten the attention of them all, she leapt onto the sled, disappearing down the driveway.

My turn now.

The stairs creaked as Robby climbed to the porch, unlatched the door, and marched inside.

35

Vessels

The tunnel on the other side of the tomb looked just as Abby remembered: the rotting wooden ladder she'd used when she'd followed Miss Winters, the brackish pool fed by tiny beads of sea water, the passage leading to the tree-filled courtyard at the center of Whispering Hill. *Bringing me there was just a distraction,* Abby realized. *Otherwise, I'd have found the tomb.*

The tunnel narrowed as they climbed. Ahead, a harsh red light spilled across the ground where the passage opened into the grove.

"Abby?" said Daisy warily.

"I see it."

"What does it mean?"

"Probably nothing good." She held out a hand to stop the others from following, then crept forward, clinging to the rocks. Miss Winters stood at the center of the clearing, shadowed by the bare branches of the ancient oak. Tina lay pale and motionless at her feet. It looked as if Miss Winters had just finished draining the last of her powers. Olivia cowered next to her, eyes widening as they took in Abby.

Olivia mouthed a silent warning just as Miss Winters turned. In one hand, Miss Winters clutched the coven's six wands. Her eyes were red orbs where the whites should have been.

"You came," Miss Winters said. "How convenient. And here I thought Olivia's little improvisation would only be another annoyance." Olivia clawed to her feet and stumbled toward Abby, who caught her just as she collapsed.

"She... wanted us... all here," Olivia said. Her voice was little more than a gurgle.

Abby ducked back into the tunnel, dragging Olivia with her, aware that she only had a second or two before Miss Winters would be on them. She locked eyes with Piper. "You were right. We shouldn't have come."

"It's a little late for that!"

"We have to leave *now!*"

Delphi squeaked. Daisy grabbed for Amethyst's hand.

"I'm afraid it's far too late for that." Miss Winters stood before them, a dark silhouette in the scarlet light. Long narrow fingers slithered over Miss Winters's shoulders and darted toward Abby and her friends.

No, not fingers, Abby realized. *Branches.*

Miss Winters stepped aside as the tree hurled the girls into the clearing. Abby landed on her stomach and skidded to a stop next to Tina, tasting blood as she struggled to her hands and knees. She clawed at the snow for something to use as a weapon—a stick, a rock, anything—but she was still scrabbling when Miss Winters slammed a boot into her chest.

Thick roots clawed out from the frozen ground, coiling around Abby's wrists and ankles, pinning her in place while another branch snared her, then wrenched her across the yard, thrusting her against the trunk of the ancient oak so hard she saw stars. Blood trickled down her forehead.

Miss Winters waved her wand, and the night became still once more. Olivia slumped to the ground just out of reach, propped up by the roots even as they coiled around her wrists and ankles. To Abby's left, Amethyst kicked and grunted uselessly against her restraints. Abby could only assume her other friends were bound to the giant tree, just out of sight. She thought she heard Piper gasping.

"What... do you want?" rasped Olivia.

"It's some kind of twisted revenge fantasy," Amethyst growled.

Abby blinked as the edges of her vision blurred red again. *Blood*, she thought. *It always comes back to blood.*

"Do you honestly think I would waste so many lifetimes on something so pedestrian as revenge?" Miss Winters asked.

"What, then?" Amethyst demanded. "Power? Immortality? Eternal youth?"

My life for theirs, Abby thought. All this time, she'd assumed Miss Winters meant she would give her life to protect Abby and her friends. But that was never it. It was about her sisters. Everything Miss Winters had done—all the lives she'd ruined, the years she'd spent hunting down her descendants—she'd devoted her life to one purpose. She wanted to bring her sisters back.

Miss Winters raised her wand above her head. A thunderclap shook the grove, and then the reddish light faded to a glow like the dawning of a new day. The snow melted to heather and rock and then wet, decaying muck. Leaves flickered onto the branches, first the yellows and reds and browns of autumn, then green like summer, then the new buds of spring, and then back to the bareness of winter.

"What's happening?" shouted Delphi.

The scene repeated itself, seasons spiraling backward at a frenetic pace as the years flickered by, the sky swirling like a kaleidoscope. Soon, torchlight and voices mingled with the wind, angry shouts and desperate cries filling the air. The cycle of seasons slowed to a stop as the world settled into place again.

"What is she doing?" yelled Daisy.

"The Pleiades," Abby said. "The veil between life and death. She's plucking her sisters from the past and bringing them to our present."

"Clever girl." Miss Winters smiled. "Full marks."

"But how?" demanded Amethyst. "Why do you need us?"

"I should think that's obvious by now," chided Miss Winters.

Abby stared ahead at a vision of the six sisters on the gallows—panicked, bound, nooses wrapped tightly around their necks, suspended in time on the razor's edge between life and death. "We're the vessels," she said. "There are six of us because there are six of them."

"She's bringing them forward to take our bodies," Amethyst realized.

Abby looked away from the gallows. "And she's sending us back to take theirs."

36

The Seventh Sister

The glow from Robby's phone carved a faint path through the corridor as a low rumbling echoed from the belly of the house. Robby quickened his pace. Abby had at least a half hour's head start. She was probably with Miss Winters already.

A flicking sound behind him, like steel against stone, broke the silence. He wasn't alone. He turned as a small light flared to life at the other end of the hall. Bishop emerged from the darkness. He looked Robby up and down and then nodded.

"You look just like her," the old man said.

"Like who?"

"Your mother." Bishop closed the distance between them. "You have the same sharpness in your eyes. She was a clever woman. Too clever."

Robby retreated a step. "Don't come any closer."

"You have nothing to fear from an old man like me, boy."

Robby met Bishop's gaze. "You knew my mother?"

"I knew her well. She was Joanna's favorite pupil."

"At Oxford?"

"Joanna recognized the spark of magic in your mother immediately." Bishop's pupils constricted in the harsh light of Robby's phone, two tiny circles in hollow sockets withered by age. "They became more than student and teacher. They became friends. I believe Joanna felt great affection for her."

Robby's stomach churned. "But she killed my mom, didn't she?" His cheeks burned with anger. *"Didn't she?"*

"I wasn't there that night," Bishop rasped. "I know they kept in touch after your mother returned home from Oxford, however. I know that marrying James O'Reilly was a most unfortunate coincidence."

"My father doesn't have anything to do with this."

"He has everything to do with it! If they'd never come to live in Willow Cove, if your mother had never met Agnes Vickory and learned of the Order, she would never have heard the stories of Joanna Greylocke. She would never have pieced together the truth about the woman she'd met in Oxford or realized that woman was the monster who destroyed the lives of six young girls in this town a century earlier." Bishop swallowed. "As I told you, boy, your mother was too clever for her own good."

"She confronted Joanna with the truth."

Bishop lowered his eyes. "To her sorrow, yes. I think she hoped Joanna would convince her that it was all a misunderstanding. Instead, Joanna tried to turn your mother to her cause. Her plans were too far along by then to be stopped."

Robby fought the urge to punch something. "What plans?"

Bishop pursed his lips. He looked defeated. "Follow me and I'll show you. But hurry. There isn't much time."

Robby trailed him through windowless halls, the silence punctuated only by the muffled rumbling. When Bishop turned to face Robby again, his breath came in shallow gasps.

"You helped Abby," Robby said into the silence. "She told me you took her to Tina. Why?"

Bishop's shoulders sank. "I'm old and tired. Too old, that's the truth of it. This was never meant to be my time."

"You want to die."

"I want to be released. That cannot happen as long as Joanna walks this earth."

"She mentioned you in her diary. 'Bishop suspects us already.' I didn't make the connection before, but that was you, right? You've been with her since the beginning."

"I was her uncle's servant. I helped her escape the village after…" He let the thought trail away. "Anyone with a conscience would have done the same. She was just a child herself, and *with* child. But the weight of her guilt changed her, twisting her mind."

"What guilt?"

Bishop began walking again, slower now. Somewhere along the way, they'd left hallways and wooden floors behind, and now they walked steadily downhill across dirt and stone.

"What guilt?" Robby repeated.

"They died for her sins." Bishop sighed. "I can still see their faces." He shook his head. "Joanna was good, you must understand. Lovely and kind, but driven—always so driven. I wonder sometimes if things would have been different had I not gone with her. So many lives destroyed over the centuries because I saved her, but how could I have done any differently?"

He motioned to a cleft in the wall ahead, where snowflakes swirled in the wind, silhouetted in scarlet. Robby felt the chill—and something else. The prickle of magic on his skin.

"Here we are," Bishop said. "But I'm afraid it has already begun."

Abby saw Robby out of the corner of her eye, as though he were standing on the other side of a funhouse mirror—twisted, blurry around the edges. A flickering dome overhead stretched to the edges of the grove, but Robby pushed through it before it solidified again behind him. He turned, touched it, and then shook his hand in pain.

No, thought Abby. *No, no, no. Robby, you shouldn't be here!*

Bishop appeared briefly behind him, shadowed and bent. Abby nearly called out a warning, but then the old man said something, and Robby dropped to his hands and knees before slinking away from the opening. Darkness filled the space behind him as Bishop disappeared again. And then Robby vanished, too.

Abby struggled against her restraints again. Miss Winters was still speaking, but Abby barely listened, her eyes darting around until she spotted Robby again. He was crawling toward Tina. Abby met his eyes and he raised a finger to his lips. She glanced again at Miss Winters—still no sign that she'd seen him.

I've got to keep her talking, Abby thought. *Distract her while Robby does… whatever he's planning.*

"You have no idea how long I have waited," Miss Winters shouted. Her face had been stripped of the last traces of gentleness. "*My* blood flows through your veins! *My* blood gives you girls your magic. And now I have need of it."

"You want blood?" growled Amethyst. "Let's start with yours."

"As you wish." Miss Winters dropped the bundle of wands at her feet and turned her own wand toward her free hand. With a sharp swipe, a thin red line opened across her palm. Then she raised her wand to Amethyst's face, and a gash appeared across Amethyst's forehead.

Miss Winters pressed her hand to it. Amethyst struggled against the twisted branches at her wrists and ankles, but Miss Winters had already moved on. She raised her wand again. Daisy screamed from somewhere just beyond Abby's vision.

When Miss Winters had done the same to the others, she returned to Abby, close enough that Abby could see the sweat on her face. "You girls pieced together quite a bit on your own," Miss Winters told her. "You, especially, Abby. You deserve some credit."

"I pieced it *all* together," Abby yelled. She needed to keep Miss Winters's focus. "I know who you are, Joanna Greylocke."

Miss Winters moved closer. She considered Abby for a moment before pointing her wand at her forehead. Abby twisted away, but Miss Winters grabbed her chin with her free hand. She traced a ragged line across the air. The pain seared along Abby's forehead as her skin parted and blood trickled down her face.

"I haven't been Joanna Greylocke in a very long time."

"But that's who you really are," Abby shouted. "I know your story. Robby told me about your diary. Jeremiah Winters, the baby, the witch trials. I know what happened."

Miss Winters pressed her free hand against the open cut. Blood mingled with blood. "You don't."

"I know you weren't always like this. I know you changed long ago. You can change again. You don't have to do this."

Miss Winters closed her eyes, shaking her head. When she opened them again, Abby caught a glimmer of regret. "I'm afraid I already have."

A murmur stirred inside Abby's head, growing louder as Miss Winters stepped back to watch her handiwork.

Sister…

Please…

It was the whispers from the tomb, buzzing now around her head.

"You can hear them," Miss Winters said. Her voice quivered with anticipation. "I can see it in your eyes. They're with you now. Inside you." She stroked Abby's face, wiping away a streak of blood. "It's almost over now, Abby. Soon your body will belong to Catherine. She was always my favorite. I will think of you when I look at her."

"Why train us?" Abby demanded. Her head throbbed. The

voices buzzed louder. Thoughts that didn't belong to her hurtled through her mind, one voice after another until she could barely distinguish her own from the others.

Joanna…

Rest now…

Abby gritted her teeth. She shook her head, squeezed her eyes shut, struggled against her bonds. Finally, she opened her mouth and screamed. "Get out of my head!"

Sister…

Mustn't…

Not for us…

"Please…" Abby opened her eyes and stared straight ahead. The sisters in her vision twitched in the air at the end of their nooses, clinging to life. "Get out."

Rest now…

Please…

Abby gasped. She felt like a ragdoll, helpless, tossed about in the wind. She breathed shallowly through her mouth and forced her thoughts into words again. "Why not… just sacrifice us… when you first came for us?"

"Because my sisters were never witches. That's the irony of it. Jeremiah recanted his accusations against me. I think he must have loved me, in his own way. But by then, the village demanded blood. If not mine, then those closest to me. I didn't have the courage to save them. I didn't understand how to control my power. Like a coward, I ran while my sisters hanged. I needed you six to help me weave this spell. Only six together can create new magic—I taught you that. And now, when my sisters return, they will no longer be powerless. Your bodies—my bloodline—will ensure that."

"I trusted you," growled Olivia.

"I am sorry for that, Olivia. You girls are not the first, of course. I failed in the past. Blood magic is never easy, and the veil only opens this wide every hundred years. To say nothing of the physics involved in crafting a spell of this scale." She paused, considering. "That took some time to work out. But I have what I need now. The blood, the stars, the thinning veil… and you."

"Were you… always… this loony?" croaked Amethyst.

"Enough." Miss Winters raised her wand. "Another word, and I will make certain you suffer."

Abby gulped for air, hoping the worst was over, but something new clawed at her insides, squeezing in alongside her consciousness—another soul pressing into the space occupied by her own. *Catherine.*

Trying to push Abby out.

Abby struggled to bring her hands to her neck, but her restraints were too strong. A noose circled against her skin like a slow and sinewy vice.

The world around her grew blurry. She could no longer see Miss Winters, Amethyst, or the others. *Robby!* She searched for him through the thick haze. She called out for him or tried to—she couldn't tell if her voice was still her own or Catherine Winslow's.

Robby…

Sister…

"Get out," Abby rasped.

Joanna…

"Get out."

Robby…

"Get. Out!"

Sister…

Joanna…

"GET. OUT. NOW!"

The voice went silent, leaving a stubborn pressure pulsing against Abby's temples. Her breath came in huffs as she scanned the ground for her best friend and found him still huddled over Tina. Again, the soul of Catherine Winslow pressed at her from inside. Whatever Robby was going to do, he needed to do it soon.

She wasn't sure she could hold onto herself much longer.

Robby crouched in the high grass, just low enough to avoid Miss Winters's attention. He took Tina's hand and searched for a pulse. Her chest moved, but shallowly.

"Tina?" he whispered. When she didn't respond, he crouched closer until her breath warmed his cheeks. "Tina, wake up."

She opened her eyes. "Robby…? What's going on?" She tried to sit up, but he held her low to the ground.

"We have a problem."

"Don't we always?"

"Fair point." He peeked through the grass again. Miss Winters was shouting, but Robby couldn't make out more than a stray word over the howling wind. Abby was buying him time, though. "Miss Winters—Joanna Greylocke, I mean—she's doing something to Abby and her friends. They're pinned against the tree, and…"

Tina grimaced as she turned her gaze toward Miss Winters. "The two of us against her?"

"Not just us." Robby dropped his backpack to the ground, unzipping the main pocket. Two yellow eyes stared back at them. "I brought a friend."

The little iguana skittered toward Tina, leaping onto her chest and licking her face.

"Piper figured it out," Robby whispered. "It's Perseus, right? He's your familiar?"

Tina turned to look at Robby, her eyes wide. "I may have just enough… left… for this."

"For what?"

"Perseus… will know… what to do."

She placed a trembling hand on the iguana's head. Her lips began to move wordlessly. Robby couldn't tell if he wasn't meant to hear them or if she simply lacked the strength to speak.

"Tina, what are you doing?"

She smiled weakly and looked at him with sad eyes. "Proud of you, Robby… Tell your father…"

"No!" Robby said. Too loud, but Miss Winters still hadn't heard him. He ducked lower. "What will happen to you?"

"I'll… rest… easily…" she rasped. Her lips began to move again. Robby glanced around, frantically searching for another idea, another way—*any* other way. He covered her mouth with his hand and pulled the iguana away from her. She tried to sit up again, but he held her down.

"I won't lose you."

Tina struggled against him. "There's… no other… way."

But there had to be. He squeezed his eyes shut, thinking, clenching his fists in frustration. His hands tingled from the pressure of it. Or was it something more? "Protons," he said with sudden understanding. "Electrons. *Science*!"

"What?"

How could he make her see? "Positive and negative charges get out of balance and they build up a charge—and then they have to be released," he explained. "Static electricity. The building blocks of nature."

She stared at him, confused.

"You rub your socks on the carpet and you start to collect extra electrons, right? They just—They cling to you until they can be released. Then you touch someone and there's a spark." He raised his left hand. In the tips of his fingers, he could still feel the flicker of a spark he'd first noticed when he touched the hexagram inside the tunnels. "I've been exposed to magic all night long—at Amethyst's, in the tunnels, the witches' seal. It's all over me. Clinging to me like stray electrons. And now I think I'm... positively charged."

Tina reached for his hand and clasped it in her own. A hint of a smile appeared around the corners of her mouth. "My brilliant boy."

"Tell me what to do," he urged her. "What to say—"

She brought his hand into contact with Perseus. "It's faint, Robby. You don't... have much. So just... picture him..." she said. "Remember who he was... and then imagine him... changing back."

The iguana's scales were rough against his fingers. Robby did as she told him, but nothing happened. Maybe they were wrong. Maybe magic simply ignored the laws of physics.

But then something electric surged through the tips of his fingers—one fast sharp shock, a pinprick over as soon as it began. He winced as another more powerful force overtook him. "Ah-ah-ah... Ah-CHOOOOOO!"

When he looked again, a black Labrador retriever panted at him where the iguana had been, its huge mouth hanging open in a canine smile. Perseus licked Robby's cheek and then bolted toward Miss Winters and the oak tree. Abby screamed Robby's name, but his focus was entirely on Miss Winters now, who'd turned to face him. Anger radiated from her as she raised her wand.

"What did you do?" Miss Winters screamed.

Robby knew what was coming. He just hoped he'd done enough. Crossing his arms, he snapped, "It's called science."

Her wand flashed and the world went white. Every cell in Robby's body burned, and then he fell to the ground and felt nothing at all.

37

The Unbreakable Bond

Abby screamed Robby's name again as he crumpled to the grass. Crimson wisps trailed from the tip of Miss Winters's wand.

She struggled against her bonds, each branch like a dagger cutting into her flesh. Somehow, there was a black Labrador inside the grove now. At first, Abby thought it must be another one of Catherine Winslow's tattered memories. But why did the dog look so familiar?

Perseus! But how?

The dog scampered toward Miss Winters, then darted aside, zigzagging around the grove. He feinted one way and then the other to avoid blasts from her wand before reaching the foot of the tree and scooping up the girls' wands between his teeth.

"Perseus!" Abby shouted. "Here, boy, here!"

The roots of the great tree coiled around him like a snake, but Perseus squeezed out just in time. Miss Winters raised her wand again. The dog flung the bundle toward Abby, and a familiar warmth spread through her hand as the wands settled between her fingers. Energy swelled through her. The branches retreated.

"*Libertas!*" she shouted, angling the tips of the wands at the constraints around her ankles. Her bonds exploded in a cloud of splinters. The world spun and then righted itself. To her right, Perseus lay in a silent heap. Catherine Winslow's thoughts grew dimmer with every step Abby took, and for the first time since she'd entered the grove, she felt fully in control of her mind and body.

Miss Winters raised her wand again. Abby ducked as a blast flew past her head, searing a hole into the tree and filling the air with the smell of smoking wood. She dodged around the massive trunk, then pointed her wand at Amethyst's bonds. Her friend slumped to the ground, finally freed. Abby threw Amethyst's wand toward her.

"Help the twins," she shouted over her shoulder as she sprinted in the opposite direction. Piper was snared against the trunk, muttering through bloodied lips. Abby angled her wand at the branches and caught Piper as she collapsed into her arms.

"That was… It was… The voices…"

"Come on." Abby pressed Piper's wand into her hand. "We have to fight."

She found Amethyst staggering away from another of Miss Winters's blasts, holding her wand outstretched to protect Daisy and Delphi. Abby tossed their wands to them.

Only one other wand remained in her hand beside her own. She hesitated for just a second before freeing Olivia and tossing the final wand to her.

Amethyst and the others were already forming a ring around Miss Winters, their wands outstretched, when Abby and Olivia took their places in the circle. Tina tottered toward Robby. She felt for his pulse and then staggered to Abby, nodding reassuringly.

"You've lost," Tina rasped. She clutched at Abby's shoulder for support. "Six wands… against one. An… unbreakable… bond."

Six wands, Abby thought. *Six of us now. Six of them then.*

She remembered that night at the lighthouse, which seemed so long ago now. Miss Winters, a swirling storm of faces in the dark, and these six wands clattering to the floor, one at each point of the hexagram. Abby squeezed her wand between her fingers. It still thrummed with energy, but now that she'd felt Catherine Winslow's presence, she understood what she'd sensed that first night

"Wands down." Abby stared at Miss Winters, whose face was unreadable, and then at her friends. She pushed her wand into Tina's hand.

"Abby, no."

"Trust me," she said. "Wands down!"

She entered the circle, her hands open at her side. Miss Winters stared at her. She looked young and vulnerable, her dark hair clinging to her face and neck. Her wand arm hung by her side.

She'd rather die than fail her sisters again, Abby thought. *My life for theirs.*

Abby stopped two paces from her and raised an outstretched hand. "Give me your wand, Miss Winters."

"She won't!" shouted Amethyst.

"We have to finish her," agreed Olivia.

"Abby," warned Tina.

"We can't beat you like this, can we?" Abby said. "You made these wands. You imbued them with the essence of your sisters. They can't be used against you."

Miss Winters studied her wordlessly.

"Is this really what you want?" Abby asked.

"I wanted…" Miss Winters began, and then went silent. Her eyes looked hollow.

"You wanted to bring them back. But they were victims, not killers. They wouldn't have wanted this."

"They would have *wanted* to live." Miss Winters's eyes flared again with anger. She raised her wand.

Abby took another step closer. "Not like this, though. Not

with blood on their hands. Listen to them."

Sister…

Please…

Mustn't…

Not for us…

"Listen," Abby urged.

Miss Winters gasped. She raised a hand to her mouth, stumbling back. Abby closed the space between them again.

"I think you wanted us to stop you," Abby said. "I think *that's* why you trained us. That's why you told us about the six sisters that first day on Willow Hill. It's why you didn't kill Robby when you had the chance. You've been giving us clues this whole time because you knew we could save you from yourself. I think you *do* care about us—and you don't have to be alone now." Abby held out her hand. "Just give me your wand, Miss Winters."

Miss Winters looked at the wand in her hand, and then back at Abby, as if seeing both for the first time. She raised her free hand—somewhere, Amethyst screamed a warning—and touched Abby's forehead where the open cut still seeped warm blood. Her fingers were like ice.

"The things I've done. I'm too far gone now."

"I don't believe that." Abby wrapped her fingers around Miss Winters's. "Forget what you've done. Think about what you can still do now. You were good once."

"I was many things, once. Now I'm just… *this*."

"Nobody is just one thing," Abby said. "You told me that."

Miss Winters's expression softened. "You always were a good student." She placed her wand in Abby's open palm. "Maybe I did one thing right after all. Goodbye, Abby."

"No!" Abby shouted, but even as the word left her mouth the skin around Miss Winters's eyes began to wrinkle and stretch like old parchment. The streak of gray widened, spreading until it covered her entire head. And then the gray hair began to fall from her in clumps. She clutched at it, staring wide-eyed at her hands as the flesh shriveled to the bone.

"It feels good… to finally… let go."

"What's happening?" yelled Olivia.

"Keep your wands ready," said Tina.

Moonlight filtered into the grove again. Miss Winters stumbled under the weight of her own body. Abby caught her and gently lowered her to the ground. The skin around her mouth had yellowed, pulled back to reveal decaying teeth. Abby clutched at her, shaking her head.

Miss Winters clasped Abby's hand. Her wand, pressed between them, thrummed frenetically. "Abby…"

"You could have stayed," Abby cried. "You could have started over with us."

"Abby…" Miss Winters whispered again, faint as a breeze. "Listen to me."

Abby leaned closer. Her eyes watered, her nostrils burning from the scent of decay.

"Remember what I told you…"

"Miss Winters," Abby cried. "*Joanna.*"

"What I told you… about the Council." She was paper-thin now. What little of her body remained was swallowed by the scarlet folds of her cloak. Only her eyes retained any hint of her past strength. "Abby," she wheezed through thinning lips. "It was all… true. Remember… don't… trust… the Council."

Her mouth widened in a final gasp, and the last of her strength fled. Her body collapsed in on itself and then turned to dust inside her cloak.

"No!" Abby screamed. "You don't get to leave. There's still so much you could do!"

Miss Winters's wand vibrated in Abby's hand as if it still had a pulse of its own. Abby had just enough time to tuck it inside her shirt before her friends rushed to her side.

Amethyst pulled Abby upright. "We won?"

Abby nodded numbly. She staggered toward Robby, who was climbing to his feet and touching his head gingerly. A few paces away, Tina crouched near the foot of the tree and cradled Perseus in her arms. His chest moved up and down in hollow breaths.

"You all right?" Robby asked when Abby reached him.

She wrapped her arms around him. "I told you not to follow us. You never listen."

"Good thing."

Abby fought back tears. "I know," she said, then, scanning the grove worriedly, she asked, "Where's Zeus? Becca?"

"They're fine. They helped me get past the chimeras. What happened to Miss Winters?"

Abby rested her head on his shoulder and hugged him as hard as she could. He wrapped his arms around her and squeezed her back.

"She's gone."

EPILOGUE

"It doesn't fit," complained Amethyst.

Abby closed her book and rolled to the other side of the bed. In the doorway, Amethyst's legs and torso stuck out from beneath a tight yellow sweater about two sizes too small. Her head was stuck in the collar.

"Plus, you know, the color," Amethyst added. She pulled off the sweater and then stuck her finger in her mouth in a mock-gagging gesture.

"Try the other one."

Amethyst tossed the yellow sweater onto a growing pile near the foot of Abby's bed. "It won't fit, either. It's like your entire wardrobe was made for a ten-year-old boy. You don't *look* that tiny."

"I'm not tiny. I'm athletic."

"How about this one?" Amethyst suggested.

Abby leapt from the bed and snatched the top in question before Amethyst could stretch it out. "That one's off-limits."

"Oh, *right*." Amethyst grinned. "Got to look good for the boys."

"Not all the boys. Just one."

"First dates are so exciting," said Amethyst.

"It's not a date! Zeus and I are just hanging out."

"Do you have butterflies?"

"A few."

"Then it's a date. That still doesn't solve *my* problem, though."

"Mom says we'll go shopping for you tomorrow." Mrs. Shepherd had volunteered her office for Amethyst's bedroom, and she'd already started the paperwork to have Amethyst live with them permanently. That hadn't left much time for shopping, though. Amethyst mostly lived off hand-me-downs and thrift store rejects in the week since her house burned down, although it looked like the insurance money would be a sizeable amount when it finally came through.

"Well, I'm taking *these* hostage until I get some normal clothes." Amethyst grabbed Abby's favorite jeans and slipped into the hallway before Abby could send another object hurtling in her direction. "I just need two minutes," she called over her shoulder.

Abby returned to her bed and shoved her pillow aside. Miss Winters's wand lay there, out of place on the white sheets. She stuffed it into her back pocket and then crossed the hall to knock on Amethyst's door. "They're probably waiting for us," she said.

When Amethyst opened the door, she'd managed to cobble together something presentable out of Abby's jeans and an old shirt donated by Olivia on the condition that Amethyst never wear it where someone might see her. Spooks peered out from behind Amethyst's legs. Abby pretended not to see him— technically he was supposed to live at Tina's veterinary clinic now—and then they fell into step down the stairs and out to the driveway. The other girls were already there. Robby, Zeus, and Becca huddled with them.

"I still don't see why we have to do this," said Olivia, gripping a gardening shovel between her hands. Piper wiped mud from the soles of her boots and murmured her agreement.

Only the twins, who carried a willow sapling between them, seemed happy to be there.

"We don't have to," Abby said, "but I think we should."

Robby and Zeus took the sapling from Daisy and Delphi, and then they all set out down the path. The ground crunched underfoot, a few stray leaves drifting in the wind like crispy snowflakes. When they finally reached the top of Willow Hill, Abby cast a subtle warming spell on the soil until it softened enough for Robby to plunge the shovel into the earth and begin to dig.

Robby and Zeus unwrapped the sapling and lowered it into its new home, shadowed along the crest of the hill by its six sisters. Zeus stepped back. Abby shared a smile with him.

"We should say something," Abby suggested, turning back to the others. Olivia coughed. Delphi shuffled her feet. Piper gazed straight ahead, eyes frozen.

"All the world is a stage," Daisy offered. "Her play was a tragedy."

"She nearly made ours a tragedy, too," Amethyst pointed out.

Abby pulled Miss Winters's wand from her back pocket. It still thrummed. "I hope you're finally at peace," she said under her breath before placing the wand in the hole among the roots and rocks and then sweeping fresh dirt to cover it.

After they'd filled the hole, Abby watched in silence as her friends trickled down the path toward home. Robby hung back with her, stamping the dirt around the tree with the blade of the shovel.

"You're worried about what she told you," he said, planting the shovel in the soil and crossing the space between them. "About the witch's council."

"I can't stop thinking about it."

"Why would you believe her?"

"I don't know. She was different at the very end, Robby. I think she really did care for us after all."

"Tina trusts the Council."

Abby exhaled. "And I trust Tina. Obviously. It's just… What if Tina's wrong?" She studied the fresh dirt around the base of the sapling. Faintly, just below the surface, Miss Winters's wand hummed as if in answer.

Robby followed her gaze. "That's why you didn't tell her about the wand?"

Abby nodded. "It's our secret—you, me, and our friends. Maybe we'll never need it, but if we do, we'll have a piece of Miss Winters on our side."

"Whatever happens, we'll face it," Robby said. "All of us this time. Together."

"Together," Abby agreed.

Their friends grew smaller on the horizon. Abby allowed herself one final look at the willows, and then she and Robby left Joanna Greylocke and the Winslow sisters behind.

ACKNOWLEDGMENTS

My thanks, first and foremost, to Emma Nelson, Hannah Stiles Smith, Olivia Swenson, and the entire team at Owl Hollow Press for believing in this story and giving it a home. I'm so happy to be a part of your flock.

I owe a huge debt to Barbara Campbell, Julia Richardson, and Jenny Bowman for their guidance on my early drafts. Likewise, I'm grateful to my first readers, Eric Griffith and Sarah Pascarella, and to my mentor and friend, Dr. MaryKay Mahoney, whose relentless encouragement kept me going through the muddiest parts of the muddy middle. Thanks also to the incomparable Alison Weiss, whose keen insights and razor-sharp suggestions helped me arrive at the best possible version of this story. Alison, this book is so much better because of you.

I can't say enough about my beta readers—Rebecca Moody, Dana Nuenighoff, Kirsti Call, Sydney Call, Laura Cooper, Marti Johnson, Keri Demers, and Madelyn Demers—or about my critique groups in Andover, Newton, and Beverly. You are my people and you inspire me every day.

A huge thanks to my mom, of course, for making a point of reading all the same books I did when I was a kid so that we could talk about them afterward. I'm a reader and a writer because of you. And thanks to my dad, too—writing this book sometimes felt like taking one of your famous "shortcuts," but I think I managed to enjoy the scenery along the way.

I'd be remiss not to mention Sally Merrick, my high school English teacher, who I promised to include in the acknowledgments of my first novel. It took longer than I expected, but here we are at last. Thank you for starting me on this journey all those years ago.

Finally, to my wife Penelope and my children, Ethan and Madeleine: I could not have written this novel without your support and encouragement. I'm lucky to share my life with you.

JOSH ROBERTS is an award-winning travel writer and editor who has written for publications as varied as *USA Today*, *The Boston Globe*, and *Business Insider*. These days, Josh writes the kind of middle-grade and young adult novels he always enjoyed when he was a kid growing up in a spooky Victorian funeral home.

He is currently at work on the second book in the Willow Cove series, *The Curse of Willow Cove*.

find Josh Roberts online at www.willowcove.com

#WillowCove
#TheWitchesofWillowCove